THE MATTER OF DESIRE

The MATTER *of* DESIRE

Edmundo Paz Soldán

TRANSLATED BY

Lisa Carter

A MARINER ORIGINAL

Houghton Mifflin Company

BOSTON • NEW YORK

Visit our Web site: www.houghtonmifflinbooks.com.

Library of Congress Cataloging-in-Publication Data
Paz Soldán, Edmundo, date.
[Materia del deseo, English]
The matter of desire : a novel / Edmundo Paz Soldán ;
translated by Lisa Carter.
p.   cm.
ISBN 0-618-39557-1
I. Carter, Lisa   II. Title.
PQ7820.P39M3713   2004
863'.64 — dc22   2003067769

Book design by Melissa Lotfy

Printed in the United States of America

MP 10 9 8 7 6 5 4 3 2 1

To Debbie Castillo, Shirin Shenassa,
and Luis Cárcamo-Huechante,
for Ithaca in Ithaca

A Gabriel, mi hijo, por ser, por estar

Is there then any terrestrial paradise where, amidst the whispering of the olive-leaves, people can be with whom they like and have what they like and take their ease in shadows and in coolness? Or are all men's lives like the lives of us good people . . . broken, tumultuous, agonized, and unromantic lives, periods punctuated by screams, by imbecilities, by deaths, by agonies? Who the devil knows?

— FORD MADOX FORD,
The Good Soldier

No siempre uno puede ser leal. Nuestro pasado, por lo común, es una vergüenza, y no puede uno ser leal con el pasado a costa de ser desleal con el presente.

— ADOLFO BIOY CASARES,
El sueño de los héroes

THE MATTER OF DESIRE

1

I APPROACH THE window a few times and, surreptitiously, search the faces in vain, looking for Uncle David. There's still the possibility that he's waiting for me outside, reading the paper in the shade of a *molle* tree — after all, he's a bit of a misanthrope and avoids contact with people whenever he can. I can't help being annoyed that he might not be here: he said he'd come to meet me. This is my city, but I would still feel like a stranger if there were no familiar face to help me, a glance to save me from my frequent forays into the depths of solitude at the slightest blunder into reality. This is my city, but the airport is new, recently inaugurated, smelling of fresh paint and plastic covers, and the view outside changes and is ever more distant from me. This is the price you pay for leaving: objects don't stay where you left them, friends forget you as soon as you turn your back, relatives don't come to meet you because the fragile bonds have stretched with the distance and broken. The map of Treasure Island is lost. It happens to everyone because everyone, sooner or later, leaves for someplace else. It's happening to an espresso-skinned girl who looks at her watch every ten seconds, then lifts her eyes to the windows behind which people crowd, looks for someone and he's not there.

The luggage arrives. I light a cigarette, wondering whether there'll be a shout to put my hands in the air, a shove that'll knock me to the ground, making the pack of Marlboros fall, an arrest and six months in a federal prison. Nothing happens. The act doesn't lead to hysteria here; you're free to damage your own lungs, change the color of your own teeth, and damage everyone else's lungs in the process. Secondhand smoke kills, so the magazines say. I'm not the only one smoking. There are a couple of young kids who look like brothers. The smell of their cigarettes is unmistakable; they're smoking marijuana, *maría, bayer,* what other names have been invented during my absence? Earrings, Bob Marley sweatshirts, Birkenstocks: they left wearing shirts and ties and this is how the North sends them back. We come back with full pockets, new knowledge, and old things forgotten, contaminating and willing to contaminate, so that what is disappears faster than it ordinarily tends to, so that the reign of the temporary sinks its claws into this world once and for all.

The ash falls onto the cream-colored tile floor. *And at that moment they knew in unison, once and for all and forever, that they would soon be that which they had been born for and which a thousand permutations had hidden: ash.* Like in the Villa de Ash. Like Ashley.

A wrinkled old skycap in a dark blue uniform approaches and asks if he can take my bag. There's only one and it's not heavy, but I recognize him and say yes. He's been working at the airport ever since I started to travel fifteen years ago (when the airport was one barnlike terminal and the bathrooms smelled of urine; it should've been easy to forget, but it wasn't). He's very small and frail; I've often wondered how he does it, like an ant, capable of carrying twice his own weight. He leaves with my green canvas bag while I carry my briefcase containing a tangerine-colored iBook, magazines, and *Berkeley,* Dad's novel, which I'd reached out to again when my problems began (that sleepless semester I'd taught it and kept it close by, on my desk, but it's one thing to read in order to teach and another in order to escape from the world). It's a first-edition paperback, full of coffee stains, notes in the margins, and phrases underlined. I bought it at a used-book stall near the post office a few return trips ago. On the cover, silvery tones and Ansel Adams lighting, there's a photo of the signpost of two streets that converge to form that mythical corner, Bancroft and Telegraph. The telegraph: that marvelous invention for coding messages. It's a photo that manages to summarize the central themes. A masterful 132-page work through which Dad finally discovered that he could be more successful as a writer than as a politician — not in the end, but, rather, at the same time. And then came the military attack on the Unzueta Street apartment, where the leadership of Dad's party clandestinely met, and his savage, bloody death, as well as that of Aunt Elsa, Uncle David's wife. His brother was the only survivor (apart from René Mérida, the traitor who informed on them and so didn't come to the meeting). Dad, who left me when I was young, and I, who strive to find him in a novel.

I walk on polished tiles toward the main exit, amid the rejoicing of my travel companions and those who receive them. Through the loudspeaker a woman's singsong voice announces flight delays, the escalators operate incessantly, the sounds reverberate sonorously on the high yellow walls with neon signs advertising Coca-Cola, McDonald's, Entelnet, and several hotels. There's a large photo of President Montenegro — affable, triumphant, not at all dictatorial — and a plaque saying the airport was opened during his administration. I stop at a kiosk bursting with Argentine and Chilean magazines, the covers featuring the sentimental crises of models and the salary figures for today's soccer players. I buy newspapers — *El Posmo* and *Veintiuno* — and M&Ms, place two dollars on the counter. The salesgirl is watching a Mexican soap opera on a miniature TV and barely glances my way. I get two candies as change.

On the front page of both papers, big headlines announce that the government has officially approved Jaime Villa's extradition to the United States. Villa, that legendary drug trafficker who thought himself a Robin Hood but was really more like Al Capone. In *El Posmo*, a full-color photo of an effusive Villa in a mariachi's sombrero and white suit, like García Márquez when he accepted the Nobel Prize in Stockholm. In *Veintiuno*, a photo of the drug trafficker with his cousin, that military Minister of the Interior who in 1980 planned the Unzueta Street massacre. Welcome to Bolivia.

As soon as I leave the terminal I hear the voices of taxi drivers offering their services. I miss the kids looking for handouts. They must not let them come into the new terminal: the price of modernization, I suppose.

I stop at the edge of the sidewalk, anxious. Am I to be punished by a migraine, one of those that force me to hole up in a room with the lights out and damn my fate? The restless trigeminal nerve, the neuropeptides, the pressure behind the right eye: the Migraine, that mythical animal I only just domesticate with Imitrex. No, it's not. Just a pang this time. I inhale the dirty air with relief, and now, seeing the cloud of dust floating over the city, the washed-out blue sky, feeling the aggressive heat of the sun, so far from the snow, I recognize Río Fugitivo, smile faintly, and know, at last, once more, I'm home. Everything stops for a few seconds and I'm the child, the young man who never left, the one who planned on following in Dad's footsteps, the idealist who wanted to dedicate his life to politics in order to change the country once and for all and forever.

The skycap asks where he should take my bag. End of the rapture.

"Leave it here," I say, and give him a dollar.

Uncle David isn't anywhere in sight. Maybe he's running late. Or maybe not — at least not here, where everything is so nearby. How often had I waited to hear the roar of a plane's engines before finally leaving for the airport? How long should I wait? Half an hour? Twenty minutes, no more. Or should I call him? No, I don't want to go back into the terminal.

I sit down on my bag, take my glasses off, put them on again. I take out my Palm Pilot, turn it on, stare, not knowing what to do, and put it away again. I don't feel like playing blackjack, I'm tired of losing at chess, and I have to reorganize myself for a new game of Dope Wars (where you head up a drug cartel, have to build your empire to fight against other cartels, and are chased by the DEA; true, its not at all educational).

I quickly flip through the newspapers and then look in section two of *El Posmo* for one of the things I miss most about Río Fugitivo: the Cryptogram, the crossword that Uncle David sets (they don't put it on the Internet version of the newspaper — big mistake; how many times have I had to have it sent to me from Bolivia?). Firmenich's nickname. While waiting for him I'll solve his verbal labyrinths, find out about the latest things he's seen and read, discover the extravagant ramifications of his education. Joined Hungary and Bulgaria. Horizontal and vertical phrases that intermingle, blank spaces that need to be filled in. Astronaut on Friendship VII, five letters. Some were born to leave hieroglyphics behind them; others, to decipher them, to clarify the world another strives to make opaque. I belong to the latter, and I'm convinced that our work is no less honorable, no less deserving of recognition, than that of the creators. Without us, without our answer to their threatening, secretive challenge, they could not exist.

Pioneer of French aviation. Defeated Spassky. Creator of Hermann Soergel. Coach of the Brazilian team defeated at the Maracanazo. Catalan painter mentioned in *The Crying of Lot 49*. So he's been reading Pynchon? How dare he use such a specific clue when so few of his followers even know who Pynchon is? But I guess it's not so bad, you don't have to know everything to do a crossword. It's a matter of having a nose for it, analytical and deductive abilities, and being generally knowledgeable. It's also a matter of good dictionaries and encyclopedias, having a talent for looking up information on the Internet, friends who share the fervor, and patience. Above all, that: patience.

Half an hour goes by. My uncle doesn't arrive, nor do I finish his crossword. I get into a taxi.

In the back seat of a white Toyota, being tortured by the sound of Enrique Iglesias and the smell of home-brewed *chicha*, I wipe my mouth on the sleeve of my T-shirt and tell myself again what I got tired of thinking on the plane, while dozing next to a gay Chilean reading *Look Homeward, Angel*: that I came to Río Fugitivo with the excuse of looking for Dad when I really came to escape a woman. Ashley. Beautiful, sweet, cruel, wild Ashley.

Finally, in the taxi, as we drive alongside the stagnant waters of the river that winds through the city, the pain of Ashley's absence overwhelms me. I miss Madison, its leaden sky in the heart of

New York State — centrally isolated, closer to Canada than to Manhattan — the intolerable snow, the cheap motels on Route 15, and the rooms with MTV on at full volume to drown out our boisterous lust.

Catalan painter, four letters.

I ask the taxi driver if he can turn off the radio. He replies with a simple no. Welcome to Río Fugitivo, where the customer is not always right.

Uncle David was waiting for me at the door of his house as if nothing had happened. His hands were stained with ink or grease. He greeted me wearing slippers and a threadbare blue-and-white-checked robe, gave me a brief hug, and made no mention of our telephone conversation, no attempt to excuse his absence at the airport. It was as if the words spoken into the phone a few days ago, that booming voice, had been just another form of static, noises that disappear once emitted, invisible frequencies you swear exist but need complicated experiments, chemical or alchemical formulas, electromagnetic radiations, to prove.

"How was your trip? Come in, come in. So many hours stuck in a plane. There's no way you could make me get on one, even though I admire the Wright brothers and all those who followed. *The Spirit of . . .* where?"

"Saint Louis."

"Well, well. The house is small, but the heart . . . This is your room; it's not very clean. I don't have a housekeeper. What for? So they can steal from me? You'd like a shower, I suppose."

"I'm fine," I said, looking at the single bed in a corner, the paint peeling off the walls, the nondescript night table and narrow chest of drawers where blankets smelling of mothballs were piled. I put my bag on the floor and opened the light blue curtains, and light timidly entered the room from the interior patio. Nothing to write home about. In truth, I wasn't fine. I needed a desk and more life on the walls. But what could I say? I had brought all this upon myself.

I'd lived here during my childhood, from time to time, but didn't remember much (or better: my memory's reconstruction of the house wasn't very helpful). I wanted to sniff around my new territory, like a dog, but felt that my uncle, his tall, thin figure in the doorway, wanted to be left alone. Maybe I had interrupted him in the final stage of setting a crossword. Sure, he'd spent all night working, that was why he didn't go to the airport. That explained the bags under his eyes and the bloodshot left one. (His right eye was glass; he lost it when a paramilitary's bullet went through it that evening on Unzueta Street.)

"Breakfast?"

"No, thanks. I had breakfast in La Paz, at the airport."

"Then rest and I'll call you for lunch. You'll eat here, right? Nothing special, I cook myself, so don't expect miracles. A girl comes in on Mondays and leaves meals for a few days. The rest of the time, it's just whatever. You've gained a bit of weight."

"Age," I said, patting my stomach. "I've started going to the gym, watching what I eat — although this isn't the best place for that. One of the things I miss most about here is the food. *Parrilladas* are so much better than barbecues in the States. I tried to do your crossword. I'm almost done. They're increasingly difficult. Catalan painter . . . ?"

"Four letters. Who else? Remedios Varo. But don't ask me again because I don't like it, that's cheating."

"I thought she was Mexican?"

"That's what most people think."

"So, Pynchon."

"In Spanish. It's too difficult in English."

"For anyone. Even in Spanish it's commendable."

"It's easier than his reputation suggests. And very entertaining. *Vineland* most of all."

"I didn't read it. I loved *The Crying of Lot 49*. Read it a long time ago, in Berkeley. I should read it again."

"So many things to read again."

The conversation wasn't going anywhere. My uncle closed the door and left. I cleaned the accumulated dust off the night table, got rid of a spider web on the lamp, lay down on the bed. The day's warm air and the smell of the lemon tree in the patio drifted in through the windows.

I'd called to ask if I could stay for a couple of weeks; I hoped to find an apartment during that time. Mom wasn't here. She'd been traveling in Europe for the last few months with an Italian who had money to burn, looking for a love that was stable and self-destructing at the same time. Maybe I should have imposed on Federico or Carlos, or even Carolina. Or I should have gone to a hotel. I wasn't a student any longer; I was now a professor at the Institute of Latin American Studies at the University of Madison, someone who, because of an article on the political situation in the region, had become (to the fury of some older and more prestigious colleagues) a figure whose opinions were sought by *NewTimes, Latin American Affairs,* and other American magazines and newspapers interested in the topic (not many, it's true). What would my editors say? Surely they pictured me in some local version of the Hyatt or other international hotel chain. I was in a period of transition. My new life required more expenses, Italian silk ties and clothes that make the man — like those of my Chilean and Peruvian friends on Wall Street — but I still hadn't lost my frugal student habits. My one small step up: from the Gap to Banana Republic, casual elegance at a relatively low price (sometimes I went to an outlet mall an hour outside Madison and bought flawed Polo shirts and sweaters). My only weaknesses were colognes and electronic gadgets — Palm Pilots and MP3 players (Ashley's influence, I should add).

Who should I call? I wasn't anxious to call any one of my friends. Each of my previous visits had served to prove, painfully, how life was separating me from them. The only ties that bound us were common memories of a time shared during our youth and maybe a night or two of getting high during my vacations. Even those memories were fading. Sometimes I wondered how we had ever shared something as intimate as a case of gonorrhea, thanks to the same whore. Married, yuppies, divorced and living with their parents, winners big and small, nine-to-five jobs and all the while searching for an easier way to get rich, at home in a world that I hadn't found yet, certain of their greatness and not knowing how small they really were. I wasn't the only one to wonder. Surely they, too, asked themselves what had bound them to someone so apparently similar but deep down so different (someone without much certainty, someone who at least knew how small he was).

It was typical of me to think this way: starting at one extreme and then heading to the other before ending up in the schizophrenia of both extremes at once. Soon I'd be with them, drinking and helping to settle their lives between spouses and lovers, between Nokia and Motorola (Nokia, always). Cosmopolitan though I was, this was my truest world, and I had to admit that. If I'd stayed here I wouldn't have been out of place — I'd have a paunch and a couple of kids, be importing tampons from Brazil, deciding whether or not to open a video store, planning Friday night out, Saturday's *parrillada* and Sunday's Italian soccer game on cable while the wife sleeps and others confess their sins only to begin again that same afternoon (the motels full at any hour).

To relieve my tension in a shower with lukewarm water and no pressure, I masturbated, thinking of Ashley naked on the carpet in my apartment, desire and tenderness in her eyes.

The house was one story. At the entrance there was a well-kept garden with pretentious carnations and a creeper on the rusted bars of the wrought-iron grille. Was it true that as a boy I had caught butterflies here? A hallway had old maps on the walls — the Americas in several Renaissance versions — and photos of famous people with the background digitally altered: Sartre at the Palacio Quemado, Franco at the White House, Walt Disney in the Potosí mines, Evita in the Café Deux Magots, Cantinflas as director of the U.N. General Assembly, Pelé playing soccer in the Chicago Bulls arena. My uncle certainly amused himself. To the right of my room was more hallway and then the living room.

When I reached the door to the living room, I stopped and for an instant saw bouquets of flowers scattered all over the floor and two coffins side by side: Dad's and Aunt Elsa's wake. But it hadn't been that way at all. There was no wake; their corpses were never found and are likely now cracked bones in some communal grave or under the Police Headquarters patio (where they play futsal every afternoon). Can you imagine something forcefully enough that you finally impose it on reality? Aren't we weaker than we believe, don't we yearn deep down to give in to our desires?

The flowers disappeared and then the coffins, replaced by a couch and a couple of chairs around a glass table weighed down by stacks of books, magazines, and dictionaries. In the corner an obscene forty-inch television demanded unconditional veneration. To my left was a wooden cart piled with bottles of whiskey and *singani*, glasses, a cocktail shaker, and an ice bucket. All around the room, against the walls, as if in a museum, were antiques on wooden pedestals: obsolete Smith Corona and Underwood typewriters, phonographs dating from the early twentieth century, a Sinclair Spectrum computer, a monstrous Blaupunkt radio from the forties (jealous of the TV's presence and yet confident that, sooner or later, this too would come to keep it company). When I came to Madison there was a Smith Corona factory nearby. The last time I drove past, a couple of months ago, the factory had closed. The sight of so much desolation in buildings once full of workers had moved me.

"What do you think?" my uncle said, looking at me proudly. He had a glass of Chivas in his hand, ceaselessly rattling the ice. "This room is too small. There's more, much more, in the storage room."

"Chapter Thirty," I said.

An idea stolen from or a tribute to *Berkeley*, I thought, remembering Bernard's Museum of Media. I admired the Underwood up close, touched its cold keys, the bulky case. Invented for the blind, it had been adopted by philosophers, secretaries, and writers. On one of those machines Dad had written the 132 pages of his novel, not counting the multiple revisions, the errors, the pages started anew. Exhausting just to think about. Quality of the work aside, all those who had sat down to compose their works key by key, without the ease of a word processor, were admirable and deserved recognition. To say nothing of those who had done it by hand, or those who still do — more than one of today's writers would have felt at home in a medieval monastery.

"It's a bad habit of mine," he said. "I collect what others disdain. So much history in each one of these machines."

He had an intimidating voice: he seemed to be shouting even when speaking quietly. They say Dad's could also be intimidating, gravelly like that of a chronic smoker. His was a captivating voice that elegantly ordered obedience. Or so they say. I remember hardly anything about him. He's just a blurry figure that rushed in and out of my childhood, him not paying much attention to me or me to him. An unknown stranger I saw so few times in person, someone I had to reconstruct — I'm still doing so — through photos, his novel, the memories of others. The most salient image comes from one of my birthdays. There's going to be a big surprise, Mom had said, and I waited anxiously. When it was time for cake, someone in an old red leather mask and a feather headdress jumped out of the cupboard. I was frightened even though I knew who it was. He took off the mask, approached, and hugged me, and everyone clapped. Now I remember the mask, vividly, but little of the face behind it.

"It's a new hobby?"

"Uh-uh, I started a long time ago."

Maybe it wasn't an idea taken from *Berkeley*. Perhaps, with the Museum of Media, Dad was paying homage to his brother, and that was why the room was a kind of return to the beginning. But I didn't remember it from my childhood.

"It's just that now I can apply myself more seriously."

I wasn't surprised by his attraction to relics like these: he would've liked to have invented one. Apart from his verbal ability, he was very good with his hands. The doorbell, different tones from classical pieces — from Bach to Stravinsky — was his invention, as were the multiple speeds of a blender for preparing cocktails, a lawnmower whose motor was an extravagance of wires and screws, and the connections thanks to which he watched cable TV for free. "Poet and mathematician," he often said. He'd studied industrial engineering but hardly practiced his profession. He wanted to be an inventor despite the lack of funds and support for his crazy projects. Dad had made fun of him and called him a "conceptual inventor." There were more inventions left half-done than finished. They say that as a kid he spent his time taking radios apart and putting them back together, studying their wires and diodes, trying to improve on the original product. He and his wife had suffered many privations because of his multidirectional passion, constant in its inconstancy. He had the intelligence to succeed at any profession he chose, just not the discipline. He'd moved from job to job, failure to failure, and ended up, convinced by Dad and Aunt Elsa, involved in politics. He'd been fanatical about crosswords since adolescence, but his dedication to creating them came later in life. He's been doing it for five years now, and I often ask myself when he'll abandon them. But he seems finally to have discovered something to hold on to. Sometimes it's bad to be good at everything; it's better to have a talent for just one thing, be it knitting alpaca sweaters or designing the Guggenheim in Bilbao.

"Whose is this?" I said, pointing to the light green Smith Corona that occupied center stage.

"Your dad's. He wrote parts of *Berkeley* on it. A collector wanted to buy it from me for a lot of money. Did he think I was crazy?"

I admired it in silence: a small machine, portable, more suited to a professional or a busy executive than a romanticized writer.

"I saw your iBook," he said. "I don't like the color, prefer something more subtle. I have a Mac too. Until just a while ago I had a Commodore 64 that I'd made some adjustments to, to make it faster and run current programs. I finally got tired. It was too much work."

"You don't collect any other type of antique. They all have something in common."

"Yes. They allow communication at a distance. Because, you know, that's the best way to communicate. At a distance. The presence of people only blocks communication."

"And what we're doing now?"

"Sometimes it can't be helped." He finished his whiskey in one long swallow and put the glass down on top of a dictionary on the table.

I looked at him to see if he was joking. He wasn't. I felt the cold radiating off him. The prominent nose, the furrowed brow, the elongated, austere face, the wrinkles etched deeply into his cheeks, the immovable glass eye. He had given me puzzles and played chess with me when I was a kid. He also taught me to do acrostics and crosswords, revealed the secrets that all crossword setters invoke of the periodic table and Morse code. He knew how to do implausible tricks with coins and cards, but I never could learn them. Then a chasm opened up between us: at times I blamed him for having survived instead of Dad. We had become closer again in the last few years, but our relationship was purely intellectual, based on the crosswords. When I returned on vacation I saw him only rarely, contented myself with a few obligatory phone calls. That was enough for him as well. It had been a mistake to ask him to put me up.

"The chicken should be ready," he said, and headed into the kitchen.

I followed. I was hungry.

I check my e-mail on Yahoo. *NewTimes* asks if the latest peace accords in Colombia will last long. NO WAY, I reply, and then a conventional phrase, one of those I know by heart for each country, more for Colombia, civilized as few are and at the same time a tragic summary of the continent's greatest ills. A touching goodbye from Yasemin. One more of the sarcastic and petulant messages Clavijero sends to all the professors at the Institute. Ashley still hasn't written the incendiary e-mail I deserve. Maybe she hasn't yet heard that I left (I doubt that).

I read the headlines from *El País* and the *New York Times*. Nothing grabs my attention.

Carolina came to pick me up at four in the afternoon on a yellow Kawasaki racing bike. She'll never change. At fifteen she raced in a rally as her dad's co-pilot, and since then her life has accumulated more risks than the lives of all my friends put together. She thrives on hang-gliding, mountain climbing, and river rafting. She was wearing a blue aviator jacket, parachute pants, earrings and gloves, purple lipstick, and mascara on her long lashes. A ring indented the skin above her right eyebrow. She looked radiant; the new haircut, almost to the scalp, flattered her angular face.

We hugged.

"You've gained weight," she said, smiling, not knowing how much she hurt my vanity. I took off my glasses to show her my best side.

"And you, so thin. You look younger all the time."

"Appearances can be deceiving." A mischievous glance. "At least you're finally learning to combine colors. And got over your obsession with pinstripes. You dress better than before. Although formal, as always."

"If Berkeley didn't change me, Madison isn't likely to. Can you picture me in tie-dye? Black on black, I'll stick with a sure thing. Doesn't that hurt?" I asked, pointing at her pierced eyebrow, reminded of Yasemin and her five earrings.

"Sometimes. They say there's no pleasure without pain."

"You're philosophical."

"And you smell very nice."

"Swiss Army. Fresh, for daytime, although you can also use it at night. I bought it at duty-free in Miami."

I got on the bike, Carolina took off, and I clung to her. She was thirty years old. Five years ago we were together for a few months during one of my vacations. It was an intense relationship, full of trust and multiple ways of spending time together without getting bored, from losing ourselves in the country on weekends to inventing pornographic stories (we created a recurring character, Dick Top, a bisexual cop). What also united us was a certain emptiness in the relationships we had with our parents. Her mom had died of lung cancer when she was a kid; her dad lived in Buenos Aires and didn't try very hard to maintain a relationship with his daughter. (In that regard, I should say that my mother was perfect during my childhood and adolescence, but as soon as she felt she'd complied with her formative duties, she took me off her list of priorities and made time only for herself.) My return to the U.S. had cooled things off. On my next vacation we came to be very good friends who included, without any commitment, sex as one of our friendliest activities. Girls I dated were jealous of her. Not without good reason, because sometimes I spent more time with Carolina than I did with them. Even though I swore our relationship was platonic, they didn't believe me and said that she didn't look at me like a friend, that it was obvious she wanted much more. Could be. I chose to feign ignorance. Two years ago there was an unexpected jealous scene and tearful confession at her door. On my most recent trips I tried to create some distance, tried my hardest to avoid caresses and sex. I wasn't entirely successful.

Now I'd wanted to call someone, and no one other than Carolina came to mind. I didn't want to stay at home and wallow in melancholy. I needed to forget about Ashley.

We passed over Suicide Bridge — narrow, with low, rusted iron railings — and over the mouth of the river with soothing eucalyptus trees on the shores. I realized that this legendary place was Dad's inspiration for the fateful role bridges played in *Berkeley:* the entrance from one life to another, the preferred place for power, in its many incarnations, to get rid of its enemies, in their many incarnations.

I exchanged dollars with an overweight moneychanger. Then we went to the Twenty-First Century Mall. There were lots of people, out more for a stroll than to shop; the Benetton sweaters and Polo shirts in store windows were admired and abandoned. I ran into a couple of acquaintances; we said hello and promised to call (we wouldn't). On the escalator I commented that the young girls of this new generation, milling around the stores, seemed more self-possessed than our generation had been.

"They go to the gym like you wouldn't believe," said Carolina. "We didn't do that in our day. And they know everything. We picked our noses when we were their age."

I kept looking at a girl who wasn't even fifteen in a tight white tank top, stomach bared. Soft skin that perhaps hadn't yet been caressed or maybe only inexpert hands had touched, hands that didn't teach much but helped her to enter, bit by bit, the territory of restless skin and failed morals that I had entered a long time ago and found hard to leave.

In the Mediterranean Café, surrounded by photos of stars from Hollywood's golden era — above all Bogart and Bacall — we ordered a latte for her, a cappuccino for me, and two cheese-filled *cuñapés.* A Ricky Martin song could be heard from the music store next door. Two young people passed by us speaking Portuguese.

"There's not much new," she said. "I told you almost everything in that huge e-mail I sent about a month ago. The one you replied to with two lines, by the way."

"E-mail isn't for long letters, it's for chatting back and forth."

"We have a new airport. It's very nice. Late, but we got it."

"To think that the decree for its urgent construction was signed in 1949 . . . No one can accuse us of rushing into things. And Montenegro took all the credit, as if he'd been ultimately responsible for its construction."

"The mayor blew his own horn too. But in the end, that's how politicians are, right? There's a recession, a bad one. At my brother's optical store, for example, sales are forty percent lower than a year ago. You missed the trouble in April. Three weeks of campesino blockades, teacher strikes, shortages. Chaos. You couldn't go anywhere. A couple of people were killed at a demonstration in the main plaza. Of course, what happened here is nothing compared to Cochabamba. Truth is, a lot of people are tired; they say this country isn't viable and are applying for a visa to the North. I even have friends who've gone to Arica or Lima."

"And it's going to get worse. The government has serious liquidity problems, exports have decreased considerably, and the balance of payments . . . The solutions have merely been patches, nothing long-term. The war on drug trafficking left us without a cushion of dollars to protect us. The hangover after too much out-of-control neoliberalism."

"You know more than I do about what's going on here."

The waiter arrived with the coffees and *cuñapés*.

"I told you I left my job at the government."

"About time. I never could believe you worked for Montenegro."

"I think you're the only one who remembers he was a dictator. Even the guerrillas who fought him are now his allies."

"Not all of them."

"Almost all. It's been three decades. Let him be. He's almost done with his term and it doesn't help to complain. We elected him now, didn't we?"

"You can't erase the past so easily."

"In this country, everything can be erased. I'm amazed you don't know that."

Carolina had worked for two years in the government's public relations office at the Ciudadela. She was in charge of general image, of making sure the government's work was broadcast via different media and received positive coverage. It was her job to do things like teach the Minister of Employment to smile at the precise moment he announced there would be no wage increases for the next five years.

"As I was saying, I left my job. It's one thing to help them better their image and another to lie in order to achieve that. I lied for a long time, felt bad, and left it."

She drank her coffee. Ricky Martin gave way to Shakira and Shakira to Matchbox Twenty.

"And now," she continued, "I help build Web sites — personal pages, for companies, whatever you want. There's no recession in this business. Everyone wants a Web site. If you don't have one, you don't exist."

"I didn't know you knew anything about computers."

"I learned along the way. I have a business partner, Estela — opened an office with her. My area is more graphic design. She's the expert in HTML, Java, all those. She writes programs to recover erased e-mails. Did you know that all the e-mails we erase are really stored in some secret corner of the computer? So you better not go around sending compromising messages."

I thought about the e-mails Ashley and I had exchanged, erased as soon as we'd written or read them. If Patrick used Estela's services, he'd recover them and have proof of our correspondence. But what use would they be if he couldn't decipher the most compromising ones? Ashley and I had many secret codes — simple substitutions, codes that led to other codes — and Estela wouldn't get to those as easily as she could the messages.

"Also," continued Carolina, "I'm really involved in a magazine that's going to come out exclusively on the Internet. Sort of like *Salon.*"

"You know more about the States than I do."

"You don't live on another planet. It's called *Digitar.* In the first issue there's an exclusive interview with Jaime Villa. I got to meet him. Ricardo, the editor of the magazine, asked me to go with him, and we became friends."

"With Ricardo or Villa?"

"Funny. With Villa."

"He's probably flirting with you. All prisoners are like that."

"You pronounce the *l* and *r* worse all the time. You're becoming gringified."

"The years take their toll."

"Well, maybe 'friends' isn't the right word. Let me know if you'd like to visit him. He has an incredible personality. You can feel the energy as soon as he enters the room."

Carolina was given to psychics, personal energy fields, and changes in personality based on the position of the moon. She believed in the Christ who cries tears of blood in Cochabamba, said she'd had a couple of out-of-body experiences. Once she told me she wanted to contact her mother through a medium and that every once in a while her mom speaks to her in dreams and gives her advice. Now she was wearing a silver chain around her neck, a pendant engraved with the image of Cristina, the fifteen-year-old who is said to have transcribed six books dictated by God in Latin and had become a phenomenon of popular devotion in Río Fugitivo. I never understood that side of Carolina.

"Of course I'd like to," I said, thinking about the possibility of an article that might end my dry spell. "The more firsthand information I have, the better."

The coffee was better than at Starbucks but not as good as at Common Ground. That's where I saw Ashley for the first time. It was August, and she was sitting at a table with Patrick, the tall, blond Dutch man she was going to marry in December. As I was passing by the two of them, she stood up and asked if I was a professor at the Institute. I said I was, holding on to my copy of the *New York Times.* She had very long red hair, almost to her waist, and round, fixed green eyes that made me nervous.

"Nice to meet you," she said, extending her hand and smiling, showing her braces. "I'm Ashley, your future student. This is my first semester here. I'm taking the 'Politics and Dictatorship' class you're offering. I've heard very good things about you."

"It's nice to meet you too. Don't believe everything you hear about me."

"I read one of your articles in *NewTimes*."

"I'm so sorry."

"More professors should do that, write for newspapers and magazines. Otherwise the university will continue to be insulated from what happens in the real world. Who reads those boring journals they make us publish in anyhow?"

"The university is the real world too. And while I'm glad you think that way, you'd be better off thinking about twenty-page articles for those journals. Newspapers and magazines won't get you too far."

"This is Patrick," she said. The Dutch man nodded his head and held out his hand without moving from his seat.

"You're very young to be a professor," said Patrick, in neutral, accent-free Spanish.

"Thanks for the compliment," I said, and smiled.

"Is something wrong?" Carolina interrupted.

"No. I was listening."

"Didn't seem like it. You were somewhere else. Very serious."

"You were talking about Jaime Villa."

"He's the worst, but people are tired of their government doing what the gringos tell them to do. Wipe out coca crops, extradite Villa . . . Incredible. Even leftist politicians have come out in defense of Villa, not because of him but because of the fact of extradition. They say he should be tried here, which doesn't seem like such a bad idea to me. Although there's always the danger that in a flash he'd buy even the Supreme Court judges."

I knew all that. It was my job to be up-to-date on things concerning Latin America. Newspapers, magazines, and television, continual searching on the Internet, and a vast network of friends kept me in touch with people's perceptions regarding their governments, future leaders, the economy. Just three years ago I was a bright political science doctoral student with a promising thesis on the role of the left during the dictatorships of the seventies. My professors and classmates had high expectations for me. But at some point I lost my way and let myself be seduced by the role of professional commentator in magazines and newspapers, with a ready response for any occasion ("If Argentina accepts the dollar, the country will sink" or "Zapatistas are papier-mâché guerrillas, unexceptional and therefore superficial"). I had lost interest in my little academic world of paused, continuous reflection, of exhaustive work on a very narrow subject area, and I quickly abandoned it. No wonder some of my colleagues — Clavijero, Shaw — mistrusted me.

"The government has already approved extradition and the situation is unstable. Groups have called for the defense of national sovereignty. A bomb exploded last Friday at the post office," Carolina explained.

Not one group had claimed responsibility for the bomb. It was strange to arrive and know more about the country than its inhabitants did, incapable as they were of suspecting the magnitude of the crisis that was coming. The government needed economic assistance from the U.S., so they had no recourse but to hand over Villa and continue eradicating coca crops. Carolina kept talking. I amused myself by making anagrams out of her name. Aanilorc: a planet in *Star Wars*. Oilancar: a brand of car oil.

Carolina paid the bill. As we went down the escalator she commented that I was very quiet.

"And what's new about that?"

"Nothing, to be honest."

I had perfected the art of listening, of letting others reveal themselves so that I wouldn't have to. This was one of the reasons I got along better with women than men: women like confessing, and one of the things they value most in a man — or in another woman — is the ability to listen to them hour after hour, or at least appear to listen, nodding the head at the right moment, a blink of the eye or a facial expression to give signs of life.

But it was true that I was more introverted than usual. Ashley swirled around and in me all the time, her mole-speckled back arching under my tongue's soft caresses. Her absence hurt, her absence was anguish, and at times I asked myself whether I had done the right thing by leaving Madison in order to calm the waters and let everything return to its normal course. The most intelligent plan of action is not necessarily the best.

"How long are you here? The usual three months?"

"This time until the end of the year. Eight months. I got a research scholarship." I had my answer prepared. "I want to write a book about my dad. About the novel, the armed struggle . . ."

"Interesting," she said, and looked at me with delight, maybe happy to know she had more time than she'd thought. Three months wasn't enough, eight might be.

2

∞

ARRIVED IN Madison, a white, Anglo-Saxon, self-proclaimed
liberal town, after getting my Ph.D. at Berkeley. ILAS, the Institute of Latin American Studies at the University of Madison,
had hired me as a specialist in modern and contemporary Latin
American politics, with emphasis on the Southern Cone and An-
dean regions. They were typically insular academic compartments
that prevented me from speaking confidently about, for example,
the Mexican Revolution, for fear of being thought to have invaded
a colleague's territory (the dream was to be a specialist on one single day in one single country, such as September 11, 1973, in Chile,
or July 19, 1979, in Nicaragua). My classes focused on the sixties
and seventies, providers of endless dramatic material that would
prevent my students from falling asleep. I planned to write my first
book based on my thesis.

ILAS had its offices in the same building as LSP, the Latino
Studies Program. It was a four-story building, the gift of a university graduate who had made his fortune in Silicon Valley. With ivy
on the walls, crenellated towers, and stained-glass windows that
filtered the soft afternoon light, the architects were able to maintain the nineteenth-century spirit of the other university buildings
(a spirit with roots reaching back to medieval times and Greco-
Latin antiquity, as if Americans, so adept at looking toward the future, needed even artificial traces of the past to legitimize themselves as a nation). Despite their proximity, ILAS and LSP ignored

each other. If Elián González and his family lived in Havana, they fell under our jurisdiction and we studied them. But if they escaped in a boat and arrived in Miami, the Latino Studies Program studied them. It was comical. ILAS and LSP concurred only in that both desperately wanted to become departments but remained programs because of a lack of support from the administration. Our classes were bursting with students, and yet the university bureaucracy, skilled at espousing a hypocritical discourse of inclusion, preferred, when it came down to it — when approving the budget — to support the departments of European studies, which agonized over their lack of student interest. The Latino migrant and demographic explosion did not necessarily translate into the symbolic acquisition of cultural weight that could convert Latinos or things Latin American into something as worthy of study as things French or German. "Eurocentric" is a worn-out epithet, but if there were any way to return it to its former glory, no better candidate could be awarded the description than any administrator in charge of the fate of ILAS and LSP at the University of Madison.

The Institute had, apart from the many floating professors who taught courses on Latin America in other departments, a reduced permanent staff of colorful colleagues who wasted their lives on infighting and played at politics like kids, perhaps knowing that their acts and omissions lacked any repercussion from the administration and the outside world, which circled and encompassed the academic world and at the same time forgot it. The director of the Institute, Helen Banks (tall, wore dark glasses that covered half her face, a specialist in indigenous political movements — this semester she taught "Marcos and the Postmodern Guerrilla"), had stuck her neck out to hire me. Albert Shaw (or Shadow, as the students called him) taught Caribbean studies and hid behind his Nietzschean mustache to propagate unfounded rumors about the colleagues he thought might overshadow him (I was the most recent incarnation of such colleagues, not owing to any particular personal talent but simply because I was the newest). His courses, such as "Caribbean (Homo)sexualities" or "Puerto Rican Women on the Edge of a Nervous Breakdown," were very popular. He wore black leather pants, and his Jamaican boyfriend was a doctoral student in agricultural economics.

I tried to keep out of the politics, but it wasn't easy. Along with Sha(do)w there was an older Cuban professor, Clavijero, dedicated to the nineteenth century. He came to the United States in 1959, escaping Castro, who had appropriated large tracts of land from his upper-class family. I had been indifferent to him, round-faced and conservative, from the start because he felt that guerrillas — self-styled adventurers — weren't worthy of academic study (thus he didn't get on well with Helen Banks either). He began to resent me in the fourth semester when he found out that I "wasted" my time giving opinions to popular magazines instead of applying myself to the research work for which I'd been hired. I knew I'd have problems with my third-year evaluation. For the time being, I tried to ignore them.

In truth, it wasn't my fault. The first year I was lucky enough to publish two chapters of my thesis (one on Operation Condor in the Southern Cone and the other on the fragmentation of the left in Bolivia) in well-respected specialized journals. But the minimal impact after so many hours of work had frustrated me: years of research that were going to a journal with five hundred copies in circulation, destined primarily for university libraries and colleagues. Plus, when results didn't support my theory, I didn't have the patience to discard it and begin again. All academics have to struggle with this, assume the insignificance of their contribution to society and dedicate their lives to archives, even though by doing so they won't obtain more than suppositions that will never be entirely proven. I couldn't accept this and asked myself whether I had chosen the right career. The world of books and research fascinated me, but I wanted to be more relevant. Not necessarily a politician like Dad (I didn't think I had the heart for it), but maybe a strategist for some political party, or an influential analyst in newspaper opinion pages.

I had started to wonder whether I should have stayed in Bolivia when, at the end of that first year, I met Silvana at an NYU conference. We became friends over cocktails and hors d'oeuvres, and I ended up with a contract for a five-hundred-word article on the political situation of the area. While writing the article and having to keep it brief, I discovered my talent — if you could call it that — for phrases that captured and simplified an entire situation. The article caused a sensation. Americans, always anxious for someone to simplify the world with an image or thirty-second sound bite, turned me into an important commentator. Requests from other magazines began to arrive. My fame with students grew, my reputation with the majority of my colleagues suffered. I lost interest in the academic world, and the rest is history.

I began the first semester of my third year at ILAS with heightened expectations and at the same time ready for a period of calm, of dedication to my classes and research, to not being overanxious at the evaluation I would be subjected to (my contract was for six years, with an evaluation in the third). After a long vacation in Río Fugitivo — where I thought coldly of Madison, thanks to the long winter that buries all other seasons in memory — my return was surprisingly wonderful. The August days were hot, the sky was clear, and summer shone from the leafy trees that were about to turn autumn's many colors. Students wandered about the campus or played Frisbee in shorts and flimsy skirts, squirrels suddenly appeared on paths and then were lost in tree branches, and I thought that perhaps it was all a question of time, that maybe Madison would soon earn a place in my heart (dominated as it was by those two sunny paradises: the Río Fugitivo of weekend *parrilladas* and soccer, and the Berkeley of bookstores and cafés).

That semester I would be teaching a freshman introduction to twentieth-century Latin American politics and a seminar on the sixties to doctoral students. I hoped I would have more time to prepare for both classes, since by then Jean had disappeared from my life — the blond, freckled graphic designer who for two years was the reason I went to New York every other weekend (a relationship that never stopped being casual but nevertheless lasted longer than planned — or maybe lasted so long *because* it was casual, suited us both, didn't require much of us; it all ended because of a lack of interest, of not wanting to make the effort to travel, of restless affinities and passionate disagreements). The seminars would be given in the basement of the neoclassical Randolph Jones

Arts Building. At the entrance, a statue of Randolph Jones himself, the bearded, eccentric founder of the university who had made his fortune on a patent derived from the invention of the telegraph and who, among other things, spent Sundays in prolonged spiritual sessions.

I was happy to see more than ten students in the first class and meet up again with some who had become my friends: Joaquín, a Venezuelan of unhurried speech — that rarity — and Yasemin, a mocha-skinned German — her parents were Turkish — who wasn't interested in traveling to Latin America, preferring to keep it as a magnificent abstraction that served as a point of departure for her endless and sophisticated theorizing. She breakfasted Benjamin and Bordieu, lunched García Canclini and Brunner, and dined Said and Jameson. In her spare time she was an obsessive e-mailer (writing to her boyfriend, who lived in Frankfurt).

My introduction lasted only twenty minutes, during which I felt eyes that wouldn't turn away, eyes that traveled over my face and body. It was Ashley, the new student who had precipitately introduced herself to me at Common Ground. She blatantly scrutinized me from one side of the room, her hands playing restlessly with her pen. I was happy I had put my contact lenses in, inveterate first-day-of-class vanity when I didn't know all the female students and preferred to show them my best side — the one I thought best — until we became friends and our trust grew. (Some said my glasses suited me better, but I didn't believe them; I felt very formal, intellectual, bookwormish with them on.)

After class I went for coffee with Joaquín and Yasemin. We crossed the Arts Quad, surrounded by buildings with Latin phrases on porticos and the ghosts of the first inhabitants — the university was built on land won from the Indians in ferocious battles. Randolph Jones bought this wasteland from the government for a paltry sum. He had a mansion built in the middle of nowhere and moved there to escape gossip: the woman he had just married, a pale redhead named Vivianne Jones, was only fifteen years old and his first cousin. They lived together for only three months: Vivianne couldn't withstand the first winter and died

26

from a sudden and devastating case of pneumonia. Legend has it that Randolph Jones closeted himself in the mansion and spent his fortune on building a university around Vivianne's tomb (as well as paying every charlatan who promised him any contact with her in the hereafter, a few words or a sigh). The small cemetery next to the bell tower in the middle of the campus is now used for an annual service in memory of Randolph and Vivianne and for the students' Halloween pranks.

At an outdoor table, under the shade of a large oak tree, Joaquín told us about his research in Caracas, part of his project on the deeper reasons behind Chávez's populist phenomenon: vast socioeconomic inequality, authoritarian culture, marketing, postneoliberal hangover (when he used this phrase without batting an eye, I knew he had a great future in academia). Chávez's Latin American rhetoric, Joaquín said, was one of the main reasons the masses supported him.

"All the malcontents jump on Chávez's bandwagon," he continued, pronouncing his words so slowly and gravely that it seemed that Spanish was not his mother tongue. "Those who are thought to be guilty of toppling Venezuela's traditional parties and those who point the finger at globalization."

"Ah, globalization," I said, trying to lighten the conversation, "how many sins have been committed in thy name?"

"It is our fate," said Joaquín with characteristic solemnity. "Bucaram, Menem, Chávez. The system's inherent crisis has given way to a rhetoric of crisis. It is a providential man who will be able to interpret the words of Bolívar and lead us out of this depression. A strong man, because otherwise we don't understand. Someone who hears the poor and marginalized, the powerful voice of the voiceless. Or we must unite in order to confront the colossal North — we are spirit while they are matter. Ariel and Caliban. Those who know how to handle this rhetoric, adapt it to the historical conditions of their country, will reign over the kingdom of Earth."

With Joaquín there, it was hard to touch on topics that weren't academic, intellectual, serious. He ardently lived because of and for ideas.

"I have a title for your thesis," said Yasemin. "'Beyond Latin Americanism.'"

"Wouldn't that be a better title for you?" I said, trying to provoke her. "You take more courses outside of the Institute than in it, you haven't even been to Mexico . . ."

"You still don't understand," she replied, "that someone can be interested in quote unquote Latinoamérica from a conceptual point of view, as a sophisticated intellectual game. Es la única manera de estudiarla: as a great abstract that hides more than it reveals. Look, you guys, what are the similarities between a Venezuelan and a Bolivian? Nada, except for language. Not even soccer."

"You're going too far, Yasmincita," said Joaquín. "There are differences, but they're not that extreme."

"You both do exactly what you criticize others for," replied Yasemin. "If I did this with Europe, looked at it as a great concept worthy of theoretical exploration, it wouldn't seem so strange to you. But with Latin America, the commitment has to be emotional as well. With the quote unquote subalternos. Because you, Joaquín, you act as if you were taking a politically incorrect position by criticizing un líder populista, but deep down what bothers you is that he's fooling the quote unquote pueblo. You hide it well, but you're another great defender of the people."

They were about to begin their usual argument when Yasemin noticed the disillusioned expression on my face and quickly changed the subject. She mentioned an affair she had had with a woman during her vacation, "just to see." I realized how happy I was to have that degree of friendship with Yasemin and Joaquín. They had made my stay in Madison tolerable. My youngest colleague, Helen, was two decades older; it wasn't hard to understand why I felt closer to the students.

We talked about movies that were worth seeing or weren't and books we'd recently read.

"Your class has promise," said Yasemin. "Muy hip, muy cutting-edge."

"So it would seem," I said. "Deep down it's very traditional: reading about the seventies from the point of view of certain peripheral but no less important personages. Michael Townley, Pedro Reissig, Captain Ástiz, Domitila Chungara."

"Reissig is your dad, isn't he? That's nepotism! I've never even heard of his novel."

"When have you heard of Bolivian novels? They deserve more recognition. You'll see why. And I promise it isn't just a matter of filial loyalty."

"Better not be," said Yasemin, with a mischievous smile. "If you make me read a bad novel, I'll never forgive you."

"But you don't complain about reading bad theory," Joaquín said.

"That's different. Theory is theory."

"Theory is also a type of fiction," I commented. "To be used when we need it, and not let it use us, which is happening more and more in the academic world. Right, Yasemin?"

"To each her own."

I said goodbye to them and went to the parking lot to get my car. Minutes later, as I was driving down the steep hill on Woodworth Street, I saw Ashley on the right-hand sidewalk with her Walkman on, looking at the ground as if lost in a song or her thoughts (or both). A squirrel crossed in front of her, and she continued on unperturbed. The yellow pack on her back made her look like a schoolgirl; her long legs said otherwise. The sun's rays filtered through the branches of the tall trees and at times filled her with light.

I hit the brakes even though I risked causing an accident. She didn't notice me until she heard the beep of a horn, looked to the side, and found me there. She took off her earphones and approached the window. I told her to get in, I'd give her a ride.

"Thanks," she replied, and got in.

"I hope I didn't interrupt serious thought," I said. "Or a good tape."

"All my thoughts are serious these days," she declared, making a tired face. "It'll pass. I liked your class a lot, and I'm not just saying that because you're here."

"It wasn't really even a class. I hardly spoke."

"But the project sounds really interesting" — a sibilant, interminable *s*. "The syllabus is intriguing. I don't know anything about the subject, but it really caught my attention, you know?"

I was nervous and so was she. This feeling was ridiculous. Where did it come from? Out of the corner of my eye I looked at her bright red nails, rings on all her fingers, pearl earrings. Her perfume suggested a strong sea breeze and was permeating my Toyota.

She gave me instructions on how to get to her house through a labyrinth of side streets I didn't know. On the way I asked how she liked her first weeks in Madison. Not bad, but she missed Europe.

"It was a very brusque change."

"Where in Europe?"

"Es una historia larga. You see, I met Patrick, my fiancé (you remember him, from the café), in Chiapas, where he was doing his fieldwork for a Ph.D. in anthropology. Yes, Chiapas, of all places. I had finished my master's and went as an assistant to one of my professors. Then I went to Barcelona, where I made a living working in an art gallery. I kept in touch with Patrick, and when he got back to Amsterdam I decided to visit him. I hope I'm not boring you?"

"Go on, go on."

"Patrick wanted to do a postdoc. I was tired of the real world, so I decided to do a Ph.D. Patrick suggested I do something related to Latin America. Since I love everything related to Latin America, me dije why not. Barcelona is full of South Americans, did you know? Madison was the only place that accepted us both. Si debo ser sincera, I would rather have gone to California. This is too close to home for comfort. I'm from Boston and the East Coast bores me."

"So you're here because you really want to do a Ph.D."

"Sí y no." Her accent was enchanting, a mix of street and sophistication. Her Spanish was mostly accented with English, but the *s* was definitely from Spain. "I didn't want to work after my master's. I was in Chiapas, wanted to do something humanitarian. Chiapas was an incredible experience. And then Spain . . ."

"From Chiapas to Barcelona."

"I really wanted to go to Bosnia. Don't look so shocked. You must think I'm pretty confused. A friend told me she could get me a job with Doctors Without Borders. I arrived in Madrid, went to Barcelona, loved it and stayed. I worked at a gallery until I got tired of it."

I realized she wasn't telling me the whole story. I saw her as a free spirit who could as easily be studying in Madison as living in some town in El Salvador or some little village on the Costa Azul. She was here because the trip must continue and some other city must come after San Cristobal de las Casas, Barcelona, and Amsterdam. But Madison would soon bore her — who wouldn't it bore? — and it wouldn't surprise me if she left again after a few months. That is, of course, if she wasn't very much in love, in which case maybe she'd end up subordinating her wandering spirit for the stability of the relationship . . . I should've given up on the pop psychology. After all, I wasn't a novelist or filmmaker, one of those who have to have an explanation for every human act or the narration suffers and so do the readers.

We arrived. She opened the door, put one foot outside. She was about to say goodbye, but stopped and looked at me without saying a word, as if deciding whether or not to tell me something I should probably know. I told myself I should look at her as I had looked at all female students since my second year at Berkeley, when I was a teaching assistant and one carefree affair ended in a scandal that almost cost me my job.

"We were crazy to come," she said, at last. "We should have waited at least a year. But when we applied, it wasn't in our plans. Did you know we're getting married in December? December twenty-first."

"Congratulations," I said. "Excellent news. Where?"

"Here, there, what does it matter? In Boston."

"You must be very happy."

"It's not good to be happy," she said, and then, slowly, as if she had rehearsed her reply, "Happiness is a very simple sentiment."

She left without giving me a chance to respond. I sat there for about five minutes with the motor running, my eyes fixed on Ashley's porch with all its hanging plants, thinking about her final comment.

3

EXT TO his bedroom, my uncle had a large study smelling
of dark cigarettes and old papers. A G4 was on the mahog-
any desk. The furniture and carpet were covered in atlases,
dictionaries, and world almanacs. There was a black-and-white
TV, a VCR, and a bookshelf with the books he'd read most recently
(*Vineland,* some by Perec and Schnitzler, one by Brian Winston
on the history of media). This was where he set his crosswords.
Wearing a robe and slippers, a glass of Chivas in his hand whatever
the time of day (now and then a cocktail made with *tumbo* or pas-
sion-fruit juice), he sat with the G4 to his right — Louise Brooks
and other silent movie stars parading by on the screensaver —
placed a white sheet of paper on the desk, made a grid twenty-one
by twenty-one, and began his work. At times he would put a jazz
CD on the stereo — Miles Davis was his favorite, or contemporary
artists like Joshua Redman — or put a movie in and work with the
television on. His left hand moved across the page quickly and
forcefully, constantly breaking the tip of his pencils.

Sometimes he worked in the study and other times in a rusty
container (the kind used on cargo ships) that he had put in the patio and that functioned as a research lab. Occasionally he even
slept there. Between his bedroom and the bathroom there was also
a small living room, where he kept his main library collection,
the shelves crammed with books. He slept four hours a night at
most and would get up very early, make coffee in a contraption

he said he'd invented — he shouldn't have admitted that, because the coffee was weak, terrible — and pace the living room and hallways with heavy sighs. His footsteps echoed in my room and kept me company on the increasingly frequent nights when I couldn't sleep. He was like a tortured soul, a ghost in a Gothic mansion, unable to find peace and close his eyes. His mind never ceased working. His thoughts crowded in on one another, falling between the coordinates of space and time only to expand, ramify, and intertwine with everything in their path.

In only five years, the popularity of this hobby had motivated *El Posmo* editors not to rely exclusively on those that the famous Benjamín Laredo sent from Piedras Blancas. It had been an editor friend who knew of my uncle's verbal skills and extensive knowledge who had suggested he set crosswords. My uncle laughed at first, then grew to like the idea. He had always loved solving them, so why not write them? He studied Laredo's crosswords and discovered that the most important thing was to have an immediately recognizable style. If Laredo's style was to use photos for some clues and a phrase that snaked the length and breadth of the crossword, then my uncle would hide a secret message scattered through several definitions. (For example, if one definition read City in France, and another required One of the colors of the rainbow, and another Spanish city bombarded in the Civil War, the secret message was Picasso, for his *Las señoritas de Avignon,* the blue period, and *Guernica.*) His love of hidden messages was a family trait.

He scorned the genre at first, then came to think of it as a great art, one that could unite intellectual and popular culture like no other. He respected Laredo but also thought he was somewhat elitist and relied too much on the periodic table and other easy tricks. My uncle's crosswords — baptized Cryptograms — were more complex and sophisticated than Laredo's and were causing a stir among an increasingly large number of followers. In that small corner of the Friday paper one was showered with the greatest accomplishments and personages from the twentieth century, information with which to surprise your friends at the *parrillada* on Saturday. First radio station in the U.S.? Poet who wrote

"The Keeper of Sheep"? Invented ENIAC? Who put the @ in e-mails? Struggled against Enigma in World War II? Female miner who started the strike of 1977? Crosswords were a great democratizer: wars and politicians and actors were mercilessly trivialized; inventors, athletes, and actresses were placed on equal footing in the grid. A century had just ended, and the most noteworthy and unusual facts from it and other centuries began to amass in an immense place of mourning and amnesia. It was up to crossword setters to remind us of the many battles where blood was once shed, the many lives that once shone, the many people now dead and decaying. It was both funny and sad; perhaps it was sadly funny.

From the living room, surrounded by dismantled telephones and radios that were incapable of emitting a sound or capturing any frequency, I could hear him laugh — a sign that the words were obeying his orders and linking in an embrace from which they would never escape. When the laughter stopped and he turned off the radio or TV, it was time to worry because those were signs that the crossword refused to come together. He was then liable to sweep books to the floor and shatter his glass or any other object within reach. But that didn't happen very often. He generally knew how to overcome the obstacles, escape the straitjacket he himself strove to create with his definitions. **True inventor of the radio (8 letters)? Country where Howard Hughes went into exile? Original Comandante Cero? Guerrilla leader from the sixties in Brazil? Inventor of the crossword?**

At night I went out with Carolina or sometimes with friends (Carlos and Federico, the only friends I really had left). During the day I fired off missives to the North ("I'm sorry, Bolivia will never get out of the coca circuit!") and reread parts of *Berkeley*. Dad had filled the text with hidden meanings that came to light only — if at all — after multiple readings. The Cuervos Anacoretas were enigma-producing machines, the treasures of Captain Kidd. Lately, for example, I had remembered Ashley's first comment when she finished the book ("Your dad was crazy about salamanders"), which didn't mean much to me at the time. I now searched and found seven references to salamanders. In one, the salamander was called Milvia; in another it "walked through the garden without haste"; in yet another he described it as a "Euclidean" frog. Milvia, Haste, Euclid: the salamander was a symbol that connected seven streets in the city of Berkeley. Why those streets? And why the salamander? I pictured myself walking down Milvia collecting salamanders, while from a house I could hear the voice of Ginsberg talking about some supermarket in California or Kerouac intoning his song to the crazies.

I tried to concentrate and continue unearthing symbols, but I couldn't: Ashley and Uncle David slipped into my thoughts and distracted me. I checked my e-mail every so often, hoping to find a few lines from Ashley, knowing I didn't deserve them (but still surprised by her silence). There were only administrative messages from the Institute, jokes from friends, notes from Yasemin keeping me up-to-date on the rumors — she hadn't seen Ashley since I left — and requests from *Latin American Affairs:* What would happen in Brazil if the stock market continued to fall? Mexico, up or down in the *nuevo sexenio*? Would FARC manage to take more municipalities in Colombia? What would be the result of Chávez's popularity? What would investors say to the study by Transparency International listing Bolivia as one of the most corrupt countries in the world?

I didn't want to write Ashley first; I would only open myself up to insult. Not that I didn't deserve it.

I couldn't stop thinking about my uncle either. I wondered, above all, about his strange relationship with Dad. During our first lunch together, I told him about my "project" with all the seriousness I could muster (deep down I knew that writing an academic book, with its research and footnotes, was far removed from my ability and my desires). I even asked him for help, to see if he could put me in touch with Dad's classmates or friends from his days as a political activist.

He listened without saying a word, then said, "When you were young you looked a lot like your mother. The expression in your eyes most of all. Now you look more like Pedro. Your smile, your gaze . . ."

"People still say I look more like Mom."

"They don't know what they're saying. Nobody knew Pedro like I did. Come, I want to show you something."

He stood up, and I could smell the alcohol on his breath. We went out into the back patio with its burnt grass and lemon tree, in sharp contrast to the pristine carnations at the front of the house. The container was in one corner. He took a key out of the pocket of his robe, opened the door, and asked me to wait. I looked in through the half-open door. The floor was covered in broken radios, keyless typewriters, and phones with their insides hanging out. The lemon tree was sharply fragrant.

"Come in, come in," he shouted.

I picked my way through the appliances. There were drawers filled with tools, nails, and wires. He explained his ambitious inventions: a machine that used a photo to sculpt the bust of an individual in a block of limestone; a camera that could simultaneously take fifty photos from fifty different angles, thanks to multiple mirrors. I kept looking at the machine that sculpted busts from a photo.

"It's not finished," he confirmed. "In my mind it is, and that's enough for me. Finishing it would take months and in the meantime a new idea comes to me, then another . . ."

"You've never thought of approaching an industrialist and offering him your ideas?"

"Here? You're crazy. They wouldn't be interested. These aren't economically viable projects."

It seemed to me he was afraid to finish his machines, afraid some industrialist would force him to continue developing the invention. I wondered whether his real fear was of failure.

"But that's not what I wanted to show you."

A folding screen divided the room in two. On the other side I came upon a framed photo of Dad on the wall, a cigarette between his lips and the furrowed-brow pose of an intellectual/politician worried about the fate of his country. There were several editions of *Berkeley* on a bookshelf to the right, some of them knockoffs. A rickety table was covered with notebooks.

"You scared me with your project related to Pedro," he said. "Luckily, mine is different."

He picked up a notebook, opened it at random, and put it in my hands.

"A dictionary for understanding *Berkeley*. Page by page, an explanation of all the symbols in the novel, all the definitions and places mentioned, et cetera. For example, on page forty-two, when the narrator arrives at the Villa de Ash and is dazzled by 'a landscape of a factory chimney built in 1910,' who knows that this is an allusion to Kandinsky? Because in 1910 Kandinsky painted *Landscape with Factory Chimney*."

I flipped through the folder, barely able to read the minuscule, tense script that crowded in on itself, as if hiding, waiting for eyes sharp enough to decipher it. *Berkeley* was a cult novel, one of those impenetrable texts that writers from the twentieth century had insisted on writing, a tribute to their extensive knowledge, to the overwhelming quantity of information the years had accumulated and that would soon explode in all directions thanks to new technologies that could process and store it. The members of this cult were few, but they were obsessively devoted, competing to show who was the most faithful follower. With his dictionary, my uncle put himself at the head of the pack. I remembered a comment Borges had made about a book that explained *Finnegans Wake*, to the effect that it was unfortunately necessary if one wanted to understand Joyce's work. My uncle's book was also "unfortunately necessary"; even though, in my case, my absolute ignorance of more than half of the allusions and symbols that Dad played with had never diminished my pleasure in reading it (but there would be greater pleasure in cracking the code, and for that I needed a book like my uncle's).

Of course, the dictionary was only a start. More to my liking were the coded messages a dictionary couldn't pin down, the layers hidden behind other layers, the magic word that would suddenly reveal the harmony of the text, of the universe itself. That was my first passion, one that reminded me of my childhood, when I would invent and decode secret messages with friends. That was my greatest connection with Dad, who wrote the following phrase, repeated three times using the first letters of each chapter: "The best way to hide a book is in the library." *Berkeley* was, after all, a long letter from Dad to me. By discovering the message he had hidden in the words of the book, I would discover him — or at least that was what I thought (I chose to forget other things I had discovered about him).

"There's still a lot left to do," he said, masking his pride. "I've only just finished the first thirty pages. I hope to put it on the Internet. Create a site dedicated to the novel, containing all the details there ever were or will be."

"In any case," I said, running my hand along the spines of the different editions on the shelf, most of them paperbacks, "just wanting to do it is admirable. I didn't know you liked the book that much."

I leafed through the blurred, photocopied pages of a knockoff, one aimed at university students without a cent in their pockets. Dad was no longer here, but something of him remained — right now in a book, but soon, surely, in multimedia (an American Express banner across the top of the page, a link to Amazon on the left). It was admirable. I would die and no one would remember my passionate affairs, the wonder in my voice when I taught my classes, my skill at acrostics and anagrams, the expression of my mouth to show interest or disdain, my crude attempts at not leaving my childhood behind, my transgressions. Feeling as if the book were burning into my hands, I set it on the table.

"They were always inventing rivalries between Pedro and me," he said after a long pause. "The truth is, there wasn't, isn't, never will be anyone who admires or respects him more than I do."

Later, in the living room, I thought about two brothers of above-average intelligence. The younger of the two was extremely charismatic and got all the attention; the other bit his tongue and swore that, sooner or later, his time would come. Both tried to escape their literary fate — one through politics and the other through inventions — but weren't entirely able to. The first wound up writing a great novel and the second became a notable crossword setter (a kind of literary fate after all). There was a lot of talk about rivalry at one time. It was even rumored that my uncle's wife was in love with Dad, that my uncle had gotten involved in politics not out of conviction, but to be closer to and watch over them. I didn't quite believe it, but I was keen to find out more about this complex fraternal relationship.

"You know who you should talk to?" Uncle David said, appearing in the doorway, startling me with his booming voice. "Jaime Villa. He was in the same class as your dad, his best friend at La Salle. They were a year behind me. Inseparable. He's a pedantic, intolerable sort but doesn't deserve what's happening to him. If you want my opinion, we have to learn to air our dirty laundry at home. Why send him to the gringos . . . ?"

Villa? Once his best friend? Villa, whose entry into drug trafficking was thanks to the same dictatorship that murdered my dad? The author of *Berkeley* never ceased to amaze me.

I walk along the sunny streets of Río Fugitivo listening to They Might Be Giants through the headphones of my Nomad. The music in my ears intensifies my experience of these narrow streets; the sharp noise of old bus horns and street vendors' shouts becomes only a murmur. This intimacy is revolutionary: my universe in the midst of the daily bustle, my nervous system moving through the urban landscape to its own soundtrack. I am insulated by my MP3 player without having to stay in my room with the door closed. Like when I would drive to visit Jean in New York over the long winter, with the windows of the car rolled up, the crepuscular landscape all around, and Queen on at full volume inside the bubble.

At one time I owned these streets. I didn't need to know them all to know they were mine. From my ever changing neighborhoods — the houses that Mom lived in, my uncle's house — I dominated the diverse cities that were taking shape at that time: the poor area in the south full of migrant campesinos, squeezed in between the train station, the weekend marketplace, and the hills; the residential neighborhoods in the north, trees shading their placid streets; the old quarter, hemmed in by new buildings that began to usurp its quiet splendor of republican façades, colonial churches, and huge houses with interior courtyards; and the turbulent, snaking Fugitivo River, with its ever lower water level, garbage accumulating on its shores, and beggars under its many bridges.

A pregnant woman changes dollars for me in a small plaza with a statue of Bob Dylan (a guitar in his hands and a crack in his forehead, behind him the hill that hides the Ciudadela). The frenzied contrast ends at Avenida de las Acacias, teeming with jacarandas and well-tended gardens. More and more buildings grow roots downtown, their walls filled with advertisements. There are shiny new malls but few customers. The number of parks with peaceful fountains multiplies (as does the number of drug-addicted children who sleep there at night). The mayor does everything within his power to beautify the exterior of the city. It is, it seems, the only thing he worries about. Meanwhile, there are more peddlers on every block — offering cartfuls of knockoff brand-name clothing, razor blades, and videos — and entire campesino families from Potosí beg on corners and sleep in church doorways. Day after day we dream up new ways to highlight both our progress and our misery, until all it takes is a single street to display our contrasts: people crowd in front of jewelry store windows but shop at peddlers' carts.

I walk through the crowds thinking about Ashley, who downloaded these They Might Be Giants songs accessible only in MP3 format. At a video arcade the young and the not-so-young stare intently at their screens. A drunk is passed out in one corner of the main plaza. The newspaper vendor reads out the bloody tabloid headlines. A woman is robbed in plain sight and chases the thief in her uncomfortable high heels. A young man in a black suit jacket has a purple cell phone stuck to his right ear. The walls are covered with posters of Montenegro and the mayor in an effusive embrace. The graffiti on the posters speaks of the oppressed nation that will rise up and devour the white nation. Someone offers to sell me stolen Suzuki headlights. Near the cathedral, they're selling images blessed by the teenager who writes books dictated to her by God in Latin. The cacophony of taxis and buses is everywhere.

Here, in this plaza full of retirees on benches and pigeons surrounding the shoe shiners, a couple of people were killed in April when an army captain fired on a group of defenseless demonstrators. He (Robinson is his name) wasn't even forced into early retirement. Ten people were killed in Cochabamba, a few more in La Paz. Every now and then the country wakes up; every now and then a group says that's enough, that such poverty, such injustice, such corruption can't go on. The government quickly looks for answers, but the underlying problems are never solved; they're only postponed for a future occasion when the people's patience again runs out (the government trusts there will always be a bit more patience and resignation). There will be other protests, other demonstrations, other deaths. The dizzying, chaotic wheel on which the country turns doesn't stop, cannot be stopped, will never stop.

I approach a crowd of people outside the door to *El Posmo*'s main office, where the majority are holding their half-finished Cryptogram from the newspaper. Information is being bought and sold: names of Argentine torturers are exchanged for those of British spies. There's a blind man whose hat fills with coins, thanks to his prodigious knowledge. Questions come and answers go. The finished crosswords are deposited in a large letterbox at the entrance. There'll be a raffle among those who've discovered the secret message. It's a familiar scene — as a child I used to meet near the plaza to trade soccer cards and foreign bills — and yet it's a very strange scene. It makes me feel very proud of my uncle.

This isn't my city anymore. I'm a stranger, a foreigner here. It escaped my grasp and left me behind, moved on without me toward its splendorous and unfortunate future. I never completely gave up my plans to return here definitively one day, but I did manage to find excuses to postpone my return. Like a mirage that continually moves away on the horizon, Río Fugitivo comes within reach but then always drifts away. I push the city away, afraid as I am to return to it. Or maybe the city I want to return to no longer exists — I left it behind the day I first went away.

Luckily I can still escape to Río Fugitivo when the North overwhelms me or, as in this case, when I need to catch my breath after a period of loss. This city isn't mine anymore, and wearing the headphones of my Nomad I feel protected. Still, there's an unmistakable smell in the air — a mixture of food (roasting *pollo al spiedo, chola* sandwiches) and carbon monoxide from the ancient buses — and a particular shade of blue in the sky. I recognize these as being part of what was mine, of what, imperfect and all, might still be my real home. I want to give myself over to them, merge completely with them. But that lasts only a few minutes, and I quickly emerge unsatisfied from my utopian dream of fulfillment.

Six blocks from the cathedral, in a small, unkempt plaza, is a statue of Dad. Even though I hadn't headed in that direction, my predictable steps led me there. I walk around it, shoo the pigeons away, turn off the Nomad. Dad is standing on a pedestal, looking steadfastly toward the future; someone has left roses at his feet. He could easily be mistaken for a patrician founder of states. The stone doesn't shine the way it did more than fifteen years ago, when a well-intentioned president inaugurated the statue in homage to one of the best-known heroes in the long struggle to regain democracy. I look at Dad and look at him again. I wish the stone could talk, that it could tell me what I yearn to hear.

Silence. The pigeons soon forget their fear and return to reclaim their lost territory.

I turn on the Nomad. Ashley liked to make love with They Might Be Giants on at full volume in the room.

Carolina came to pick me up at ten P.M. Black leather pants and jacket, prominent cheekbones, and the ring over her right eyebrow lent an air of danger that hid an absurdly romantic, naïve, and vulnerable woman. Though she wasn't beautiful, she did stir me. I was going to tell her so but decided to keep quiet. I asked where we were going.

"For a spin and then to El Marqués, a brand-new club. They say it's like the everything-goes gay *antros* in Miami and San Francisco. We'll meet up with Fede and Carlos there. There's also a surprise for you. Hey, what the hell are you doing wearing blue contact lenses?"

"I've always wanted them," I said, blushing. "I realize I didn't buy them because of what people would say. To hell with it, who really cares?"

"It's obvious you don't live here anymore. Half the city thinks I'm a drug addict because of my eyebrow ring."

"And you're not?" I got on the bike.

"Funny."

"No need to lose your sense of humor. Don't worry, I only wear them now and then."

"Blue contact lenses, enough cologne to drown in . . . You're more of a flirt than all my girlfriends put together."

"This is Envy. Perfect for nighttime."

It had happened as quietly, as unobtrusively, as on previous vacations: in just two weeks Carolina had meddled with my life in such a way that she became indispensable. When I mentioned that I wanted to lose a few pounds, not only did she sign me up at a gym, but she also offered to go with me (it was there I discovered that looks did indeed deceive, that her thighs had gotten heavier). She invited me for dinner at her apartment, rented videos so we could watch them together — she knew my antiquarian weakness for old black-and-white movies — and came to pick me up the moment I mentioned I wanted to go to the municipal library to look up some detail or other for my book. I didn't know whether she just naturally adapted to my way of life or whether she wanted to please me in every way out of some ulterior motive. Sometimes, in those rare moments when I flashed back to the carefree air of previous vacations, I was surprised to realize that I was still single and railed at the maturity that was taking over despite my best efforts. I thought (bothered, cynical, spoiled) that Carolina's indiscriminate presence would scare away any suggestive woman with good (or bad) intentions. Maybe that was a good thing; the last thing I needed was another emotional complication. I thought I had solved my problems by taking a semester off to write the book, when really I was escaping from Madison, and all I had done, I slowly realized, was bring my problems with me.

El Marqués was one big, dark room without tables and no air conditioning. The music was deafening. All the waiters and bartenders were blatantly gay males wearing T-shirts with cut-off sleeves. The walls were papered with the front pages of *El Posmo* and *Veintiuno* — alarmist headlines, the occasional Cryptogram (Flew over the North Pole in the blimp "Norge"? For which movie did Joanne Woodward win an Oscar? Last name of the guerrilla Tania?), and one of those digitally altered photos of celebrities that were popular a while ago. At the back was a stage. There was barely room to walk, and it took us a while to find Carlos and Federico. It was one of those clubs people go to for some strange feedback effect, not because they like it but because it's in fashion. I had been to many similar clubs in Río Fugitivo and San Francisco (when I lived in Berkeley), but never in Madison. I was a professor there and had to keep my distance, couldn't meet my students in those kinds of places (I could, however, meet them in cafés or cheap motel rooms). Maybe clubs hadn't changed and the music had always been deafening, the smell of cigarettes and sweat oppressive, the room impossible to walk through; maybe I was the one who had changed.

"The happy couple," Federico said sarcastically when he saw us. He was drinking a Cuba Libre and had his Startac to his ear. I ordered an Old Parr and a San Mateo for Carolina.

"Yeah, hurry up, che," said Carlos, an Old Parr in his hand. "You're way too happy together, you better get married. You came dressed to kill, Caro. And those eyes? Holy shit!"

"What's happening on *The Sopranos*?" said Federico. "Oh, I forgot. You're hopeless when it comes to pop culture. You must be an academic. Probably haven't even seen the latest Will Smith movie."

Federico was one of the few single friends I had left. Tall, dark, he was a co-pilot with LAB who, despite that, or maybe because of it, indulged in drugs and alcohol. He complained about the Brazilians who had taken over the airline, saying they were cheap with parts — "Any day now there's gonna be an accident, che" — and was irritated that they controlled his smuggling — "Before, they let us bring anything, che." Carlos, short and blond, was married and had two kids but acted as if he were the most unattached man in the city — when he went out on weekends, it wasn't with his wife. He was also very good at lying about how well he was doing in business, and making us believe him.

"I have my crossword in the car," Federico said. "Maybe you can help me. Tell your uncle not to fuck with us so much. *French philosopher of feminist writing?*"

"He must have his book of answers in some trunk," said Carlos. "If you find and photocopy it, you'll make good coin. You can win two hundred bucks a week uncovering the secret message."

"Nobody forces you to do them," I said. "Move over to Laredo if you can't handle my uncle."

"Easy, che. Just kidding. I'm happy just doing the crossword, the message is another story. You make me nervous with those blue eyes. Let's go to the bathroom and I'll take them out for you, if you like. While we're there I've got some coke."

I looked at them uncertainly. Yasemin and Joaquín should have been there with me; they were more like my current world. I pretended to listen, my smile intent, but in reality I was looking at the eighteen- and nineteen-year-old bodies that surrounded me, that walked unworriedly through the darkness, sheathed in light dresses or wearing jeans about to burst, sometimes moving to the rhythm of the music. The shape of their faces was still undefined, their makeup excessive, desire in their eyes. They were eighteen- and nineteen-year-old bodies that I had increasingly less right to. No matter how I denied it, I was moving further away from them — or maybe they were moving further away from me. The day would soon come when I would be breaking the law by searching them out. I'd be one of those aberrations judged guilty by their peers, someone who has to go about in darkness and in secret, behind everyone's back — the way most things are done in our society, since there's very little that people allow and applaud.

Carolina had a look of controlled anger about her; maybe she'd noticed my wandering gaze. I put my arm around her and took her to dance. The DJ went easy on us with an interlude of disco music. The girls had sparkles on their faces and the guys had earrings and short, streaked hair. I thought about the Argentine soccer player who started that hairstyle and once missed three penalty shots in a single game. Out of the corner of my eye, I looked at myself in the mirrors to see whether I could compete with them, with so much youth. I could. Sure I could.

"So what's the surprise?"

"Have you heard of Berkeley?"

We had to shout.

"The book? The city?"

"The hottest Bolivian rock band right now is called Berkeley. Don't laugh. You know all about politics, but you don't know anything that really matters. In homage to your dad, I guess. They're playing here tonight."

"No way. What do they play? Protest songs?"

"Not at all. Their videos are pseudo-political, I don't know if you've seen the latest one or not. But their songs are one hundred percent romantic, like Luis Miguel on acid. Sometimes they use traditional instruments, the way Octavia does."

"I haven't seen their video."

"It's a surrealist version of what happened on Unzueta Street. Homage to Buñuel and everything."

I was intrigued, thinking about the proliferation of that name which meant so much to me. Thanks to Dad, there was now a Berkeley Café in the Bohemia nightlife district, a Berkeley bookstore by the state university, and a rock band called Berkeley. I went to study in Berkeley years ago, motivated by the desire to find some key to understanding Dad (I wound up more confused and understanding him even less, but at least I had found myself, or that's what I thought, or that's what I thought I thought). Maybe if there'd been such a proliferation of that name earlier I wouldn't have had to go to Berkeley.

I pictured myself walking through Sather Gate on my first day of classes, coming back from Dwinelle and on my way to Sproul Hall, two stone Chinese dragons flanking the door. The smell of marijuana was overwhelming along the esplanade: fifteen students in a smoke-in, preaching the virtues of grass in front of three bike cops in shorts. A white-haired man was standing on an upturned bucket, Bible in hand, announcing the coming of Christ. There were tables of Chicano, bisexual, Republican, anarchist, and communist students. Birkenstocks, tie-dyes, disheveled women with

46

hairy legs, tattoos and rings perforating bellybuttons and tongues. I would never be like them, but I applauded their awkward search for freedom (losing themselves in the search). I signed a petition to lift the embargo from Cuba and felt happy. Far off, from the stairs to Zellerbach Hall, you could hear the rhythmic beat of drums.

"I really want tonight to last forever / I really wanna be with you."

"I love ELO," I yelled. Ashley listened to songs from *Discovery* all the time: "Confusion," "Don't Bring Me Down," "Shine a Little Love." Ashley listened to *music* all the time. That would allow me, she had said, to hold on to her memory when we broke up, if we broke up: I could go to a classical music concert and Bach would bring me back to her; I could turn the television on and every video on MTV would carry her with it; Claydermann's music in elevators; Shakira in Spanish or English in malls . . . It was ridiculous, pathetic.

"I can't hear you."

I brought my mouth to Carolina's right ear and said it again. She nodded. I imagined Ashley wearing a turban, like the guy on the cover of *Discovery,* looking at a neon red, yellow, and blue record, but instead of "ELO" in the center it read "P&A."

The song ended, and we went back to where Carlos and Fede were standing. They teased me so relentlessly about my contacts that I decided to take them out. I went to the bathroom with Federico, took them out, and put them in their case while he snorted coke. Then I put on my metal-framed glasses and hated the face that stared back at me from the mirror.

"Want some?"

I didn't, but said I did. No point in offending your friends.

"You're gonna get some action tonight, aren't you?" he said. "Wanna take some with you, blow her mind?"

"Nothing's going to happen."

"Fuck off, she looks like she can hardly wait."

I told him that a student had rocked my world and I wasn't interested in anyone else. I told him about Ashley and asked him to keep it a secret.

"A student, how delicious. Fresh, right out of the oven. Her panties still smelling of piss. But I guess screwing Caro wouldn't really be cheating."

"I don't want to find out. I'd rather not complicate my life."

"When did you turn so prissy? Hard to believe. The States is softening you up, che."

When we got back to the others, still thinking about what Fede had said, I casually asked Carolina if she could take me to meet Jaime Villa. I had to keep myself from noticing her leather pants.

"Sure. When do you want to go? I'll talk to Ricardo."

"The sooner the better. I want to ask him a few questions for my book." *For my book.* It was laughable.

"Academic. Who would've believed it?"

"Web designer. Who would've believed it?"

"Don't take it the wrong way. Another whiskey? It's just strange, when you think about it. I don't have friends who are professors."

"It was in my blood. In my genes. My interest in writing, I mean."

"Then you'd be better off writing a novel. It would be more entertaining."

"Doesn't interest me. For that . . . you don't need an education. Or maybe you do, but a less formal one. Don't you think what I do has merit?"

"Not the same. Artists reach more people. Who reads critics?"

"What I do is also an art," I said with conviction while she looked at me incredulously. "I'm an artist too."

That was when my mood changed. I kept looking at the young faces and bodies around me, hoping someone would approach me and say, "It's not too late for you." Meanwhile, some of the envy I once felt for Dad had resurfaced, the envy that had become unconditional admiration because he had deservedly achieved the recognition that was denied me (mine would be short-lived and matter to only a few). Love can grow out of intense hatred, but a love like that can never bury all the roots that gave rise to it. I had to face it, accept it that on that day at my uncle's, in the container, while he told me about his dictionary project and I was looking at the editions of *Berkeley*, I was very proud, but also felt a stabbing envy that was hard to admit. Maybe my uncle felt that way too; maybe I'd wind up identifying with him and understanding him better than I understood Dad.

The DJ finished at two A.M. and Berkeley came on. There were four of them, their style somewhere between hard rock and grunge, suggesting their familiarity with music from the North and their desire to appropriate styles at will, taking meanings out of context. What was that mop of hair à la Poison doing with those ripped jeans à la Nirvana? Even the guitarist's *chullo* was from a Stone Temple Pilots video and not one of our campesino hats. Worthy of both applause and disdain.

The women screamed and the men clapped. The smell of marijuana filled the place. Everyone crowded together; it was hard to breathe. I ignored a big-breasted girl who offered me Ecstasy at twenty dollars a pill (the recession hadn't hit El Marqués). Berkeley started out with Marilyn Manson and Third Eye Blind covers — pretty good, but the drums sounded like a glorified tin can. The singer had long black hair and a stage presence that made women scream his name. He was handsome in a conventional way: full lips and a Roman nose.

"Losers," said Carlos, with typical male envy. "They think they're God's gift, but they're barely good enough for a backwater like Markacollo. Maybe they think someone's gonna discover them at this dive?"

"I like them," said Caro, contemplating the singer with delight. "They've got rhythm, style. What more do you want?"

"Originality," said Federico, his jaw trembling, his eyes red.

"You're just jealous."

"Right. I want to be a rock star. And they can fly my plane."

"The way LAB pilots fly," said Carlos, "I wouldn't be surprised if these guys *were* in the cockpit, Fede."

The originality came later. When they started to play their own songs, I was surprised to find that, except for us, everyone in El Marqués knew the simple, banal lyrics by heart. I felt removed, as if a cult had just gone into session in the catacombs, excluding me just like that.

"This is the song I was telling you about," Carolina said. "'Donde vayas te seguiré.'"

The words were not at all original, a bolero with a rock beat. "Donde vayas te seguiré / donde vayas te llevaré / eres mi religión privada / contigo el cielo no lo necesito / no, no, no." I was disappointed. It wasn't worth even trying to uncover a message about the Unzueta Street attack. I'd have to see the video.

I amused myself by watching a blonde with a dizzying neckline who, taking advantage of the dark, let a boy no older than sixteen fondle her. I kept watching them, wanting to change places with the boy.

I put my hands to my head. With a complete lack of subtlety, a migraine announced that it was on its way — a monster creeping along my cerebral cortex, waiting to attack.

"Doesn't look like you're having much fun," said Carolina, a touch sarcastically.

"Enough noise for one night," I protested, breathing deeply, letting the expanding waves of pain in my head subside. A new wave would come again soon.

"If she wants to go, you can stay with us," said Fede. "We'll drop you off later."

"No, it's OK. Caro will take me."

"What's with you?" Carlos asked. "Maybe you've got a gringa girlfriend and gone all soft? Jesus!"

"Pedro's such a gringo," said Fede. "Don't they close everything down before two and everyone has to go home? They have no idea how to party in that country!"

I smiled and said goodbye. As soon as I turned my back, I heard Federico murmur, "I'll tell you later." I looked at him and covertly ran my finger across my throat. It was no use; we were on different wavelengths. I shouldn't call either him or Carlos, I shouldn't go out with them again. That was the right thing to do. And yet I had to admit that I didn't want to lose them. Or maybe I didn't want to admit that I had already lost them. There are couples who go out for a long time and then suddenly realize that things were over years ago. It hurt me deep inside: Federico and

Carlos were my adolescence, and losing them was to lose another of the fragile bonds that still held me to Río Fugitivo.

I turned around to face them, then hugged them tightly.

"Just what we needed," said Carlos. "He's gone all sentimental on us."

"Or it's gone to his head," Fede finished. "Cheap drunk. American beer is like water."

On Carolina's Kawasaki, holding tightly to her, the pain like a drill in my temples and the pressure building behind my right eye, I imagined I was holding that gringa girlfriend who wasn't my girlfriend. And I felt such despair at the desire that had threatened to surface, desire I had wasted by allowing my weak flesh to get excited at the thought of those budding young women when, in the distance, in the Madison of oppressive gray skies, there was a real woman. Despair because Ashley lay sleepless in bed, next to a man she was indifferent to, trying to decide whether it was possible to love me after my cowardice, or whether it was better to hate me, or whether she should forget me once and for all. Despair because I was afraid to call her, and she hadn't called me, and right then there was nothing I would have liked more than to get home and hear the telephone ring, that goddamn bearer of misfortune and wonders.

"I'll pick you up at eight to go to the gym?"

"No. I'm tired. I want to sleep in."

"If you want to lose weight . . ."

"Missing one day isn't the end of the world."

"That's how it starts."

"I'll call you tomorrow about Villa."

I gave her a quick kiss on the cheek and ran to my room. I took an Imitrex and threw myself on the bed with my hands on my temples until there was a pause that I held on to with all my might.

My uncle was wrong. The phone could help communication, but insurmountable distance was not the best way for two people to find each other.

∎ ∎ ∎

My first few weeks passed during a time of political unrest that had the country holding its breath. Bolivia, up or down? Down. The symptoms of recession had worsened, and bread and gas prices rose. Accusations of corruption tainted several public officials — facing the deplorable state of finances, politicians chose to take their share before it was too late. On TV, a campesino leader from Achacachi and another from the coca plantations of Chapare, both Aymaras, called upon their armies to block highways and became leaders of the general malcontent. The leader from Achacachi, less settled than the other on a specific problem, espoused an aggressive argument about the "two Bolivias" and the need for the white, superficial Bolivia to give way to the more profound Bolivia. There were huge civic protests in Santa Cruz and La Paz, strikes everywhere, marches by workers from different unions. Effigies of Uncle Sam were set on fire (they blamed the U.S. for meddling in internal politics). Insults were hurled at neighboring Chile and Brazil for having taken advantage of the privatization fever and for now controlling the country's main strategic companies. Effigies of Montenegro were burnt at the stake. The authoritarian head of state, who had managed to disguise his authoritarianism as benevolent paternalism during the first few years of his term, wavered between continuing with the charade and controlling the unrest by calling in the police and the military (or perhaps Montenegro had never wavered, it was just that now he had meticulous image consultants and an efficient marketing team).

In Río Fugitivo, teachers and coca plantation owners mobilized by blocking avenues and roads. One morning it happened in our neighborhood. We lived to the north, near the soccer stadium where the River Boys lost every Sunday and at the foot of La Atalaya, the nouveau riche district on the hill above the city. I spoke with a few furious neighbors, remembering that when I was a kid there weren't many houses in the area, the streets were unpaved, and Uncle David's house, surrounded by willow and eucalyptus trees, had been on the outskirts of Río Fugitivo. The city had grown, it had reached his door, bringing businesses and labor movements to disturb his peace and isolation.

"Protest, but somewhere else," said a wrinkled, white-haired woman, trying to move the stones that impeded access to the block. "They're a nuisance here."

"That's why they do it, Señora," I said. "Do you want a protest that doesn't bother anyone?"

"Who do you think you are?" she protested, irritated. "Do you agree with these dirty Indians?"

"It's not about agreeing or disagreeing. Just put yourself in their place. You'd do the same if you were one of them."

"Don't insult me, young man. And it's easy for you to put yourself in their place. So well dressed, you're just looking in from the outside."

I shut up. I wouldn't get anywhere arguing with her.

One Friday around noon, when I was at the municipal library reading newspapers from the seventies — actually, I was doing the Cryptogram — an explosion could be heard in the distance. Curious, people went to the windows or ran outside. The uproar had caught me at Russian, true inventor of the television in 1908. I had the third and fourth letters: *si*. I got up, went downstairs with the Cryptogram under my arm, and went out into the street. A policeman was directing traffic. There was a crowd of people three blocks away at the door to a blue building. Curiosity got the better of me and I headed over there, stopping at a police barricade half a block from the building. A red Jeep had been destroyed. TV cameras arrived, and a dark-haired reporter in a black blazer and tie began her live report, questioning passers-by in a shrill voice. I found out that a bomb had exploded outside a television station.

"Very, very strange," said the reporter with a telegenic smile that didn't match her worried tone. "Channel Veintiuno plays music videos and covers entertainment news. What motive could there be for putting a bomb here? What degree of social chaos have we reached? Luckily, we do not have to report any loss of life, only material damage — a Jeep and great deal of broken glass."

I left the area.

Uncle David told me later that he was sure the bomb had something to do with Villa. According to him, the catalyst for all these protests was the government's decision to extradite Villa. I wasn't so sure. Many groups were taking advantage of the reigning chaos to put their demands on the table: low wages that didn't rise with the continuous cost-of-living increase, massive layoffs, political instability, desperate poverty. It was a new millennium, but the problems the country was facing were almost the same as those it was born with a couple of centuries before.

The government had already approved extradition, but they still hadn't put Villa on a plane to Miami for fear of a new outbreak of protests. The drug trafficker languished in his mansion on the outskirts of the city under house arrest. I hoped to meet him soon; Carolina had promised me.

The subject fascinated my uncle, and he had incorporated data from Villa's legendary past into his crosswords. We would sometimes go for a walk in the neighborhood, and with his dark cigarettes smelling of chocolate and his hands gesticulating, he would repeat his argument: we needed to be more nationalistic, say no to the gringos once in a while.

"Now the gringos want us to eradicate coca plantations and the government does so without protest, not a single worthy argument about cultural identity. Someday they're going to tell us to change the name of the country and we will. The thing is, Montenegro has a guilty conscience. He's so worried he'll be remembered as a dictator that he does the most incredible things to show how fair he is. It's not going to do him a lot of good. We all know it's just a front and that deep down . . ."

His voice was mellow. He'd been drinking since breakfast. I wondered whether the smell of chocolate from his cigarettes might be to hide the smell of alcohol on his breath.

"You have to look at things on a case-by-case basis," I dared to say. "I'll always remember Montenegro as a dictator, but I think it's a good idea for them to take Villa. If he stays, he'll end up running his business from prison and a few judges and police will fill their pockets. Our legal system is one of the most corrupt."

My uncle looked at me. His corpulent figure and immovable eye were intimidating. He smiled.

"I like it when you contradict me. I saw your name in a Yankee magazine. 'According to Pedro Zabalaga, assistant professor of Latin American politics at the Institute . . .' Who would have imagined, Pedrito. Can't argue politics with you anymore."

"It's easier than it looks, Uncle David."

When we got home I asked him who the Russian inventor of television was.

"You're taking advantage of me. Boris Lvovitch Rosíng. During the cold war the Soviet Union was famous for having fabricated the story that almost all the great scientific advances in technology were made there first. That makes Rosíng suspicious. But his is one of the few that are undeniable, even though the British disagree."

My uncle was likable despite himself. He was a bear with an unsociable exterior that allowed only glimpses of a reticent tenderness. He asked me whether some definitions were too easy (Stephen Albert's profession, Trotsky's assassin) and excitedly brought to my room a new motor he was building for his lawnmower, one that still used too much electricity because it lacked resistors. He said he noticed I'd been serious, worried; it was his way of starting a conversation, of allowing me to unburden myself. And I told him that, yes, in truth, I was serious and worried. But I was the one who shut down: I didn't mention my problems with Ashley in the turbulent days before I left Madison or indicate that I wasn't very sure of how to face the book about Dad. When two weeks had passed and I told him it was time I left, lying that I was going to rent an apartment on the Avenida de las Acacias, he suggested I stay for another month. I happily agreed (I didn't want to go, I was starting to like his company). He opened up bit by bit. Sometimes he told me stories about Dad, or commented on his progress with the dictionary, or showed me the extensive site he had begun to design with Carolina (she came to the house the odd afternoon for him to approve her ideas — sometimes even when I wasn't there — and the ten-minute visit would lengthen into a couple of hours; they got along very well).

Sometimes he talked to me about his inventions. One day he surprised me by telling me about his elaborate project to invent a radio that could capture the voices of the dead. Voices, he said, that were floating someplace in the past, it was just a matter of finding out how to reach those frequencies.

"There's no reason for media to aim only at the present — that's limiting. The past and the future have to be thought of as well, they have to be reached."

He was talking about technological spiritualism, and I thought how ironic it was that progress had also come to the supernatural. I asked him to be more specific.

"Do you think the past disappears completely? That the future is formed out of nothing as soon as the present dissolves? Somewhere, in different coordinates, the past survives intact and the future is waiting for its entrance."

I looked at him and tried to hide my incredulity. No wonder he got along with Carolina, taken as she was with the idea of souls wandering restlessly in the cosmos. A song from the Police, "Spirits in the Material World," came to mind. But my uncle and Caro weren't alone; maybe I was the one who was alone. I was, after all, on a continent of witches, shamans, *callawayas, yatiris, macumberos,* and ordinary people who said they spoke effortlessly to spirits. And it wasn't only here in the South. I remembered having read an article in *People* that said seventy million Americans believe in the possibility of communication with the hereafter. I also recalled the parade of mediums on *Oprah, Montel, Jerry Springer* — whispers that came from the other side in distress or comfort, voices that took over the mind of a landholder in Mexico or a teenager in Kansas, ordering the first to be faithful to the girlfriend of his youth and the second to kill petty teachers and bullying classmates.

He said he'd show me the plans for the radio. He went to the container and came back with a notebook, then decided not to show me. He was a bit paranoid: he refused to reveal more details about his project for fear that I would steal his idea. Or maybe he thought I'd make fun of him. He could talk to me in confidence about the dictionary, but the radio was secret. Ah, "conceptual inventor." I ate my soup and looked at him half in amusement and half seriously: amused because a radio such as the one he'd described was better suited to a science-fiction movie, yet serious because he didn't normally joke. I had always believed that you measure people not by their success but by the nobility of their dreams. It was better to fail when trying to realize something of overwhelming proportions than to triumph at things that are at only half of our true capabilities. Carlos had once said it more precisely: "If you're going to be a shit, try to be a big shit."

In any event, I told myself that success or failure was secondary. The important thing was that more people than you might guess believe that the line dividing life and death can be crossed with a bit of effort, and I was open to that. I would've liked to have had that faith, not always hide behind easy skepticism, not be ironically opposed to everything.

4

A S A STUDENT, Ashley wavered between enthusiastic and apathetic. From one side of the classroom, her long hair falling in disarray around her face as if she'd just woken up, a lock covering one eye as if in intentional parody of and homage to Veronica Lake, she sometimes asked searching questions that required me to use the full extent of my mental agility — not so much for the exact answer as to find a quick way to postpone doubts, at least until the next class. At other times I could picture her counting the minutes until the end of class. Her weekly assignments were a strange mix of sophistication and a tendency to make Latin America exotic, to view it as a faded Macondo where people were innocent and should be saved from corrupt Western civilization. She reminded me of several friends from my days at Berkeley: Robin, who wanted to work at a Colombian newspaper sympathetic to FARC; Kate, who had turned the Andes into a fetish and who saw my nose — somewhat big and hawklike — and hairless chest as conclusive evidence that indigenous blood ran in my veins (something I knew nothing about, but which didn't mean much in any case: we all know the lengths our ancestors went to to whiten their past); and Denise, who had gone to Nicaragua with an international brigade to plant coffee. There were academics who behaved similarly: Chandra Wickley, my thesis advisor at Berkeley, who designed theories to explain the fundamental importance of campesinos in Latin American revolutions, and Helen, my colleague, who was leading efforts to close the School of the Americas — she would be going to a massive protest at Fort Benning at the end of the semester — and was an unwavering defender of Subcomandante Marcos. Maybe by studying the continent, by committing to it and idealizing it, they were making up for their fellow citizens' indifference. Maybe by loving a continent that was so different from their own they were able, in a way, to transcend our natural instinct to reject the other, that which is not like ours, those who are not like us. There was something both admirable and pathetic in their voluntary efforts to help us.

There was a degree of reserve to Ashley's interest, as if her time could've been better spent on more fascinating discoveries than my class, as if I hadn't quite convinced her of the value of my work. She was obsessed by the period's utopian leftist discourse — more specifically, the Sandinistas — while I studied the period in a much longer context, relating it to the messianic proposals for change and social revolution that had existed since colonial times. My approach was more pragmatic and materialistic: study the errors of the left in a volatile situation, emphasize the wrong moves, the false manifestos that weakened it even further in an already extremely difficult situation. Perhaps my disenchantment had something to do with the way Mom had brought me up, as if Dad had embodied the errors of the Left — the One left that had always been fragmented into Many. By voicing this criticism I was publicly distancing myself from Dad. Doing so protected me and allowed me to admire him in secret.

It was, after all, very difficult to guide talented people only a few years younger than me, people I felt bound to, above all, because of a shared perplexity at the world. How could I blame Ashley for her lack of conviction about my work when even I wasn't convinced? Those were the days when I had come to recognize my complete lack of interest in the academic world. Discontentment had quietly grown throughout the previous year, when I spent most of my time on journalistic articles. Now I had come back from vacation in Río Fugitivo — three months of forgetting my academic responsibilities — without the slightest desire to continue my research, not even any ideas for articles. I was teaching from memory, without much conviction.

But my other students didn't resist me as much as Ashley did. Maybe that was why I initially approached her. My insecurity has always led me to befriend everyone, seek approval. Growing up, I never belonged to just one crowd but moved from group to group, and while I was able to connect with each one equally, some looked down on my lack of commitment. It was hard for me to understand that I didn't have to be liked by everyone in order to be respected, and that someone's like or dislike of us is arbitrary, can't be explained by reason alone. That's why I was hurt by the indifference or negativity shown me by senior colleagues like Clavijero or Sha(do)w (even though they had convincing reasons to reject me, I begged more generosity from them: times change, and it wasn't all my fault). That was why Ashley's indifference weakened me as much as if it had been outright rejection. I needed to seduce her intellectually, make her see that, despite my inexperience and lack of interest, I knew more than she ever thought I could.

She would approach me in class and then later keep her distance. She never came to my office — I had a magnificent view of the campus and the pastoral town at its feet — and she didn't come with us to the usual café either, maybe because she was bored by Joaquín's and Yasemin's theoretical discussions. E-mail gave me the perfect excuse when one night after class Ashley sent me one that read: "i really liked your class today. borges deserves a whole seminar." Was this a joke? I had mentioned Borges in passing, used him as an example of how politics interferes with life, how his acceptance of a medal from Pinochet in 1976 cost him the Nobel. And what's more, given Ashley's inclinations, Borges was the antithesis of her idols.

I couldn't miss this opportunity. I replied with a long, formal e-mail, saying that I happened to be writing a paper on Borges and politics and that I'd like to know what she thought about the topic. I'd be at Madison CyberEspresso the next day, all afternoon, four blocks from my house, and if she was interested . . . She made fun of my e-mail in her reply, telling me that my writing was old-fashioned, that e-mail was not a substitute for letters but an entirely different form of communication where things like capital letters and punctuation didn't belong, something that I, more than anyone else, should know. She ended by asking me what the title of my paper was. "Borges and the Anarchist-Conservative Imagination," I invented, wondering whether I'd see her the next day.

She showed up wearing a light yellow jacket. Her hair pulled back into a ponytail made her look more serious. There was a Walkman at her waist. The Internet café was full of students sending e-mail or surfing the Web — pale faces, red eyes being constantly rubbed by fingers after too many hours in front of a monitor. A couple were kissing on the sofa next to a guy in a black coat who was playing chess on his laptop. It was the end of September; the sky was a light gray color with leaden clouds like scabs. The sun was gone; we'd see it only reluctantly until some effusive, surprising day in April. It was windy and leaves were littering the street; autumn had taken over without giving us much time to adjust to the change.

She sat down at my table next to the window and smiled, displaying the incongruent braces on her teeth. Why at her age? Was she younger than I thought? Had the aesthetic need to make her smile more symmetrical come over her at this late stage? I liked to think she was much younger. Not because I was interested in teenagers, though; it was a strictly literary fetish: *Lolita* was one of my favorite books. But that novel had already been written; it was impossible to beat it and therefore better to look for another subject.

"Sorry I'm late," she said, taking the Walkman off and leaving it on the table. "It's just that Patrick suspected something and made a million excuses to keep me from going out. If he has one fault, it's that he's so incredibly jealous he becomes unbearable at times."

"You should have told him the truth."

"That my prof me invitó a tomar un café? No way."

"I don't remember anything about coffee. It was a purely academic invitation."

"And Keanu Reeves is a good actor. This place doesn't really suit professors."

"I take my professor costume off as soon as I leave campus."

Inviting her to discuss Borges? A child could have seen through my excuse. I looked out the window: a police car chased after someone going all of forty-two miles per hour instead of the legal thirty-five miles per hour. Madison was so exciting.

I got up and went to the counter. I ordered a latte for her and a cappuccino and chocolate croissant for me.

"Strange that your boyfriend is so jealous," I said when I sat back down. "Aren't you getting married in less than three months?"

"He won't sleep soundly until we're married. No, that's a lie. It'll be worse then. He'll be suspicious all the time, and any man who comes near me will be seen as a possible rival."

"You must have done something to make him so insecure."

"Nothing, that's what's so bad. He says he knows exactly how men think and that they only ever think about one thing. Es cierto?"

"I should ask you that. Is it true?"

"Seems like it."

"So he's not paranoid, just very much in love and afraid of losing you."

"Thanks for the diagnosis. But if I'm in love too, why aren't I afraid?"

"Maybe he's given you a sense of security that you haven't given him."

"Maybe," she said in a tone as whispered as the rest of our conversation, full of winks and complicity, as if, without trying, we had naturally begun to communicate in such a way that everything we said was just the playful exterior to an ardent, furtive, underground meaning.

She told me that Patrick was doing his postdoc in the anthropology department, teaching a first-year course, and trying to turn his thesis on the phenomenon of transculturation in Chiapas into a book.

"Yo también tengo que convertir mi tesis en libro," I said. "I should talk to Patrick."

They met at a party in San Cristóbal. She was working as an assistant to one of her ex-professors and lived in the same rented house, where he organized a party for a few colleagues and students. Patrick came to the party and they met, both drunk on mescal. A few days later they were living together. He was a great sax player.

"He's interested in Latin America, he's a good musician, ¿qué más se puede pedir?"

"He also knows how to cook and give massages."

"Then he's perfect."

"You have a funny accent. As if you were pretty new to this country."

"I know. Pero some people think it's sexy."

That was one of the only times we ever talked about Patrick. Later we tried to pretend that he didn't exist, or that he existed in a parallel universe. It was as if we didn't want the two worlds to touch — maybe to maintain the purity of one and impurity of the other (which of the two was pure?).

But Patrick did exist, and the two worlds were inextricably linked. We just didn't want to acknowledge it. That afternoon, we began to imagine something so strongly that we knew it would soon burst in upon reality and alter it once and for all and forever.

I touched her Walkman. It was a shiny, little, gray metal rectangle.

"They're so small and elegant now," I said. "I remember when they first came out."

"It's not a Walkman," she answered. "It's an MP3 player. Nomad."

"Oh," I said, as if I knew. "I've read about them."

"Sixty-four MB RAM, it can even record. Además it doesn't skip like Walkmans do when you're at the gym."

"You're kind of surprising. It's as if one side of you contradicts the other."

"Technology is a fetish of mine. I Internet-trade while I listen to music on my Nomad and there's a poster of Marcos at my back. The only thing I know for sure is, acepta tus contradicciones. I have a lot of them and stopped trying to be consistent a long time ago. That'll come with time, I guess. Y si no, tough luck."

I listened to part of a David Bowie song on the Nomad. There was something sublime about the ongoing futile attempt to achieve greater clarity in sound and image: perfection backed away the closer one got to it, making the effort either infinite or absurd.

"Internet trading?"

"Patrick's grandmother left him some money. I invested part of it in tech stocks. I do it from home un par de horas al día. Really easy. You're looking at me as if I were from Mars. You're really behind the times." Her tone was ironic. "You'd better get with it."

She was right. I lived in a country where at least half the population owned stocks. A country that had made millionaires of a lot of young people in the few years that Internet company stock speculation fever had lasted. In reality, I lived in a country I had come to really care for but where a lot of things went on that didn't matter to me: ups and downs on the stock market, reality shows on TV, presidential elections.

"And when do you find the time to study?"

"I don't know. I have four classes and tons of reading to do. It's a matter of organization."

There was something about Ashley that didn't quite convince me. Despite her apparent interest in the Ph.D., she didn't have the intensity of a true student. Or maybe things had changed in a very short period of time and students had become more versatile than before, less prone to closeting themselves away in libraries or bookstores all the time. Generations now followed on the heels of one another with incredible speed.

"So, Berkeley," she said, noting my gray sweatshirt with the university logo. "How was student life?"

"I'd almost say they were the best years of my life. Not so much because of the program, although I was lucky enough to have a couple of brilliant professors and a thesis advisor who knew everything about Latin America — everything and more."

"Chandra Wickley."

"Aha. You already knew."

"I've read her name several times in your papers. It wasn't hard to figure out."

"You'll have to read her. Sometimes she exaggerates the argument a bit, pero es first-rate."

The political science department at Berkeley, on the second floor of Barrows Hall, was huge. There were about forty professors specializing in, among other things, international relations, political psychology, arms control, national security, mass media and politics, Reagan, and César Chávez. I liked Chandra Wickley's personality from the start; she was one of three Latin American specialists. She spoke Spanish with a heavy English accent, but at least she tried. She was blond, tired-looking, and anxious. Her innate shyness got the best of her in class, making her cover part of her face with her hands or play with her hair and look at the ceiling while she talked. She was a true academic, happy in the archives and uncomfortable when she had to face the public. She had been assigned as my advisor, and at our first meeting in her office — overflowing with books and manuscripts, plants, and a fish tank — she said she liked the essay that accompanied my application for admission. She commented, without knowing how close to the truth she really came, that my opinions of Pedro Reissig had the force of personal conviction.

"Now," she emphasized, "you have to transform those opinions into facts, into something that can be used to understand similar cases. That's why you're here: to give those opinions a scientific bent. Take the second word in 'political science' very seriously."

"She has a very influential book on the 'new authoritarianism' in Latin America," Ashley said, "about the military's influence on politics and society. Should I read it?"

"I like her more recent work better; it's in papers here and there. It's a project on revolutions, where she applies Theda Skocpol's methods to the region. What distinguishes the few successes from the failures? To look at this, she does a macro-causal analysis and distinguishes favorable from unfavorable conditions, then systematizes the results using Boolean algebra, which she believes is more appropriate than statistical analysis. Using this procedure, she attempts to determine the 'necessary and sufficient' conditions to produce revolutionary success or failure."

"Demasiados números. I don't imagine her colleagues respect her much."

"They respect her, but you're right, they do look down on her attempts to introduce algebra into political analysis."

"You don't?"

"Despite my quantitative skepticism, the truth is that she finally gave me a concrete method to understand what happened in Bolivia in the seventies."

I offered her my croissant; she declined. There was a pause. I continued:

"But let's get back to Berkeley. What's important is actually living there, being in an atmosphere that stimulates creativity. Walking down Telegraph Avenue any time of the day or night, going to a party full of students with eyes popping out from so much pot, looking at the bay from my room at the International House . . . Just living in a place that has so many legends helps. People look at you differently when you say you study at Berkeley."

I recalled a class when the door opened abruptly and a homeless man with a long beard came in and urinated next to the board, then left. The professor, a neurotic Argentine who put on European airs — like most Argentines, I know — barely forced an uncomfortable smile. We looked at one another with the arrogance and indifference of those who know that certain things happen only in their city. "Berkeley is unique." How many times had I heard that? Lo cierto es que it really *is*.

"You said almost."

"I also have memories of growing up in Río Fugitivo. In its own way, it's comparable to Berkeley."

"How lucky to have so many fantastic memories to choose from."

"They weren't all fantastic at the time, but they are in memory. And that's what counts."

Forgetting that I usually preferred to listen to others talk, I told her that Mom had tried to bring me up normally despite Dad's absence. She succeeded to a certain extent. As the years went by, however, the desire to come to know that person who was spoken about so reverentially grew stronger (Mom never, ever talked about him, but people would come up and ask me about him). In my last year of school I discovered *Berkeley* and read it, exalted, one Saturday morning, without getting out of bed. It was then I realized that maybe the answer to the enigma that was Dad was in Berkeley, the university he had gone to and the central symbol of his novel. I should go there, as a sort of pilgrimage to discover my roots. When I finished my law degree at the state university, a friend told me there were full scholarships to Ph.D. programs in the States. I applied to Berkeley, and that's how I finished studying for a career that, at the time, didn't interest me much.

"And writing a thesis about your dad."

"Sort of. When it was time to write my thesis, I predictably chose the seventies in Bolivia and the Southern Cone; more specifically, the way the left had confronted state terrorism during those dictatorial years. The period fascinated me: I wanted to give Dad a context in order to understand him better, or at least picture him more clearly."

"And then Chandra Wickley appeared . . ."

"Uh-huh. Guided by her, I got completely involved in the horror of the political violence that decimated a whole generation. A generation that was more nonconformist and less cynical than ours, more idealistic, but, I soon discovered, not at all ideal: they made as many mistakes as we did, or more. Of course, given that we conform to the state of things as they've been handed to us, there's no pride in saying that we make fewer mistakes. We've forgotten about utopian ideals and take no risks."

It was a morbid sight: security forces, military, paramilitary, guerrillas, terrorists, opposition politicians, students, laborers, and civilians faced a war without mercy, where no one gave an inch and deaths were answered with more deaths. In this panorama of confusion, I wasn't surprised to find that Dad had made a lot of mistakes as leader of MAS — for example, his insistence on staying independent and not forming part of a common front with other leftist parties and unions, and his desperate response to violence with more violence. Were they mistakes? At that time, were they? Once again I was critical of the left in general, but in a way I excused Dad.

For the chapters on Bolivia, Wickley's method allowed me to formulate a thesis that paraphrased her ideas on revolution: urban guerrilla warfare was destined to fail because, among other things, it didn't have the support of the campesinos — an indispensable element for success. I also did a detailed discourse analysis study in which I deconstructed the radical, intransigent, dogmatic, and sectarian rhetoric of the left, which wasn't what nonradical, common people were ready to hear or assimilate. However, as I progressed with my thesis and got into the Southern Cone, Boolean algebra started to produce inappropriate results: too many exceptions to the rule. In countries like Uruguay, Chile, and Argentina, campesinos weren't a consideration (although, exaggerating the argument, you could say that *precisely* the lack of a campesino population in these countries prevented the possibility of success through urban guerrilla warfare). A class with a visiting French professor who specialized in guerrilla warfare in El Salvador filled me with more doubts. In contrast to Wickley and the dominant paradigm analysis, he said that mobilization began in the privileged sectors of society in El Salvador, that the countryside had not been the source of the insurgence but where it expanded to, and that the popular mobilization had been less of a cause than a consequence of moving civil war out of the city. The conclusion I came to after that class was that analysis models weren't worth much, that each case had its own story, tied to particular contingencies. There were more than twenty countries in that entity known as Latin America and many similarities among them, which intellectuals, academics, and politicians took advantage of to create grandiloquent, encompassing theories. And yet we had to remember their differences, their individual histories. Worried about finishing my thesis, I made it into an administrative project: hiding results that didn't match my argument and eliminating data that didn't support my theory. In the end, my thesis was a sophisticated parody of Wickley (maybe that's one of the possible origins of my failure as an academic: my first few years as a professor were based on two derivative chapters published in prestigious magazines, and then I was left without arguments, with nothing to show). She passed me even though she hadn't liked the second half of my thesis. The beginning, however, made her recommend me enthusiastically and convinced her of my brilliant academic future.

"But now you're interested in political science," Ashley said.

"It's ideal for me. I live far away from my own country, but I'm more in touch with it and the continent than I would be if I lived there. I have the time to do what I like here. I couldn't do that there. I'd have to have six jobs just to survive — teach forty contact hours, write articles for the editorial page, and I'd wind up opening a computer import store."

"Very convenient — ser latinoamericano from afar."

"Living there is a daily act of faith. Someday I'll go back. I can't see myself growing old here. This country is for young people."

"Not always," she said, her look defiant and coquettish, the dissimulated tension we had managed to create rising forcefully to the surface.

"You're right. I came for a couple of years and have been here for ten now. I really shouldn't talk."

"Maybe deep down you've already decided that you'll never go back, that you're fooling yourself."

"Maybe." I didn't like the way this conversation was going, so I changed the subject, asked her if she liked to do crosswords.

"Sometimes. When I'm on the bus going to Boston, to visit my parents. At an airport. The ones from the *New York Times*."

"Acrostics? Anagrams?"

"No, neither. Why do you ask? What a change of topic!"

"Just curious. I love those kinds of games."

"I'm good at Scrabble."

"We should play sometime. I doubt you'll beat me."

"It's like a treasure hunt, a kid's game."

"It is. It's my way of staying in touch with the puzzles I used to like when I was young. The games of strategy I would invent. The secret languages I would create to communicate with my friends. The crosswords I still solve."

"You went from being a creator to a decoder."

"There's nothing wrong with recognizing that you're better at decoding secret languages than inventing them. One is no less deserving or necessary than the other."

"I love secret messages. Reading between the lines is my favorite sport, and university is perfect for that."

"Yeah. The other day I passed by a classroom and saw fifteen students concentrating on their books while the professor stood looking at them with his arms crossed. They looked like members of a cult studying a holy book, searching for clues. I think it was *Moby-Dick*."

I finally mentioned Borges. She confessed, her cheeks reddening, that she had lied: Borges didn't interest her in the slightest. Between mischievous laughs, repeatedly brushing her unruly long hair out of her eyes, leaning her body toward the table and letting me see the restless skin underneath her blue linen shirt, she said it would be better if we continued to talk about the realm of fantasy and I could tell her about Borges and love, Borges and women, Borges and sex. When she wanted to, Ashley could be cruel.

After that, it became our café and we adopted that table next to the window. It was risky. We should have looked for a more reserved place, not exposed ourselves to being caught, but we couldn't tear ourselves away from that talismanic table. Anyhow, the university was on the other side of the town, at the top of a hill where ever stronger winds collided, and we felt far enough away from it to continue seeing each other at that café. And it wasn't as if we were doing anything wrong.

One afternoon I was walking her to the bus stop when it occurred to me to ask her to my apartment. I asked without thinking, or maybe I'd been thinking about it the whole time without even realizing it. She touched her nose with her right index finger — a gesture I would later learn to read — and accepted my invitation without a second thought, or at least that was how it seemed. We headed to my apartment with anxious looks and hurried steps, bodies swimming in the current of time, being incessantly towed by desire.

5

INTER WAS coming — I had to get an extra blanket out of the closet in the middle of the night. Early in the morning and in the evening, the temperature hovered in that ambiguous range where it was too warm for a sweater but too cool for shirtsleeves. During the day there was a noticeable difference between the sunny and shady sides of the street.

Some nights I stayed home and joined my uncle in the living room. He would watch TV and I would get on the Internet, taking the opportunity to reply to my overwhelming list of e-mails. I had built up a network of friends and correspondents that spanned the continent and allowed me to stay up-to-date: Rafa, a Mexican who worked for the Central Bank there; Ursula, assistant director of the leading Colombian newspaper; Francisco, a Peruvian in charge of a huge welfare project for street kids in Lima; Guille, a spendthrift Argentine who worked in the Department of Inequality and Poverty at the IADB in Washington. They were some of the key sources for my articles. When I met Silvana (the Guatemalan in charge of the Latin American section of *NewTimes*) over a year ago and she asked me for a general article about the region, in the style of those that Jorge Castañeda writes for *Newsweek,* it occurred to me, in complete contradiction to my academic practice, to write it without checking a single book on my shelves or from the library. I wrote it by recycling the old but true notion that democratic societies in Latin America had been built on a foundation of deep-rooted colonial authoritarianism. To that I added my common sense, intuition, and imagination, which told me that modernization projects on the continent were obsessed with economic, industrial, and technological progress and that the region's instability was due to a complete lack of modernization in terms of racial and social prejudices. To this cocktail I added numbers and perceptions garnered on the Web and in e-mails from friends. The success of the article convinced me to continue in the same vein, leaving me a bit worried because the North American academic world did not value this type of work — especially when done by a young professor whose free time should have been spent on research. Infatuated with these quickly written pieces, I wasted no time in pushing worry aside. (I realized now that fate had helped me a great deal, that it wasn't easy to write original articles without research; soon, not only my colleagues but newspaper and magazine people who trusted me would discover that the emperor truly had no clothes — something they had already begun to suspect.)

I also went to quote.yahoo.com to see how Ashley's tech stocks were doing. Patrick had given her access to the account with the $100,000 inheritance from his grandmother so she could "play" the stocks, and now only $70,000 remained (she never said she'd lost money, just that the stocks had gone down). She had shown me how to e-trade, but I hadn't paid much attention to those graphs and indexes that excited her to the point of distraction. I did, however, memorize her password and sometimes went into her account to check her portfolio — AOL, YHOO, CMGI, AMZN, EBAY — and share in her happiness or sorrow. Tech stocks had continued to fall (they were the only ones she invested in, refusing to diversify).

My uncle had given me a file of all the crosswords published in the last six months and a notebook of unedited material. Revolutionary Bolivian politician? Author of *Las Furias*? Ethiopian athlete? Japanese admiral? Designed the Walkman? Cybernetics theorist? English writer who practices spiritualism? Town where Jaime Villa was born? I tried to finish them quickly so I could get to what I liked best: finding the three hidden clues that unified the whole. The words on the surface hid an underlying message written in invisible ink; they were the stubborn shell that had to be cracked open through sleight of hand. When I discovered the secret I was filled with the same childlike joy as when I created alphabetical codes in school that I thought were indecipherable (even though someone always proved me wrong).

One of Uncle David's main themes was the history of media. Facts about *Berkeley* and *Vertigo* were intertwined with questions about the invention of the postal system or the computer. Who said "Information should not be confused with meaning"? Invented the UNIVAC? I still didn't understand his obsession with media. It wasn't just a matter of technology, no. And I didn't entirely accept his answer either, which was that personal, face-to-face communication involved gestures that made messages ambiguous, but with media, thanks to distance, one could concentrate solely on the messages, on the information. There was more to it than that, much more, I was sure.

My uncle watched the news on his big-screen TV and was fanatical about soccer, mostly the European leagues: he was a Juventus and Real Madrid fan (right now the European league season was over, so he watched the national team matches). Also, strangely enough, he loved MTV and music video programs on other channels. What was he looking for in the avalanche of images, fast-cutting and furious montages offered up by every three-minute clip? I discovered that he'd taped a local band's video and would watch it over and over, pausing the images and taking notes. The song sounded familiar. When I read the name of the group at the end — Berkeley — I knew I shouldn't have been surprised, but I was.

One afternoon while he was working in the container, I sat down to watch a music video program with the recorder all ready. Berkeley's was the last of the show. It was shot in black-and-white and had the grainy, unsteady quality of a home movie — an elegant attempt to disguise their low budget. I couldn't follow the story and wasn't sure there even was one; there were too many unconnected images. Every now and then it focused on the band, four mop-haired guys with a listless drummer who couldn't keep up with the frantic rhythm of bass and guitar. The singer was too aware of the camera that followed his every move.

The fourth time I watched it everything started to make sense, or maybe, out of necessity, I began to impose order on that meaningless sequence. The lyrics curled up in the most euphoric kitsch of a love song. The images told another story — one not exactly of love. It was an allegory of the Unzueta Street attack. Six deaths represented by scenes of six flying geese, six trees in a park, six kids in a kindergarten playroom. A group is gathered at a dinner party — an image taken from *The Discreet Charm of the Bourgeoisie*. All of a sudden, a window is broken and pictures from World War I appear, seven soldiers jumping from trenches with bayonets fixed on their rifles (a perverse wink at Kubrick's *Paths of Glory*?). The party guests, immobile, await the bayonets. Only one of them throws himself under the table and manages to escape by dragging himself across the floor; in one confusing scene a soldier who sees him pretends not to. All of this lasts twenty seconds. The rest of the video is made up of symbols taken from Dad's novel: power lines, helicopters flying over cities, and bridges — bridges of every shape and size, bridges everywhere.

I understood why the video obsessed Uncle David. Twenty years had gone by and that fateful afternoon had become the axis around which the myth of Dad revolved. Five others had died in that attack, all of whom were now reduced to mere footnotes, trivia perhaps worthy of an appearance in one of my uncle's crosswords. Only a few millimeters had spared him from death, but he had lost the woman he had been married to for ten years. Even though he appeared calm and didn't have nightmares, some trauma, latent or visible, must have remained. And while he respected Dad greatly and admired him, surely he was afraid of being reduced to trivia too. He who lives by the sword dies by the sword. One life counts while others are lost in the sea of time and it's as if they never existed, bodies and souls without consequence, beings more ethereal than ghosts.

It was then I noticed that there were no photos of Aunt Elsa anywhere in the house. Maybe it was how he controlled the suffering, kept it at bay, stopped it from attacking him from frames and pictures hung on the wall — in the living room in her wedding dress, on the nightstand on that backpacking trip to Machu Picchu. People said they were the oddest couple imaginable: she was so vivacious and he so serious; she wanted to change the world with her flower-power idealism, while he absorbedly built appliances and took them apart. In the mid-seventies my dad got her interested in politics: Montenegro's dictatorship had to be opposed. She was enthusiastic and finally convinced my uncle to join Dad's small party — MAS (Movimiento al Socialismo), an armed, clandestine leftist group. We know how that enthusiasm ended.

The next day, after lunch, I asked him to tell me about my aunt.

"There's not much to tell," he said, picking up the plates. "Actually, there's so much I wouldn't know where to begin."

"I'm surprised there're no photos of her."

"Ah, photos. These days we need them to prove that certain things happened. It's suspicious not to have a picture of your wife in your wallet. Coffee? I'm just fulfilling a promise I made to her. 'If I die before you,' she said, 'remember me with your body. Remember my voice, my looks, without photos, without letters, without anything of that sort.' And, obedient man that I am, I comply."

He went into the kitchen to make coffee, returning in a minute.

"I met her at a party during Carnival. It was fate because I wasn't the sort to go to Carnival parties. Your aunt was. She was this mask who asked me to dance. She had the longest legs you've ever seen. Pedro wanted to take her mask off, but she refused. She laughed and laughed. Her laugh was somewhat unpleasant, strident. But something about that woman stayed with me. Before she left, she gave me her phone number, and I called her a few weeks later. She was at the university, studying sociology. I was shy and couldn't really move the conversation forward, so she ended up asking me to the movies. We started going out and I discovered, or rather I confirmed, that she was a bit flighty. She would talk about the Beatles and the Rolling Stones, Cream and Hendrix, but also about Los Jairas and Gladys Moreno, Piero and Leonardo Favio. Not to mention the Cuban Revolution, Castro, Che — all that leftist rhetoric. I thought she was a good girl who felt guilty about having so much in such a poor country. Like your dad. Like so many of our generation back then."

The coffee was too hot, so I left it to cool. My uncle had begun a monologue and it was as if he had forgotten I was there.

"In truth, she always set the pace in our relationship. I simply followed her. I was attracted to her despite our ideological differences (or rather my lack of ideology, because I wasn't interested in the left or the right, I simply wasn't interested in politics). Extremely attracted. She had a dynamic personality, and I wanted to get to know her better. That's how I fell in love. The years went by and I don't think I ever really got to know her completely. To this day."

"Are you still trying?"

"Sometimes."

He furrowed his brow, looked away.

"She was happy. What changed her, what made her radical, was the Teoponte insurgency. She lost a brother there. Agustín."

Teoponte, 1970: that tragic struggle in which sixty-three of the seventy-five guerrillas, the majority of them young, middle-class idealists — Nestor Paz Zamora, the singer Benjo Cruz — lost their lives (starved, cornered by the military). It was ELN's attempt to carry on with Che's cause, led by Chato Peredo: he had lost two brothers in the Ñancahuazu insurgency.

"I didn't know that."

"Agustín was executed there by the military. He was one of the few who didn't desert or die of exhaustion."

"They were city kids. They weren't physically up to it. It was a stupid adventure, very poorly planned. Peredo didn't learn his lesson from Che's defeat. He wanted to carry on the idea of starting a campaign in the countryside, organizing an army of campesinos able to defeat the 'other army, defender of the system.'"

"Poorly planned, yes, but not at all stupid. I think the poor planning was intentional. Those kids were true idealists, ready to die for their beliefs. It's something that, thirty years later, from your generational perspective, must be very hard to understand."

I wanted to say something more but kept quiet. He lit a cigarette and turned his back. It was as though certain images had materialized in front of him. He took a few uncertain steps, as if approaching to see them better, wanting to touch them. I was moved by the sight of his coffee-stained slippers, his wrinkled pants, his threadbare shirt.

"I think," he went on, "that those kids, who idolized Che, felt guilty that he'd died in Bolivia. I think that, consciously or unconsciously, they decided to sacrifice themselves in order to somehow redeem Che's death. They wanted to follow his example to the end and could think of nothing better than offering their lives, as Che had. In a way, it was a generation that lived for death, one that found realization in death. The highlight of their lives was transcendence through death. It's something Benjo Cruz always talked about."

I wasn't quite convinced, but at least it sounded original: I would never have thought of looking at it that way. In my world, everyone, one way or another, behaved rationally. It was hard for me to understand that foolishness is sometimes more logical than common sense.

"Elsa was so persuasive," he went on, "that she managed to get me to do things that weren't like me. Or that I thought weren't like me. Like listening to the preacher, Ruibal, who was in fashion those days. Like fighting against Montenegro's dictatorship. When Pedro came back from Berkeley, willing to follow ELN but focusing on the cities, Elsa's ideas found a real outlet. And I was swept along with them. Of course that didn't happen right away. At first Elsa went to MAS meetings on her own, to listen, to find out. Three, four years of dictatorship had to pass before we became involved in the struggle, once Montenegro showed his true colors and declared all-out war on the opposition."

He looked at me, closed his eyes.

"Learning how to hold a gun," he said, "even though my hands were shaking and I would've done anything not to have to use it. Blowing up pylons in the early morning. Kidnapping industrialists, friends of our parents, to raise funds. It all sounds so strange now, and it was so normal then. But I did those things not only for her, but because I saw that she was right — they had to be done.

We had hopes and dreams, but we were dominated by fear: fear of the military, of the paramilitary, of torture, of death. We were always on the defensive; we were so small compared to the government. And all the while we heard of friends or acquaintances who had been killed, detained, tortured, made refugees, exiled, disappeared."

The telephone rang and I hesitated to answer. But then I realized it might be Ashley and jumped up. I wanted it to be Ashley, prayed it would be Ashley.

"What's wrong? You sound out of breath."

It was Carolina.

"I was on the other side of the house when the phone rang. I had to run to get it."

"Were you waiting for a call? Anyway, estás listo? We'll be by to pick you up in half an hour. We're going to see Villa. You wanted to, didn't you? I got authorization. Remember, when the guards at the gate ask, I'm his niece and you're my cousin. We'll see if it works."

She hung up. I went back to my uncle, but he'd gone out into the patio and was staring, lost in thought, at the lemon tree. The phone call had broken the spell.

Jaime Villa's mansion was in La Atalaya, next to mansions owned by politicians who'd been in power long enough to fill their personal coffers and close to a sky filled with languid clouds about to tumble down over the city. To get there you had to pass through a heavily guarded checkpoint where soldiers were the target of insults from university students carrying placards. They let us pass once they had checked our names against the list of authorized visitors. The whole city was visible from La Atalaya: a city struggling to modernize by way of graceless buildings (construction had stopped on many of them, as if the recession had blanketed the scene in an enchanted cloak, freezing it in time). Living on top of the hill must have given residents a sense of power and also disgust — knowing there were few legal ways to get there but innumerable illegal ones. Living with that knowledge was a form of punishment for so much obscene acquisition.

Carolina had arrived with Ricardo, the editor of *Digitar* she had once mentioned. He was big, had shaky hands and a furious case of acne that belied his age. He chain-smoked and looked at Carolina as if waiting for her to finally take notice of him. It didn't take me long to discover the dynamics of their relationship: he wanted to be more than friends, but she didn't. It wasn't strange — the chances of that were greater than of there being mutual interest. The world was filled with unrequited love, hearts that beat in indifference, lives dedicated to other lives in vain, or maybe not; maybe being true to the feelings themselves was an exalted form of redemption and on a higher plane than the banal, narcissistic search for reciprocity.

"So, you're a virtual journalist."

"Not only that," said Carolina proudly, "but Ricardo works for Channel Veintiuno. He's a man of many talents."

"Where the bomb exploded? What do you do there?"

"The bomb destroyed the Jeep that was parked next to his car," Carolina said. "It happened right when he was leaving, caught him in the hallway. He was so lucky, just barely escaped."

She looked at him as if having been a few yards away from an explosion were enough to lend an aura of heroism. I looked at him as if it would take more than that.

"I'm production manager," he said, avoiding my eyes. "It's really just an office job. We don't produce much — the odd music video here and there, shorts. But I'm tired of it and going to quit soon. Once *Digitar* gets going I'll have to do that full-time."

Would he leave? The majority of online magazines in the States had large readerships but didn't generate any revenue. No one wanted to pay to read magazines on a computer screen.

"Tell me about the bomb."

"There's not much more to tell than what Caro said. I was lucky, that's about it."

"I can't imagine what a government protest has to do with a private TV station. They could have put the bomb somewhere else."

"Makes you wonder, doesn't it?"

He drove for a while in silence.

"So you're the son of the Great Leader and the nephew of the Crossword Setter," he said. "Quite the family you've got."

I could detect sarcasm in his voice.

"You can't choose your family," I replied.

"You can't choose them at first," he countered, "but once you know who they are, you can distance yourself from them."

"Anyone in mind?"

"At least you changed your last name. At least you're not Reissig."

"My mom changed my name, gave me hers. But I don't see what —"

"Don't pay any attention to him," Carolina intervened. "Ricardo has a thing against your uncle's crosswords. He says they pretend to be for intelligent people when they're really for idiots. They're all the rage — everyone's doing them everywhere. Even the dumbest secretary thinks she's the greatest when she solves one."

I didn't quite believe her explanation, but I let it go. Ricardo kept quiet. Was he jealous?

The mansion was on a corner, protected by high stone walls. Ricardo parked his Honda behind a military Jeep and finished telling me about his online magazine. They accepted submissions but didn't pay very well yet.

"Caro has told me a lot about you," he said, and I noted a hostile tone in his voice, or maybe I was exaggerating. "She says you write. Academic papers, more specifically."

"I also write analyses for general-circulation magazines. Yankee ones, mostly."

"*NewTimes, Latin American Affairs,*" Carolina finished, as if those names held any weight in Río Fugitivo.

"I don't know them."

"They aren't really distributed here. *NewTimes* wants to be, but it arrives only irregularly. They're planning a Spanish edition to come out soon. I wrote a few articles at the beginning. Even one in *Salon.*"

"That's important."

"But nothing lately — writer's block. Mostly I write opinions, the kind that helps reinforce the argument of an article. 'As Professor So-and-So of the University of Blah Blah Blah says' . . . It's not much, but it's hard to break into. It's a matter of getting on the Rolodex."

Then one could coast for a long time, live on borrowed time, on ephemeral past glories, until someone discovered the deception and took your name off the Rolodex, replacing it with another — or kept it there, never to be used again.

"You could . . . uh, have a column in the magazine," Ricardo said grudgingly, as if he were more pressured by the situation than by any desire to have me as a contributor. "It's the wave of the future. Soon there won't be a magazine or newspaper of importance if it's not on the Web."

"I'm not as optimistic," I said. "The first thing everyone does with those magazines is print the interesting articles. It's impossible to leave the material text behind."

"Impossible for you, maybe," Carolina said. "Increasingly more possible for the majority. I haven't bought a newspaper in ages."

"In the U.S.," I said, "some online magazines have even begun offering a traditional print edition as a way of financing the other. The so-called revolution never arrived."

We approached the door. There were soldiers everywhere, some with rifles and others with walkie-talkies; a helicopter flew over La Atalaya. A soldier with leathery skin and a mustache asked us for our names and identification.

"Ricardo Mérida, journalist." His voice was strangled, barely audible. "I interviewed him the other day and came for him to review the text. They're relatives."

I felt uncomfortable, didn't like pretending to be related to Villa. The soldier wrote our names in a notebook and spoke on the walkie-talkie with someone inside the house, who authorized our entrance. He held my ID as if trying to read what the State of New York hologram said, then asked me if I had Bolivian ID.

"I've lived overseas for ten years," I said. "My card here expired."

"So what do you use?"

"My passport. Or this."

He looked at me as if waiting for something. I didn't understand. Ricardo took out a few bills and set them on the notebook. The soldier put them in his pocket and gave me back my ID.

We walked along a tiled pathway through a large garden and past a pool where two teenagers and a black mastiff were lying in the sun. The house was painted white, and there was elaborate wooden trim around the windows. The architecture was confusing. The house was three or four stories high, with the second-floor terrace on the same level as the garage, which was set on a hill and reached by going up a drive bordered by hydrangeas. It was an excessive, opulent house, the kind usually inhabited only by servants because the owners are generally at one of their four or five other houses.

We came to a half-open door and passed through a living room that could be attributed only to another excess, that of bad taste: a local carpenter's interpretation of Louis XVI chairs, Persian carpets designed by someone who knew nothing about Persia, marble busts of Roman emperors, and, on one wall, an immense picture of Villa's third wife — a woman from Tarija with sallow cheeks and a nose job, twenty years younger than he was. I felt I should cross myself and say a prayer for the soul guilty of this monstrous lack of refinement.

A servant led us to Villa's study, where two soldiers stood guard. The man himself was there, with a bald, mustached man I later learned was his secretary (someone who had taken part in selling Che's diary to Cuba). Daylight streamed in through the large windows. The walls were filled with plaques from various associations, mayoralties, and fraternities grateful to Villa (a popular soccer club from Santa Cruz, the civic committee from Beni, the association of friends of Cochabamba). Villa was short, white-haired; it was hard to believe that this was the man who had outwitted the government and the DEA all those years. He was wearing a *guayabera* and held rosary beads in his hands. The table was covered with Bibles and pamphlets from every type of religious organization. Villa spared no prayer in his attempt to avoid Yankee jails.

We shook hands. In a dry voice he asked who I was.

"Pedro Zabalaga," I said, intimidated all of a sudden.

"Pedro Reissig's son," Carolina added.

He looked at me incredulously, stood up, and embraced me — in anger or affection, I wasn't sure.

"That son of a bitch!" he said. "That son of a bitch. If I ever see him again I'll kill him. Of course, that's never going to happen because he's already dead. He had a lot of enemies, understandably."

Carolina was right: even though he wasn't handsome, he was dangerously charismatic. You couldn't help but listen to him or look at him and feel that he wasn't speaking in metaphors or hyperbole, that each of his words was to be understood exactly as it was spoken. That was the Villa of legend: the one who showered money on poor neighborhoods, had whores flown in from Amsterdam, bought government ministers with what was left over from his visits to Medellín, had his enemies dismembered. He was also the first cousin of that Minister of the Interior who had ordered Dad's murder during that infamous dictatorship in which it took less than a year for Montenegro (and the — many — other dictators we were fated to have) to appear to have the most refined manners. But it wasn't Villa's fault that he was related. Or was it?

"Calm down, Don Jaime," the secretary said. Villa's wife came in wearing a tight-fitting red dress and enough makeup for a wax museum mask. What was she doing dressed like that at that time of day? What party could she possibly be going to? She was beautiful in person, had an easy smile and sweet gaze; she mumbled a hello, offered us water and orange juice, then disappeared.

"Don Jaime," Ricardo said, "Pedro would like to ask you a few questions."

"I'll ask the questions first, then he can ask me. I never read that damn novel. At least not all of it. But someone commented to me once that there was a certain Villada, 'King of Benzedrine and Other Drugs,' on page seventy-seven. I read that page. It wasn't a flattering portrait. No, young man, it was quite a joke. And no one jokes about me just like that."

"That can't be," I said, faltering. "When the novel came out, no one had ever heard of you, sir . . . You became famous only in the mid-eighties. It had to be a strange coincidence. In any event, it's a novel, not a history book or an autobiography."

"I know. But he'd known me since school. We were close, you know. We grew apart because he thought he was smarter than he was. Made fun of all of us and still wanted us to applaud him. He couldn't have been more ironic. Very cerebral, he had to think about everything. But let me tell you, young man, intelligence is not enough," he said. "So what the hell is it you want to know, exactly? My pardon to the lady here and Ricardo."

He lit a cigarette and calmed down. I watched him do something strange: he collected the ash in his palm and ate it.

"Ash contains potassium," the secretary explained, stroking his mustache. "And potassium is very good for heart problems. Don Jaime hasn't been well lately."

"The sons of bitches in government," he said. "They're to blame. That little dictator wants to earn a few points. Traitor. Gringo ass-kisser."

Carolina looked at the floor, Ricardo smiled, and I sneezed. Villa asked to what he owed the pleasure of my visit. I told him I was writing a book about my dad and that I needed statements from people who had known him.

"So you're a writer," he said with interest.

"Not exactly."

This was one of my most regrettable destinies. Because of my profession and because of whose son I was, people unfortunately confused me with being an author and told me their life stories so I could write them. As if all lives were worth writing about. As if I would be interested in writing about them.

"Like father, like son. Yes, you might be the ideal person. I could tell you a lot of things. In exchange, maybe you could do something for me."

There was a pause, and Villa seemed about to confess a great secret. He asked to speak to me in private. Ricardo lit a cigarette and left the study in disgust, followed by Carolina, who looked curious.

"Some time ago an American publisher offered me a lot of money to write my memoirs. I wasn't interested at the time, but I've been writing them over the last few years. I think my life is worth knowing more about. There've been a lot of lies about me. And some people who love me have insisted 'Don't you keep quiet' because I've done a lot for this country. A lot. There are few patriots like me. I don't have a cent in my pocket because everything I did was for this country and its poor. They say that people's affection can't be bought; well, that's what I've earned. It's not for nothing that plazas and streets are named after me in Beni, soccer teams in forgotten little towns. Because the government never made it to those towns, but I did. Nobody pays tribute to presidents, but there will always be flowers on my grave. There must be some reason, don't you think?"

"I suppose so," I said, somewhat intimidated. His tone had risen.

"Don't suppose anything. Simply believe me. Everything will be much easier if you believe me. And you have to believe me, because what I say goes and damn the consequences. I've written almost five hundred pages."

Five hundred pages? So just anyone could write five hundred pages? By the look of it, the gringos might be sons of bitches, but gringo publishers were not.

"I don't understand what you're asking me, sir."

"Don't be so formal with me. I want you to read my memoirs and tell me how they can be improved."

"You don't know me, sir," I said, unable to treat him informally. "How can you be sure I'll do a good job?"

"I can't. But that's the way things are with me. It's not too hard to judge people. I call a spade a spade. Or do you want me to run in circles like a dog chasing my tail?"

I wound up accepting his offer — I wanted to be the first to read the memoirs of the King of Cocaine. Besides, I didn't have much else to do those days.

Before I left I asked him for the manuscript. That was when I found out that Villa was also paranoid: the manuscript could not leave the house and could not be photocopied. I could read it only in the study, which meant I would have to visit him several times. I agreed. I had no other choice.

On the way home I heard a Paula Cole song — "Where Have All the Cowboys Gone?" — on the radio and thought of Ashley. Carolina talked and Ricardo listened quietly, looking at her and ignoring my presence. He seemed quite unhappy that Villa had bestowed his magnanimity on me. Obviously. After all, he was the journalist. But neither of them asked me what I had talked about with Villa. Maybe they were waiting for me to tell them of my own accord. I didn't.

That night on the phone with Carolina, after summing up my conversation with Villa, I asked her if it was my imagination or if Ricardo really disliked me.

"He was uncomfortable," she said. "I should have told you, but I didn't know if it would bother you. So I decided not to say anything. Some people misjudge him right off the bat and it isn't his fault."

"You should have told me what?"

Silence.

"Ricardo is René Mérida's son. His last name — didn't you notice how nervous he got when he had to give it at the entrance? And his looks: get rid of the acne, give him a beard, and he looks just like him."

There is nothing worse for someone who prides himself on solving mysteries than to be confronted with his own purloined letter. His last name, of course. His looks. It was all so obvious that it was hard not to see it. René Mérida, the only one of the leadership in Dad's party who had missed the Unzueta Street meeting and had therefore been saved. From that point on he was believed to have been the traitor, the one who had sold his comrades to save his own skin. Not that it helped him much: he was found dead a few days later in a putrid dump on the shores of the Choqueyapu River.

"Aha," I said. "You should have told me. And his comment

about distancing myself from my relatives? Does he have something against my dad or my uncle?"

"It's strange. I'll tell you about it someday. Not now. It's not worth it."

Sometimes I take my notebook, draw a grid on the page, and set a crossword. I used to write them for my high school newspaper. I don't have my uncle's range or his ability to find arcane or ambiguous facts. I think about my classes, not my articles, and begin to set clues: Uruguayan guerrilla. Famous torture center of the Videla dictatorship. Murdered Letelier. Inti Peredo's name. Coco Peredo's name. Roque Dalton's nickname. Spanish advisor to Allende. Led the takeover of La Moneda presidential palace. Manuel Marulanda's nickname. In charge of the Death Caravan. Bolivian Minister of the Interior murdered by his own officials in May 1973. The 1974 massacre in Bolivia. Nora Astorga's and Leticia Herrera's political party. Astiz's name. What country was DOP from? Who ordered Torres's murder? Who ordered Zenteno Anaya's murder? How many countries had an ELN? How many had an MIR? Which dictatorship helped Klaus Barbie? What country did Proceso belong to?

I'd like to show one to my uncle, but he'd think it was the work of an amateur. Carolina would say I'm morbid. Without finishing it, I throw it into the garbage.

As time went by, I slowly took on the measured rhythm of those who live permanently in one place. Life was not without its surprises, but even then I was unable to vary my routine completely. I missed certain things from my life in Madison: the protective anonymity of being in a place where no one on the street looked at me as if recognizing me from somewhere, or the time I had to undertake long projects (time I then wasted on a thousand trivialities that erased what was important). I missed the *New York Times* and the coffee and the movies and the magazines and the indoor heating and the water pressure and the sensation (almost always deceptive) of being at the heart of where things happened, things that happened in the rest of the world only days or months or years later.

And yet I began to think I could live happily in Río Fugitivo. Increasingly, I got used to the political instability and the economic problems as if I had never left the country. I wasn't bothered by the constant strikes or blockades, and even though I took it personally when the indigenous leader from Achacachi said that we "whiteys" were to blame for the nation's backwardness, I could ignore it when he said we were not "true Bolivians." My migrant way of life over the last decade, my continuous coming and going between two poles, allowed me the flexibility to feel at home in both places. But there was an underlying discomfort, the suspicion that this flexibility could also mean I would never feel entirely comfortable in either place. I knew I couldn't live in the North without the possibility of escape to Río Fugitivo. Soon I would discover whether I could live in Río Fugitivo without the possibility of escape to the North. Perhaps I had already lived too long in other places and it was impossible for me to come home without wanting to be somewhere else. Maybe there was an exorbitant price to be paid for embracing the back-and-forth — one I had not yet begun to pay.

Winter came and it was harsh, especially at night and early in the morning. Still, it didn't remotely compare to winter in Madison with snow up to my knees, frost on the windows, the asphyxiating gray sky, and a wind that cut my face and numbed my ears. I spent the San Juan festivities with Carolina and got drunk on sangria: I started to recite Cryptogram definitions and repeated the first and last lines of *Berkeley* — ashes to ashes. In the wee hours of the morning I was crying at the door to my uncle's house while Carolina (patient, understanding, innocent) tried in vain to calm me down. When she asked me why I was crying, I told her it was because I missed so many things, but didn't tell her what (Ashley and my parents and San Juan when I was a teenager).

I suffered two migraine attacks that caused me to close doors and windows and hide under a blanket in my room, biting my lips and praying it would soon be over. On the radio I heard a retired colonel declare that the body of Quiroga Santa Cruz could be found buried under the Military School patio in La Paz, and I wondered where Dad was buried. I had recurring visions of his and Aunt Elsa's wake at Uncle David's house.

I saw Montenegro on TV and realized that I didn't hate him. That good-for-nothing was the man Dad had opposed? Maybe that was how Montenegro had managed to stay in power for several years and then staged a democratic comeback: because people thought he was beneath them, no one could believe that evil would have such a banal incarnation. I should pay more attention than the rest, I said to myself, and yet it was difficult. That was one of the main differences between the majority and people like Villa or Montenegro: sooner or later we dropped our guard and let ourselves be seduced by the human exterior. We got tired of seeing the wolf in sheep's clothing and were capable of pity, compassion. We were stupidly predictable in our misplaced generosity.

I watched the Berkeley video several times, trying to capture the sea of symbols that complicated what was real. I watched *The Discreet Charm of the Bourgeoisie* and *Paths of Glory* to see if they would give me any clues to the video. I reread the paragraphs in Dad's book where he mentioned bayonets and bridges and pylons. I looked up the etymology of the word "goose" in a couple of encyclopedias. In the end, I knew a lot about each symbol in the video, but I couldn't say I had made coherent sense of all that I knew. These days, it seemed my destiny to lose myself in the labyrinths of my own hermeneutical fantasies. Maybe it wasn't the text that was at fault, but what I demanded of it. Maybe it was my overinterpretation, my ability to diverge into a thousand petty details that threatened the possibility of one master interpretation. Maybe sometimes a bridge was just a bridge. Maybe. It was impossible for me to accept that. It went against my nature, which saw a conspiracy of codes all around, codes that needed to be deciphered in order to understand the world.

I spoke with Dad's friends as if I were really interested in writing the damned book. I speculated about *Berkeley* (the salamanders had not led me anywhere). I read and worked on Villa's manuscript. *Latin American Affairs* drove me crazy with the Peruvian crisis and the one in Paraguay, the country I knew least and improvised most about — generally positive things, thanks to the memory of a Paraguayan woman I had known fleetingly and with whom I'd had an intense e-mail relationship for a few months, the kind of relationship that involved fantasies of whips and silk scarves. And I spent time with my uncle, enjoying the crosswords and his progress with the dictionary, which was now on the Internet thanks to Caro.

"The home page," my uncle said, looking at the screen, Carolina by his side, "has the classic, Cortazarian photo of Pedro with the cigarette in his mouth as if chewing on it. Then the complete text, and each page has multiple links."

He clicked the mouse, again, then again: each word from the dictionary with its several reverberations. There were miles and miles of paths, inexhaustible ways of exhausting the life of a man, the life of a text.

"But that's not all," said Carolina.

"The big surprise!" my uncle finished excitedly. "She's a wizard, I tell you. I asked if it could be done and she did it."

There were links to texts from famous authors in Berkeley: Jack London ("He caught a Telegraph Avenue car that was going to Berkeley. It was crowded with youth and young men who were singing songs and ever and again barking out college yells"); Simone de Beauvoir ("I looked at the athletic-looking young people, the smiling young girls in my audience, and I thought that certainly . . . there were no more than one or two concerned with the news of the day"); Kerouac ("In Berkeley I was living with Alvah Goldbook in his little rose-covered cottage in the backyard of a bigger house on Milvia Street. The old rotten porch slanted forward to the ground, among vines, with a nice old rocking chair that I sat in every morning to read my Diamon Sutra"); Pynchon (". . . and this Berkeley was like no somnolent Siwash out of her own past at all, but more akin to those Far Eastern or Latin American universities you read about, those autonomous culture media where the most beloved of folklores may be brought into doubt, cataclysmic of dissents voiced, suicidal of commitments chosen — the sort that brings governments down"); and Philip K. Dick ("I wondered, then, what the hell I cared about Arabic mysticism, about the Sufis and all that other stuff that Edgar Barefoot talked about on his weekly radio program on KPFA in Berkeley . . . I still work at the Musik shop on Telegraph Avenue in Berkeley and I'm trying to make the payments on the house that Jeff and I bought when we were married"). Lodge, Milosz, Hass, Norris — the list was endless.

"What do you think?" my uncle said, his arm around Carolina. "What do you think? We surprised you, didn't we? Tell me we surprised you. In one fell swoop, Pedro connected to all the greats."

I was happier about my uncle's excitement than about finding my dad amid all that Berkeleyan mythology. I had rarely seen him so radiant, so full of joy.

I tried to write a weekly column for *Digitar,* but even that was difficult. I had become the king of stock phrases, and now I couldn't even think in paragraphs. I hoped, however, that I'd get my confidence back through the column and then return to writing articles that Silvana could accept for *NewTimes.* I told myself it wasn't that hard, I'd done it before. Or maybe it was true that ignorance is bliss, and now that I knew more about what I had gotten myself into — providing opinions about a tortured continent, armchair theorizing while entire countries wavered on the brink of collapse — I was frightened by the responsibility produced by my irresponsibility.

I had told myself that I wouldn't publish in *Digitar,* because Ricardo's father had been responsible for Dad's death. But with Carolina's help I tried to be fair and not blame Ricardo for someone else's atrocity. As children we carry the unnecessary and unjust burden of our parents' triumphs and failures. It was hard enough to carry our own without taking on others', however close and beloved they might be. In some strange way I identified with Ricardo. Dad's enormous shadow had asphyxiated me more than once. Extremes meet.

Still, I had asked Carolina not to call me when she went out with him. I didn't want to be near him or become his friend, even though we would surely have had many things in common to talk about. I even resorted to attachments when sending him my articles. And I didn't want to become part of a melodramatic triangle, in competition for Carolina's favors. He seemed to be truly interested in her, and I wouldn't have minded if she'd encouraged him. I just wanted to stay out of it.

My weekly column was called "Vivir en el Sur" and it was about "the strangeness of living in the South after so many years in the North" (the mediocre libraries, the strikes, the smell of nicotine on clothes after a night out at a bar or club, the fact that I smoked or that I arrived late here, while everything was the opposite there). I wanted to be witty, but it was hard not to sound frivolous. It was obvious I was lost, distracted. Sometimes I thought that everything had lost meaning since I met Ashley and that, therefore, she was to blame. Then I remembered that I had already lost interest in a lot of things by the time I met her and had used insignificance as a way of escaping the impossibility of finding something that would make my life meaningful. Maybe I had passionately given myself over to Ashley because I had seen the chance that she would provide a certain sense of direction to my vague wandering. I didn't count on the fact that my character would let me down again.

Oddly enough, the strangest thing about my column wasn't the cultural differences; it was not being able to see my articles in a printed magazine: I had to turn on the computer in order to read the final product. And this was no geographical fluke. The same thing would have happened here or there. This was due to living in a turbulent new historical era: another layer was being added to eras that were already cemented — sometimes cracked but never entirely gone. Life was a palimpsest that never ceased being written. Strange calligraphy was being superimposed on other lettering that was no less strange but had already been accepted out of habit or mental lethargy (the kind that keeps us from being awed at the working of a telephone or the fervent crisscross of planes in the sky).

On weekends I went to El Marqués with Carolina, Carlos, and other friends. We would get drunk, and I succumbed to a few kisses with Caro but quickly sidestepped in order to avoid sex or, more precisely, the guilt that would plague me after sex (it's not that I wasn't interested; I just told myself that I had to be strong, even though strength in the face of desire had never been one of my virtues). At the end of the night, Carlos would tell me to drop Carolina off and go with them to a brothel. I always declined, knowing that I had left those days far behind, even though every refusal hurt because it alienated me further from my friends. Sundays at noon we would meet at a Chuquisacan restaurant in Bohemia. A big bowl of tripe *menudo* cured our hangovers, and in between gossip and laughter we attempted to solve my uncle's crosswords. Invented the kinetoscope. Wrote the short story *"El Puritano."* University on the Thames. Spanish novelist who supported Franco. Hitchcock's favorite actress. Goalie for the 1963 national team. One of the bridges in *Berkeley*. Carlos always had a great time, and no one mentioned the writ of attachment against him that had been published in the paper (we wouldn't have been surprised to see the police show up at one of our get-togethers). Federico was the most obsessive about the crosswords. He would come armed with several dictionaries and was willing to phone his very knowledgeable brother in Santa Cruz before admitting defeat. I participated with relish, happy to have found common ground at last. But after a while a word or a gesture would remind me of Yasemin or Joaquín, and I would realize that however hard I tried to get closer to Carlos and Fede, to be like them, the fragile bonds that connected us had really been severed long ago. And so I would force a smile and avoid their eyes and it was hard to accept.

There were times I wanted to phone Ashley, or e-mail her, let her know I hadn't forgotten her. I called a couple of times but hung up before I could hear her voice — or Patrick's. I also wrote a few e-mails, the tone of which oscillated between sweet and dry, but never sent them. I wrote two using one of our secret codes. The message was to be read backward and worked on simple substitution (*xbmelomt* meant "I love you"), but it seemed stupid, childish. And I was frustrated at waiting for a sign from her. I imagined she'd decided not to forgive me for running away. I didn't blame her. Oh, if she only knew that I loved her more every day, with the whim of a heart that only knows how to surrender to the unattainable. Maybe I had left Madison to be able to continue loving her.

Days passed and I hadn't written a single line of my projected book. I had, though, taken many notes in a black notebook that Helen Banks had given me when I arrived in Madison. In the notes, classmates, friends, and political colleagues of Dad's had revealed fragments of his complex and contradictory hopes and fears. Everyone had an opinion or an image or a story about him and gave it freely. At first I suspected that this had been one of the reasons I'd stayed in the States: I could live there without Dad's presence being woven into the fabric of my days. My drowsy curiosity, which had never quite been dormant, slowly awakened. It had been wide awake until Berkeley. After that I preferred to hold on to Dad as an idealized dream and stop unearthing remains that might hurt me. It was strange how everything had unfolded. My period of crisis with Ashley had led me to look for consolation in *Berkeley,* as if hoping to find advice from Dad that would solve my problems. In order to leave Madison for a while, until things calmed down, I obtained a leave of absence for a semester to come to Río Fugitivo and write the long-awaited book about him. And even though it was an excuse and I had never really thought of writing or even researching it, now here I was in Río Fugitivo with a burning desire to learn more about Dad. I had Ashley to thank.

As with any text, I had to sort through and make sense of the notes I had taken. Dad's image revolved around superlatives and hyperbole. Most of the opinions were favorable, but some dared to be negative — as if time had finally allowed the polished surface of the hero to tarnish, given people the courage to voice what were once just rumors. Those opinions took me back to my days in Berkeley when I discovered a side of Dad I had tried in vain to forget.

His voice was gravelly, steady, deliberate. It was a voice that ordered without ordering. He heard you and was there for you, but when you turned your back, he did what he liked. No one got angry. He allowed photos to be taken, but only of his right profile (his best angle). He limped a little but tried to hide it when people he didn't know well were around. He could go without showering for a week but would bathe himself in cologne. He could spend hours staring at a wall; he said he learned the technique in Berkeley and it was his way of finding inner peace in the midst of so much chaos. He liked to mention his time in Berkeley whenever he could. He said he'd acquired great revolutionary experience there: they had killed the Vice-Chancellor, that great symbol of the establishment. He always read a few pages of whatever book he had on hand before sleeping. He slept little and very lightly; the slightest thing would wake him up and he couldn't fall back to sleep. He was a womanizer, had risked everything a few times to sleep with students who idolized him. To his closest comrades he said that the most important thing was to "transcend, become a part of history."

When he formed MAS, the idea was to become the axis of resistance against Montenegro. The group was very small, but he didn't want to make a pact with anyone: not with MIR, "good little bourgeois boys"; not with the miners and laborers, "hardly radical"; and not with the campesinos, "who left Che all alone." So he led the party into an irrelevance they escaped from only because of the fall of Montenegro. His voice was gravelly, steady, deliberate. He asked people to give more than they were able to. At times he wanted them to be able to go beyond, be steadfast in the defense of their ideals, never accept the situation. Deep down, his true objective wasn't triumph or the revolution, but keeping the struggle alive. He took the death of a comrade personally and would take time to find the family and offer his condolences. He was part angel.

When the party was ambushed or suffered setbacks, he concluded that since Montenegro knew the group's movements so well, it had been infiltrated. He discovered the traitors and had them shot, despite opposition from his brother. "Extreme times call for extreme measures," he would say. If anything went wrong he would furrow his brow and could take it out physically on any underling who got in his way. He was part devil. No one except his brother would confront him. That didn't accomplish much, though; his brother was ignored. Theirs was a strange relationship.

He liked Bob Dylan. He would lock himself in a room wherever he happened to be and taciturnly stare at the cover of a book for hours, or tie and untie his shoes, or light a cigarette and moments later throw it on the floor, as if the whole weight of the world were borne by him alone. He had defeat on his mind. Gravelly, steady, deliberate. Transcend, become a part of history. Extreme times, extreme measures. Angel, devil, defeat, death, disappearance.

I heard a lot of stories about Dad during that time, some of them new, others repeated: the time he escaped a military patrol by hiding in a confessional (confirmed); when he escaped from a jail disguised as a guard (doubtful) or jumped into a river to save a stranger from drowning (maybe); the time a bullet hit the medallion of the Virgin Mary that he wore around his neck (impossible) . . . Stories abounded, and it was easy to doubt the truth of some of them. For having lived such a short time, Dad had had a cinematographic life. That's how popular myths are created: when people believe they've been in contact with someone special, they extract part of the meaning of their lives around that contact and build it into the substance of their days, aggrandizing it in order to aggrandize themselves by association. I had to listen to the stories, take notes, and later decipher which of all the tales, all the literature, were true.

Mom seemed to be one of the few who managed to stay outside of Dad's orbit, at least the mom that I knew. They had been teenage sweethearts, and when he came back from Berkeley in the early seventies, they went out again. She got pregnant, and they were married two months before I was born. In my version of events, neither of them had been in love. They were together only rarely because he was in hiding during Montenegro's dictatorship. We spent a lot of time at Uncle David and Aunt Elsa's house. After Dad died, Mom did everything she could to give me a life where he was not an overwhelming presence. While the country created the myth, she changed my last name and gave me hers, forbade the mention of Dad at home, and paraded lovers through her bed without the slightest respect for her status as the hero's widow.

I was surprised that almost no one spoke to me about Dad's literary side. That was what really interested me, since, beyond the opinions and the stories, the true depth of Dad — his dream realized, his conglomerate of obsessions and nightmares — was found in his writing. It was as if he had written *Berkeley* in secret, in the darkness of his room in hiding, behind his political life. As if he had done everything possible to prevent the two worlds from touching or mixing. As if he were trying to go against the current of Latin American tradition, which fused literature and politics, or chose literature and renounced politics. He had chosen both and decided that the best way to keep them alive inside was to keep them in separate compartments: a project as notable as it was utopian. No wonder the book had to be published posthumously.

"*Berkeley* can be interpreted as a political critique of media," my uncle told me one rainy morning in the living room, in his housecoat and a glass of Chivas already in his hand, the ice rattling against the glass. "And as a history as well, starting with the telegraph and even, in the last chapter, prophesying the coming of the Internet . . . 'a time in space without depth.' The novel runs through the political use of these media, their manipulation by the government. If you'll notice, there's one chapter dedicated to radio, another to newspapers, and another to film. It is, of course, more ambiguous because even though the Cuervos Anacoretas are constantly being manipulated by the government and they come to their end because of it, it can also be said that, in a way, each one of them finds his small redemption thanks to these media, which put them all in touch with various forms of the hereafter. Geographical and emotional in Bernard's case, and metaphysical in Montiel's."

That was one interpretation. There was another (there were many). The fantastical saga of the Cuervo Anacoreta brotherhood, spanning space and 150 years, was, in my opinion, a great experimental text, full of linguistic fireworks and formal audacity that dared to propose something both sweet and cruel: that we each possess our lost paradise, but there's no way to get it back. Berkeley, more than a specific geographical location, became a symbol of this lost paradise, glimpsed by Bernard once and then never found again. I had identified with Bernard's search and made his nostalgia my own — so much so that I had followed in his steps, and Dad's, to the point of going to study in Berkeley.

"And how did you get involved in politics?" I took the opportunity to ask after a long pause. "I know it was Aunt Elsa. But how, exactly?"

My uncle cleared his throat. He turned down the volume on the TV — an exhibition game between Holland and Argentina. Outside, the wind blew forcefully against the walls. I lit a cigarette.

"You have to have lived in the seventies to understand," he continued. "A lot of people were happy with Montenegro, and I admit that maybe I was one of them. At least for the first few years. We had come out of a period when the country was leftist, when there was constant instability and dangerous polarizations. All of a sudden, here was someone brandishing an argument about order. And the economy was all right. But Pedro, Elsa, and their friends never left me alone. Pedro was the first; he really felt it. He came back from Berkeley with this idea of 'leading the revolution.' Nothing could stop him, not even the fact that he arrived and in less than a year was married to his teenage sweetheart. Your mom."

He paused, took a swig of whiskey, and choked. With big bags under his eyes, unshaven, his gaze unfocused, he looked worn-out, as if he were terminally ill. I had heard him pacing in the patio that night; it looked like he hadn't slept at all. The smoke from my Marlboro rose slowly to the ceiling, beginning to pollute the air. I took my glasses off and cleaned the dirty lenses on the sleeve of my sweater.

"Poor thing. She was alone most of the time. Pedro spent his time in hiding, so much so that when she got pregnant we all joked that his aim was enviable: they slept together once a year and that was all it took. They never lived together like a normal couple. That's why I don't blame her for going on her own when you were born. She was very much in love and suffered a lot, but she wanted to give you a normal life with no surprises. And she did. That's why I don't blame her for anything. At some point it had to be her turn to have fun."

He was referring to the fact that, in order to escape poverty, Mom had become the lover of various politicians. When I was a teenager I got tired of hearing her arrive home early in the morning, trip up the stairs, sleep it off on one of the sofas or the rug. Later she turned to foreign industrialists. Dad had helped many people find themselves, but Mom had lost herself thanks to him.

"You had to know your dad. He spoke with such passion that he could ensnare you. It was impossible to say no to him. His smile, the way he gestured, his ideas — it was a complete package. I grew up with him and developed antibodies. Not so Elsa, and she fell into his camp easily. Well, she was predisposed to because of what happened to her brother in the Teoponte insurgency."

"Wasn't Dad already in hiding?"

"Sometimes late at night or early in the morning he'd show up at the house in disguise. He wasn't an important leader yet, and the government wasn't watching us. Then things got complicated. I already told you I could have continued on without getting involved, that politics really didn't interest me. Elsa talked about it from morning until night: how the dictatorship was a violation of our rights. But we were living well, we had work, there was stability."

"Orden, paz, y trabajo."

"I changed jobs all the time, but the point is that there were jobs. I started to feel guilty. One day Elsa told me she wanted to join MAS in earnest; the resistance had grown. She backed me into a corner. She asked me to do it for her brother. She talked about our future children, that she wanted them to grow up free. I decided to do what she asked. Not so much because I believed in the 'popular insurrection,' but because I didn't want to lose her."

He was serious, staring fixedly at the screen. Holland had just scored a goal. You could hear the rain falling in the patio, on the container, like the continuous hammering of nails on tin.

"That's not true," he went on. "I didn't want to lose her, but I also had to admit that what she said made sense. And what Pedro said. We heard of friends who had been exiled, others arrested, some tortured. Montenegro was nothing, he never went to the evil lengths of a Pinochet or a Videla, but it's not about ranking dictators, is it? One abuse, one death, is enough to dirty the hands of a whole government, and it deserves to fall."

"Maybe your way was better," I said. "While most of your generation were born convinced that revolution was right, that it was worth risking your life to stand up to a dictatorship, you became convinced of it bit by bit. You took your time, but when you saw that it was the right thing to do, you didn't hesitate."

"Oh, I hesitated all right — a lot." He sighed. "But in the end I did it. And look how it all ended."

We both watched the game for a while. I came back with another question: "When did Dad write?"

"He wrote all the time. Life in hiding isn't as romantic as you might think. There were entire weeks of complete immobility, the angst of waiting, for what you didn't even know, interrupted by a few days of frantic activity. Haven't you noticed how many guerrillas kept diaries? Plus, the important thing was to leave a record. It was another way of transcending."

"You didn't?"

"Letters. Many letters."

I would have liked to insist on this point, but he continued:

"Sometimes Pedro wrote by hand. You'd find him concentrated in some corner, absorbed, nothing like the hyperactive Pedro of orders and counter-orders when he put a plan into action, when we would head out at three A.M. to blow up pylons — something, by the way, I came to like doing. Destruction as a means of creation. The kidnappings, not so much — innocent industrialists, pissing their pants, serving as bait so we could raise funds. Other times you'd hear the rhythmic tap of the typewriter coming from his rooms. He was very mysterious about his manuscript. I thought it was his diary — that was the most obvious thing, after all — and it was only after his death that I discovered it was a novel. I didn't even suspect it. He read a lot, but mostly Regis Debray and things like that. He did like *Hopscotch*."

Would I find La Maga? I had read that book twice without ever entirely discovering why Dad had revered it so much. I assumed it was just another generational difference.

"When Montenegro left power, Pedro became one of the leaders of the left — a minor leader, but a leader all the same. Although I don't think he ever stopped missing the years of armed struggle, when we were sure to lose. His utopian plans were counterbalanced by his strong ambition to come to power. He didn't want to make a pact with Quiroga Santa Cruz, who was the best person to unify the left. And there were historical leaders like Siles Suazo and those from this new generation, like Paz Zamora. I think your dad was always ambitious, but both things were compatible in him: he wanted to come to power in order to carry out his reforms. People were jealous of him, and disturbing rumors began to surface. They said he was a womanizer of the worst kind. Here, it's fine for a politician to be seen as a womanizer. Within certain limits, of course. And so they painted him as someone without limits — that he was my wife's lover. Which wasn't true, but can you imagine? Getting involved with his brother's wife!"

"People will say anything," I said automatically, shaking my head while wondering whether there was any truth to that rumor.

"We went back into hiding two years later, after García Meza's coup. Our movement had lost even more power because of Pedro's inability to make a pact with the other groups. We were dissolving into insignificance. Sometimes I couldn't believe Pedro was so stubborn, thought maybe it was calculated and deep down he was hoping things would fall apart . . . He was trying in vain to reorganize his power when the Unzueta Street attack occurred. In the end, and forgive me for saying this, he was the only one who came out on top. You saw how quickly the myth about him was created."

"That doesn't mean he didn't deserve it."

"No. But this is about trying to humanize your dad, show a more complex side of him. That's your job, isn't it?"

He appeared desolate. He was looking at me as if he had omitted the most important thing, as if he couldn't tell me. I decided to stop with my questions. The more I learned about Dad, the less I knew him.

My uncle took two steps and, all of a sudden, fell to the floor. He tried in vain to break his fall with his arms. The force of his landing scared me; I was by his side immediately. He lay face down for a moment, muttering swears. After a while he got onto his knees and tried to stand up on his own; he couldn't and let me help him.

"Are you all right?"

"Everything hurts," he said, puffing angrily. "It's nothing, don't worry. I just lost my balance, it happens sometimes. Sudden movements."

I felt a waft of alcohol hit my face and didn't ask any more questions.

I had another interpretation of *Berkeley,* a more complicated and unproven one. The novel was full of secret messages, cryptograms that the characters constantly exchanged. *Berkeley*'s obsession with telegraphs and computers was because they were the ideal media for transmitting coded messages, converting the world into a secret code. I thought that all those disparate messages, many of which I had managed to decipher, referred back to one code, the center that would unite the textual labyrinth. As if the secret message behind the plot were able to hide an even more secret message.

I talked about these things with Carolina. We were walking through the courtyard at La Salle, down the hallways where Dad must have once played with Villa, in search of an illusory image of the place (this scene wasn't the same as it had been when Dad was a child). She listened and then asked me to stop theorizing so much, to put my thoughts in order and sit down to write. Her high heels resonated against the school's white walls.

"Do you think you can put me in touch with the band Berkeley?" I asked her suddenly.

"Sure. What's up?"

"I don't know. I saw their video and it's as if they wanted to reconstruct the Unzueta Street events, half in code. Maybe I could write a final chapter about Dad's legacy to younger generations. Or an article."

I was lying. I was interested in finding out why this interpretation had perturbed my uncle so much. I knew I should speak to him first, ask him what exactly had happened that day, how Dad and Aunt Elsa had died. I knew the big picture, but now I needed the details, the minutiae that would differentiate this attack from the others. I had to find just the right moment, get him when his guard was down.

We were going home on Carolina's motorcycle; it was dusk, and something happened. It was her body against mine, or her perfume, or the way her hair tickled my face; the thing is, I embraced her tightly and she understood I was suggesting something. We headed toward her apartment. I was a bit unsure of what I was suggesting, but wasn't about to tell her to change direction. I hadn't planned it, it hadn't even occurred to me seconds before I held her, but once we were in her bed, naked and lit by the last of the fading sun coming in through her blinds, everything seemed so natural that I wondered why the hell I had waited so long to be with her again, why I had been so ridiculously scrupulous.

Walking home later (I hadn't wanted Carolina to take me), I remembered why. I knew I was a lowlife who could never be as good as Ashley, as good as the love between us. Not only had I escaped physically, but now I had tried to escape mentally and emotionally as well.

But that was all just an illusion: I hadn't escaped anything and was headed straight toward the whirlwind that had thrown my life into confusion.

6

THE FIRST time Ashley came to my apartment on Mayfair Street, which faced a park of trees with branches stretched skyward, empty of children, dogs, and noise, she told me that my carpet needed cleaning and that my Magritte reproductions from the Museum of Modern Art in New York (a gift from Jean) were magnificent — especially *L'empire des lumières,* with its natural juxtaposition of night and day in a forty-inch-by-thirty-inch frame.

"It's so big compared to mine," she said. "I see that professors earn a very good living."

"Not really. Although, for the amount we work, maybe."

"You need some plants. I don't know, a woman's touch."

"I don't know how to take care of plants, they always die on me. I suppose I've let you down. You expected a poster of Che on one wall or that photo of Menchú receiving the Nobel."

"Just one of your classes is enough to tell me you're not the type."

"I teach Chungara's book." I smiled. "Isn't that enough?"

"There's nothing from Bolivia here."

I showed her three small paintings of smiling indigenous women by the fridge.

"They're the size of postage stamps."

"Walls are made to hold the pictures you like, not to profess your nationality."

"I bet you don't even have any music from your country."

"I do. Savia Andina, Kjarkas, Pacha. Tons. I never listen to it. Why make myself more homesick than I already am just from not living there?"

"Homesick. Anyone listening might actually believe you."

She stood in front of my bookshelves while I opened the fridge and poured two glasses of apple juice. There were a lot of history books ordered alphabetically by author, but very few on political theory.

"You seem more like a historian than a political scientist."

"Maybe I chose the wrong profession. It's hard for me to theorize. I envy historians — the facts, the facts, the facts. Siempre tienen de donde agarrarse."

"But don't you think they have to theorize too? Postulate hypotheses?"

"Sure. But they seem more concrete que nosotros."

She took a book by Castañeda about the Latin American left and Sergio Ramírez's memoirs of the Sandinista revolution off the shelf and asked to borrow them. She sat down on the sofa, the slit on one side of her blue skirt revealing her muscled right thigh. She flipped distractedly through my video collection.

"You should switch to DVD," she said. "Much, much better. Estás muy atrasado."

"I'm a professor, remember. We like to be anachronistic."

I put the glasses on the floor and turned the TV on, leaving it on the Cartoon Network — Tweety saying "I tawt I taw a puddy tat!" and Sylvester waiting for him behind the door — and sat down next to her.

"You like cartoons?"

"Any channel is fine as background noise. I have to have the TV on."

"Watch out. Ghosts come out of there at night and steal your soul."

I looked at her without knowing how to continue the conversation, afraid to take the next step. She had taken her jacket off and her nipples pushed up against her white shirt. The house shook as a truck went by. I could feel my cheeks burning. I started to stare at

Ashley's gold engagement ring, as if hypnotized by it, paralyzed by a moment of desire. The hand wearing it became invisible. A heavy ring was suspended above my head, a woman who didn't belong to me . . . I had taken this game too far, had better stop.

"I should go," she said.

"Yeah. It's getting late."

"I hope I was able to help you plan your work. La influencia de Borges en Hollywood. We started by reading 'El Sur' and watching *Jacob's Ladder*."

"Right. Got it."

Her braces made me think of a ridiculous pickup line: "If I touch them, will I get a shock?" I didn't say it, but it was as if I had: she brought her face close to mine and kissed me gently, her green eyes wide open. That was all it took for me to throw away my scruples — my attempt at scruples — and get back on track. With the next kiss she bit my lips, and her tongue slowly made its way into my mouth.

"You gave me a shock."

"Really?"

I unbuttoned her white shirt, a man's shirt (Patrick's?), and my shaky right hand ran over her breasts, softly at first and then with more urgency. In the background, far, far away, I could hear Tweety's high voice.

A short while later, she lay back on the couch and I buried my face between her legs. I didn't stop until I felt the first tremors run through her body. Then I stopped, took my clothes off, and sought her as I had wanted to from the moment I suggested she come to my apartment. We wasted no time losing ourselves.

"You think I'm going to hell?" Ashley said when she woke up. She had fallen asleep on the sofa with me next to her, my eyes closed but awake.

"I don't think so. Are you serious?"

"Of course not," she said, laughing. "No soy muy religiosa que digamos. A bit spiritual, yes, but religious, no. Will I keep calling you Professor?"

"Now more than ever."

"You have such small ears," she said, stroking them. "Te llamaré Little Ear."

"You look good with your hair down," I replied, playing with one of her long locks. "You look too formal when it's in a ponytail."

"Sometimes I get tired of it and want to cut it all off. El moño is a compromise. Even though it does make my face look round. Will you open your big mouth and tell everyone?"

"It's me who has the most to lose. And I don't have anyone to tell anything to."

"No lo creas." Her Spanish accent moved me. "Do you promise to erase my e-mails?"

"As if you had never existed."

"This never happened, OK? Not here. It belongs to another world. One in which there's only you and me."

She regretted what had just happened and didn't want anything more between us. She would hold on to the memory of this afternoon as something special and would go back to her routine, her life of classes and fiancé and the wedding that lay waiting just around the corner.

I was wrong. She wanted to continue our relationship as she had suggested, as if ours were a reality very different from the one that overwhelmed other mere mortals. We would keep quiet, we would erase all the e-mails we sent each other, we would keep a respectable distance between us in class. I had just started to get to know Ashley and was already discovering that when it came to a lack of scruples she wasn't far behind me.

The idea frightened and seduced me. Furtive affairs call out to me — passion spent in search of a single night of fulfillment. The relationships I seek are those that have the certainty of an inevitable end, whether because of the other person or geography. I realize that I've lost true love — or not so true, after all — because of my sudden boredom after a few months of passion. I admit I'm more suited to the glittering quest for superiority than the opaque but longer-lasting shine of daily life.

And so I embarked on a relationship with Ashley, confident

that the affair wouldn't last beyond October, thinking that maybe I was doing her a favor: it was her way of saying goodbye to single life. On campus, it was as if neither of us knew that the other existed, and our e-mails were kept short, only a line or two. But at least twice a week, in the afternoons, she visited me with the excuse that she was going to the gym. She showed up wearing a black Adidas tracksuit, bringing a bag of M&Ms, Pringles, and Hershey chocolates, listening to her Nomad — Shakira, Café Tacuba, the inevitable Rodríguez and Milanés, Los Secretos, Sabina, Paula Cole, They Might Be Giants, a lot of music from the seventies, especially ELO, and the downloads of the week. La Chica Adidas I called her, and she had a long list of nicknames for me — Professor Little Ear was her favorite.

They were intense hours that left us physically and emotionally exhausted, and became the main objective of the week. We barely said goodbye and were already planning the next meeting. One afternoon she had me meet her in a cheap motel on Route 15. There, in Room 132, she gave me a rapturous striptease to the beat of a Madonna song — see-through black silk lingerie — and we made love and showered together, with MTV as background noise (I remember hearing Garbage; she loved Shirley Manson's voice and red hair). Another afternoon she had me meet her at the Holiday Inn, where she was waiting for me with a long cream-colored scarf with which to tie up my hands and blindfold me. We needed hotels, she said, so that my neighbors wouldn't suspect anything.

"We'd be in big trouble, Little Ear," she said, smiling.

"Who can see us? The retiree on the corner who spends his time on the porch? He's deaf and dumb, I think. And if he sees you, so what? How's he going to know who you are? Who could he tell?"

"Still. ¿Te imaginas si Patrick se entera? He wouldn't kill us, but it would destroy him. Well, maybe he *would* kill us."

"What do you mean?"

"Don't worry. He doesn't even raise his voice to me. But people in love do crazy things, don't they?"

▪ ▪ ▪

Reality intruded on our lives at times. One day as I was coming out of a meeting, Professor Clavijero, in his chronically venomous tone of voice, said he'd noticed I'd been distracted. We were at the main entrance to the Institute; a poster announced a protest against military exercises in Vieques and another the trip to Fort Benning that Helen was organizing.

"One of your students told me the same thing," he said. "He came to complain."

"That's not good at all. Next time, ask him to speak to me directly."

Poor guy, I said to myself: an exile, someone who maybe dreamt of a Havana that no longer existed and where it was better not to return. Is that what gave him the bad attitude he confronted everyone with, that ability to dislike everything and everyone, his talent for holding a grudge?

"I'm his advisor," he said. "He can tell me whatever he wants."

He walked away grumbling. I would soon have my first evaluation, and surely I would pay for this. It shouldn't have bothered me, but it did.

Another day Yasemin told me I'd been distant and too serious in class. We were walking through the Arts Quad. Two men were painting the statue of Randolph Jones a metallic green, brightening up his years. His eyes were sad. Had the messages to his cousin gotten through? They said he'd died of a heart attack during a spiritualist session where, through a medium, he finally heard the childlike voice of his beloved. Maybe he had tried to communicate with her out of desperation, deep down knowing he would never be able to; then, when he heard her voice — what he thought was her voice — it was simply too much for him.

"It's midterm," I said. "I'm up to here with work."

"Maybe you're up to there with something else," she commented with a glance I couldn't interpret — jealousy or complicity.

I went to Helen's office. Her desk was covered with manuscripts and piles of papers to be corrected, the computer was on, and e-mails arrived incessantly. How were preparations for Fort Benning going?

"Very well. Sure you don't want to come?" she asked, setting down the green file folder she'd been reviewing when I came in. I suddenly realized it might be my file. My whole history at the Institute was there, the recognition and complaints, the evaluations and works published. I wanted to reach forward, open it, and read it.

"I have a lot of work this semester. But I hope you film it all. It would be fantastic for my students. And you'll come to my class to speak, won't you? I've already mentioned the topic. It's incredible; very few knew about the SOA's role in our history."

In truth, as much as I hated the existence of this training camp for military repression on the continent, I couldn't see myself holding up a sign in front of its walls.

"Joaquín and a couple of other students are coming with me." I was surprised to hear Joaquín's name. "It's going to be the biggest protest in recent years. Viene Martin Sheen. Not that that really matters to me, but it's the only way to get on the news. I love him in *The West Wing*. Proof that you have to be a good actor if you want to be president . . ."

I admired her enthusiasm. She directed over ten thesis students, was on innumerable committees, and had to fight with three teenage daughters, and she still had time to organize protests. Next to her I felt useless, as if I wasted every minute.

"My evaluation is coming up," I said. "I'm a bit nervous."

"It's easy, don't worry." Her maternal tone calmed me. "Even if you hadn't published a thing these last few years and there were a thousand complaints, we wouldn't fire you. It's just to see your progress, so that you're not surprised when the real evaluation comes around."

She let out a sharp laugh. Her office was cold; the walls were bare, and there were few books on the shelves. I remembered Wickley's office, overflowing with posters and plants.

"Sometimes I think it would be better if I didn't write for magazines, that you hold it against me."

"Castañeda writes for *Newsweek* and no one says a thing."

"Castañeda is Castañeda. Yo no tengo tenure." I asked her what she thought of Clavijero.

"Why?" She adopted a conspiratorial tone. "Has he said anything to you?"

"At times he seems very aggressive toward me. As if he's not quite convinced I should be here."

"He's a great colleague, but he can be unpleasant if he gets something or someone in his head," she said. "This Institute would be nothing if it weren't for him. He was the first permanent professor. He hired me ten years ago. At that time I was working on topics like the impact of American foreign policy on the continent and he was very happy with me. One day I got tired of Kissinger and company, discovered another topic that interested me much more, and he never approved of it. We started to draw apart."

She stood up as if to bring our talk to a close.

"Don't pay much attention to him," she added. "He's going through a rough time because the dean has suggested he retire. Le está costando asimilarlo. You didn't hear this."

She asked me to keep her informed if anything happened. On my way home, I was still thinking about the green file folder.

Every now and then Ashley would mention her frantic wedding plans.

"Mom has noticed I'm not as enthusiastic as I was," she told me as we sat in a Jacuzzi, her naked body resting against mine. "If she only knew. Patrick senses that something strange is going on with me, pero evidentemente no sabe lo que es. He comments that I'm going to the gym an awful lot. I tell him it's to relieve stress, that you don't just get married every day. And anyhow, it's him who's going to benefit."

"Quite the muscles." I tried to joke but had noticed her worried tone. "All that exercise."

She didn't laugh.

I went on, "Aren't you tense?"

"I don't know what to do. What should I do?"

"Maybe it's better if . . ."

There was a pause. I caressed her mole-covered back, bit gently along her shoulders and neck. No response. The hot water had relaxed us too much.

"Maybe what?"

"Nothing. Nothing."

"Do you picture yourself as an academic for the rest of your life?"

"No way. It's an emasculating profession. I'd like to . . . do something that's more relevant to people."

"What you do *is* relevant."

"Only to a few."

"'La gente' es una gran abstracción. What you'd like is to be a populist."

"I would've liked to have had Dad's personality. To go into politics, I mean. A life dedicated to public service. Do something to change things."

"Like what?"

"I don't know, but something. We're too conformist."

"You're never conformist. So many people envy you and you still complain. Quizás that way you're more at ease with your conscience. So not everything is so easy for you."

"Maybe. But I also don't know what I'd do with my life without this."

"Maybe. De por ahí you're sterile, and so emasculation doesn't affect you."

"Un match perfecto."

"Would you like to go back to Bolivia one day?"

"I always go back."

"I mean to live."

"Don't ask such difficult questions. Sí. No. Maybe. I don't know. I didn't come here to stay, but somehow I have. I'd like to go back, but it gets harder all the time. Deep down, I think I've gotten used to missing it, to living away. I can't live without the idea of returning, but at the same time I'm afraid to go back."

"You can't go home again."

"You can go home again, but you don't know if you should."

"Podrías convertirte en un American citizen and take part in politics here."

"Never. I owe this country a lot, it's given me the chance to work at something I like, pero no lo siento mío."

"It must be strange to live in a country but not really live there."

"As a matter of fact, I like it that way."

"I want more," she whispered, her face still sunk into the pillow as I tried to control my racing breath.

"The only thing my dad thinks about are his stocks." We were lying on the carpet in my apartment, looking at the ceiling, holding hands, Sabina on the stereo. "He's so ambitious, in the most material sense of the word. He'll never respect what I study. He wants me to be a lawyer o una de esas profesiones 'more useful for society.' My mom's the same. I hope you never meet them. Son *tan* middle-class."

"And this is your way of rebelling? Getting involved with your professor?"

"One of many."

"There's nothing more middle-class than graduate studies."

"Sí. Mejor me callo." She touched her nose with her right index finger. "The intrepid traveler . . . and there's nothing more sedentary than a Ph.D."

"También tienes stock."

"But to me it's like playing with Monopoly money." She sighed. "Sometimes I miss the days when I didn't know what to do with my life and traveled in search of experiences."

"I'm sure you'll be off again soon. I love it when you touch your nose. Every time you're nervous or anxious, there goes your hand, like clockwork. That's my favorite gesture."

She asked me to show her pictures of Dad. Black-and-white photos taken in Berkeley, found years ago in an album of my uncle's. A sit-in at People's Park. A heated discussion with the police, the International House in the background. Long hair, mustache, and sideburns, his right hand held out in the peace sign. The stereotypical figure from an era my generation was nostalgic for without ever having lived it, as if seeing itself in an impossibly distant mirror.

"He's not at all like you, at least not physically."

A sort of improved version of his brother, he was tall but not too tall, had a good build without being too robust, and the lines of his face were delicate without losing their masculinity. Despite his long hair and sideburns, just looking at him made you think of harmony, order. That was the beginning of the end: it was easy to imagine him as a measured, rational being whose passions were guided by lucidity, not excess.

"Good-looking. So we're going to read his novel. Tell me more about him. Fill in the blanks."

"I can tell you about him in Berkeley. Or rather, about him and my time in Berkeley."

The official version went along the lines that Dad had radicalized his political vocation in Berkeley. That was true, but only as long as it didn't simplify his whole life. Dad had discovered many things in Berkeley. So had I.

I asked to live at the International House because that was where Dad had lived for a few years while he studied for his Ph.D. in political science. I would reach him, and through him Bernard, and Berkeley through both of them. I would walk the halls where he had walked, eat in the cafeteria where he had eaten. Of course, I didn't say that on the application form. I had Mom's last name; I didn't want them to think I was lying about my relationship to Reissig just to get one of the sought-after spaces at the I-House. It was a student residence with Southwest-inspired architecture, an inner patio, and a minaret-like cupola, located next to the football stadium. Half of the residents were foreigners and the other half Americans. I was assigned a room on the fourth floor, small, but with the advantage of a dazzling view out my window of the whole Bay Area: the city of Berkeley and the campus to my right, then the waters of the bay and the bridge on which a heavy fog sometimes lay, and in the distance, like the magical end of the rainbow, San Francisco. Light filled my eyes. The air was clear, not opaque like in Río Fugitivo.

My first group of friends in Berkeley were four classmates who started their doctorates with me: Elka, Carmen, Linda, and Tsiu. We had one class together on methodology to help prepare us for our jobs as teaching assistants, part of the work-study scholarship. In the afternoons we would meet at C'est Café on the corner of Bancroft and Telegraph — the perfect angle for Ansel Adams to get the cover photo of *Berkeley* — and watch the faces and extravagant styles, tattoos and nose piercings, Birkenstocks and patchouli, while we commented on the forced survival of a certain hippie culture in the midst of a grunge youth.

"Even though something of the sixties spirit remains," I said, "it was more about atmosphere then. There's no better way to prove that than by reading *Berkeley*."

They asked me what I was talking about, and I excitedly told them about the novel. I got them to read it and told them, asking them to keep it a secret, that my dad was the author. Not one of them understood it or was impressed by it.

"It's probably a joke," Tsiu said. "Your last name isn't Reissig and you're nothing like him."

I didn't bother to argue. Dad's destiny seemed to be as a cult writer.

On Fridays we would go to Larry Blake's for beer. It was there I first kissed Elka, my German classmate with hair so blond it faded into white.

"Spare me the details," Ashley said.

Elka was depressed. Her reading the first week of classes was an essay by Weber — "Politics as a Vocation" — that had made her realize her naïveté in viewing politics as disinterested community service.

"If politics is as amoral and pragmatic as Weber says it is, is it worth studying?"

Elka and I weren't compatible: what brought us together were complaints about a couple of professors and our amazement at walking down Telegraph Avenue among people reading tarot cards on the corner, fifty-year-olds promoting campaigns to legalize marijuana, or a man with a snake wrapped around his neck, carrying a stereo with Nirvana on at full volume.

Need also brought us together. For five years I had been with Mariana, the girl I had left behind in Río Fugitivo and thought I was in love with, tirelessly wrote long, melodramatic, intense letters to, and phoned every once in a while during those days before e-mail.

"I can't imagine those days," Ashley said.

Mariana of big brown eyes and black hair, intolerable tenderness, who waddled like a duck and had a boyish body. I had never had a long-distance relationship and discovered, with anxiety and pleasure, that the flesh is weak — that my flesh was weak. Elka also missed her boyfriend, a systems analyst named Peter. Both of us, up until then, had been completely faithful. That ended a cycle for us both and, at least for me, began another. I discovered it was easier to be swept away by temptation than resist it. It was easier to say yes than no. I entered a world that I'm still incapable of leaving behind. My efforts to do so have been halfhearted, hesitant at best.

"I know." Ashley smiled, her right hand caressing my chest.

There were a lot of Latin Americans at the I-House. Most of them studied economics or engineering: Esteban, the Argentine who could read a Stephen King novel in one night; Rafa, the Mexican who liked Metallica; Piero, the Peruvian who went to the gym all the time; Marilia, the Brazilian who went with me to black-and-white films at the PFA; Maria, the Uruguayan obsessed with soccer; Jorge, the Chilean who idolized Pinochet so much that he called him Bolívar II. We ate together, sometimes we went to the movies together, and on Sunday afternoons some of us would go to the stadium to play soccer with the Europeans. Among ourselves we could tell the jokes that political correctness, then in its heyday, prevented us from telling in other circles.

That first Halloween we went to the gay pride celebration in the Castro district of San Francisco.

"San Francisco has changed so much now," Ashley said. "Full of dot-commers. And it's so expensive. It was such a beautiful city. Well, it still is, pero ya no es lo mismo."

After watching several groups of gays and lesbians parade by in their colorful attire, still shocked by a bisexual truckers' association and another of sadomasochists — the women with whips and the men with their backs covered with welts — we went to a nightclub that had two bathrooms: one for men and another for men. There, emboldened by alcohol, I made Tania a risqué proposal . . .

"I don't want to hear it. Weren't you going to tell me about your dad?"

"Oh, yeah. Sorry. It's just that, all of a sudden, that whole time came flooding back. To think that we all went to Zellerbach when Fujimori came to the university to accept an award."

"Fujimori in Berkeley. That does sound incredible."

"Just wait. Students might be liberal, but the administration is the same everywhere and in Berkeley it was particularly conservative. Fujimori was a hero at that time, one of the real people, who had managed to defeat Shining Path and inflation. We were sitting listening to his speech when, on a balcony to our left, two women and a man stood up with a Peruvian flag and began to shout 'Long live Shining Path and the revolution!' The police got them out of there right away."

"That sounds more like Berkeley to me."

"There's a branch of Shining Path in Berkeley. The People's Republic of Berkeley. But I'm getting off-track again. Or maybe I'm not. At the I-House, a Puerto Rican secretary who had been there back then told me that Dad had won a short-story contest. I'd said I was writing a report on Bolivians who had lived there and she came up with a few names: Tejada, Petrovic, Reissig . . ."

"A Necessary Crime." I suppose that was his start in literature. It was kept in a filing cabinet and the typewriter ink was fading on the yellowing pages. It was a mediocre detective story, an unsubtle satire, very much in keeping with the times: by using the murder of the director of the I-House he was trying to comment on students' power to rebel. I thought about the truth behind the saying that genius is the result of practice, not talent.

The overweight secretary, smelling of nicotine, as wrinkled as a crushed paper bag, told me that Reissig was antisocial at the I-House. He thought that those who lived there were little bourgeois who would never dare to take part in the revolution. He hated the Latin Americans most of all, saying they would go back to their countries and become part of the status quo without having learned a thing at Berkeley.

"He was here for a year and then he went to a co-op two blocks away. It was a co-op famous for its food orgies and because several of the residents were kicked out of the university. They were against the war in Vietnam and couldn't find any better way to show their pacifism than by bombing the Vice-Chancellor. But he wasn't the only one who died; so did his wife, his twin daughters, and a maid."

That was the story Dad had told of his time in Berkeley, the one he had used to start the legend about himself. True, he had omitted the part about innocent deaths.

"Don't worry. I think that happened a year before Reissig went to the co-op, if memory serves me correctly. It was a cowardly deed. At the very least they should have made sure to kill the right person."

She showed me the only photo there was of him in the residents' book from that year. Long hair, untidy beard and sideburns, his gaze fixed, and a knowing smile: that of a man who knows he's above the rest, I thought. One who likes to appear innocent.

"Why are you so interested in him?"

After asking her to please keep it a secret, I told her. She seemed genuinely surprised: I thought she believed me.

I would later learn, thanks to university records, that the Puerto Rican had gotten her times mixed up. After going through some files, the Korean American woman who helped me at Sproul Hall told me that the co-op was closed down during Dad's year there, 1971.

"Some of the residents were arrested, accused of conspiracy and first-degree murder, and had to spend between six months and five years in jail. Others disappeared, went into the mountains or to Canada. They were radicals associated with the Black Panthers and an offshoot of the Weather Underground called May 19, in honor of Malcolm X's birthday and Ho Chi Minh."

Dad had never gotten his Ph.D. in political science, as he had alleged. And he hadn't returned to Bolivia in order to fight Montenegro's regime, as he had heroically said again and again. He had gone back to Bolivia to escape a federal arrest warrant.

Seated behind her desk, the woman took off her shoes and continued reviewing files.

"Here's something interesting," she said. "An investigation revealed that not everyone at the co-op knew about the attack. There was a group involved in subversive activity, but the majority were more peaceful protesters — sit-ins, et cetera — and didn't even know about the others' subversive activities. The majority were absolved of all blame. Among them, Pedro Reissig."

"Really?" I said, surprised and somewhat disappointed. The legend of political activism that Dad had built up for himself was crumbling.

"Really. Reissig could have continued his studies without any problem. But he left that same semester. No reasons are given; however, from his grades it looks like he wasn't doing so well."

She asked me why I was interested, and I would've liked to have told her the truth. I didn't.

My search ended there, or at least that was what I thought at the time. What if there were more lies? I was either a coward or just immature, afraid to find out about my real father. I preferred to be like the rest and keep him protectively idealized. I would keep the leader, the martyr, the strategist. Without his strong image to guide me, what would become of me? Mom would be proven right to have done everything to erase him from my life.

Bit by bit I came to think that what I'd learned about Dad could be thought of as a white lie. At a time when he was struggling for the soul of the country, his participation in the murder of the Vice-Chancellor of Berkeley had served to legitimize him as brave, as a true revolutionary. And the title of doctor had served to legitimize him as an intellectual. He knew the historical importance of intellectuals on the continent, of their symbolic role as architects of national projects, mediators between different warring factions, the moral conscience of their societies. It was a role that transcended the limited scope of his words. You didn't have to read them to trust his ethical integrity.

"Poet and mathematician," said Ashley.

"Exactly."

"You never talk about your mom."

"She's a strange woman." I put on the video *The Trouble with Harry*. Ashley wasn't bothered by my interest in the classics, but she did think it was funny to only ever watch black-and-white movies.

"Why strange? Describe her."

"She has small brown eyes and wide eyebrows, and her mouth is a bit big."

"Like you."

"So they say. She was born at the wrong time. She was raised to become a housewife, have a stable home and several children. Instead she fell in love with a man who offered anything but stability. She wanted to be like other women those days, like my aunt Elsa, for example, but she didn't have the personality or the interest to get involved in politics and accompany Dad. I think he never forgave her for that. Later, she wanted to make up for lost time, women's lib and all that, but no one understood her and she got a bad reputation. I got mad at her once and she told me to go to hell. We started to grow apart."

"Was it your fault?"

"Maybe. For a while I thought it was hers. Now I'm not so sure. It's true that she gave me everything, that she was a good mother. It's true that I was selfish and didn't understand when she did things that you can accept in other women but not your own mother. Sometimes I miss her a lot. She's obsessive about cleanliness. She washes her hands I don't know how many times a day and lives with her toothbrush at hand."

"You spend all your time searching for your dad. Maybe you should be searching for her. Don't wait until it's too late."

"Isn't that what we all do?"

"Last night I read *Berkeley* in one sitting," she said, leaning up against the sofa. "It's full of salamanders. I'll have to read it again to understand it. It has some beautiful moments — Bernard moved me and Xavier is fantastic. It's very romantic, con toda esta idea del lost paradise. But it's complicated, I think unnecessarily. Why all those chronological leaps? The story could have taken place over two months and would've been a lot stronger. Why one hundred fifty years? Characters who are reincarnated as other men but keep their names and their looks?"

"That was the style then. To the question why, te digo why not?"

"You're angry. It's a great novel, very ambitious, but . . . And there's so much technology. What was his obsession? And the political question isn't very clear. Was he really a leftist?"

"Being on the left doesn't mean you have to write a leftist novel."

"I don't know. It seems like an almost final version, but not quite. ¿Me entiendes?"

"It was published posthumously. If he could have, maybe he would've revised it a couple of times more. But that should be secondary, shouldn't it? Don't worry. I'm used to it. Nobody will react the way I do; it's that simple."

"That's not bad, is it?"

"I don't know."

"Have you ever been in love?" Ashley asked me, Charlie Parker playing on the radio — a song of pain, loss, cigarette smoke, and midnight.

"Many times. You?"

"Seriously, tell me the truth. Have you or haven't you?"

"You didn't let me tell you about my romances in Berkeley."

"Eran intranscendentes. Answer me."

"Many times."

"Which means never."

"You?"

"Just once."

"When?"

"I'm not naming names."

"Last night I told Patrick all about us," Ashley said, *A Touch of Evil* on the TV — a movie I never tired of watching.

"You're crazy!"

"Don't worry. I told him as if it were a fantasy of mine. To go to a motel on Route 15 with him and some unknown man. Make love con ese otro hombre while Patrick watched. He got excited; he loved it. There's always been a bit of the voyeur to him. He thought

I told him all this to pleasure him, as a gesture of love. If he only knew."

"Don't do it again. It's not only cruel, it's dangerous."

"Now you're going to tell me what's cruel?"

"Even the most despicable deeds have to be done with some style."

"Ladrón de guante blanco. Style or no, nobody beats your cynicism."

"That's why you like me."

"One of the reasons."

"Tell me something, but be honest," she said, serious, one cloudy afternoon. We were naked, playing Scrabble on my bed. "Do you think I'm capable of falling in love?"

"Do you think Patrick will kill me?"

"Come on."

"I think you already are."

"De quién?"

"Do I have to tell you?" It was my turn at Scrabble, and I got a long word, "granted."

"No promises, no conditions?"

"If you find the right man, yes. You'd be capable of leaving everything behind."

"And you don't think I've already found him?"

"No promises, no conditions?"

I started to stare at her gold ring (she never took it off; she was afraid of forgetting it). At some point it would all end, and given the circumstances, the sooner the better. But I couldn't end it, and I didn't think she could either. We wanted to disguise it as a simple affair, but deep down we knew we were kidding ourselves, that ever since that afternoon at Madison CyberEspresso — or had it been that first morning at Common Ground? — we were inexorably in love, living the clumsy charade of a furtive affair. The beginning of the end, we both knew, would be when one of us began to ask about the other's feelings, to wake up from the fog that prevented us from thinking rationally and attempt to take control of the facts, whether for a greater or a lesser commitment. Everything could continue on as long as neither attempted to control what was happening to us. Would love be enough to leave everything else behind? Or was it that, once she had spoken, we both knew it wouldn't be?

When we were getting dressed I told her she looked like an exclusive model for Victoria's Secret (all her lingerie was that brand). She made a face that couldn't help become a smile.

At the end of October it was Ashley who came to the logical conclusion: she didn't love Patrick and should break off the engagement. She told me in a roundabout way, insinuating, waiting for me to help her make that decision.

I got scared. What about the scandal at the university? Weren't we rushing things a bit? Reasons, goddamn reasons came to my aid. It must have hurt Ashley that I wasn't able to live up to her "no promises, no conditions," that I wasn't at the level she expected of me: her love was far superior to mine, there was absolutely no comparison. But she said nothing and continued to see me. Neither one of us dared make any kind of decision. And so the days passed.

I taught her a secret language, one we had fun using to send each other e-mails. She taught me how to Internet-trade. She talked me into investing $500; I did and lost it in two days. I never played again (money was real, but in front of a screen full of graphics it seemed like a game). Ashley felt guilty and wanted to pay me back. I thanked her for her good intentions but rejected the offer. It wasn't her money.

On Halloween I met Ashley and Patrick at a grad student party. I was with Yasemin and Joaquín; I hadn't wanted to go, but Yasemin had insisted (she was meeting up there with Morgana, the woman she had been sleeping with lately).

"I don't recognize that cologne," Yasemin said.

"Boss. Relativamente nuevo. I bought it on the Internet. You like it?"

"Too sweet. You wear cologne every day, don't you? Con razón you always smell so good. And I've discovered your secret. You wear contact lenses to parties. Y para algunas clases y reuniones. You're so vain it's not even funny."

Joaquín told us about his planned trip to Fort Benning. He was going for anthropological reasons, out of curiosity, and to "explore forms of transcontinental alliance between North and South."

"The last one is the real reason," Yasemin said. "Here we have the great reformer of the profession. With Joaquín, enter post–Latin Americanism and post–area studies. Mark my words: sooner than we think, this guy will be working at Duke y tendrá poder para enterrarnos."

"I'm not that naïve," Joaquín said. "We won't manage to close anything down with this protest. And even if it does close here, another will open somewhere else. But I think it's a worthy cause."

I agreed with Joaquín: Fort Benning was an emblematic reminder of military abuses on the continent. It was an excellent cause. I told myself that I, more than anyone, should be there, first in line. But I also couldn't lie to myself: that sort of thing wasn't for me. What would I do in the middle of the turmoil, there with so many well-intentioned gringos and Latinos carrying coffins and holding candles? I could applaud their attitude; I could condemn the School of the Americas, but from afar. Maybe in an article in *Salon*. Maybe I'd be more effective that way.

In the darkness of a living room filled with people dressed up as mummies and vampires, with the deafening sound of Limp Bizkit, I coldly greeted Ashley, dressed as a witch in a very short black skirt, and Patrick, who had let his beard grow and had painted fluorescent orange and yellow on a black sweatshirt (the paint had stained his hands). His affability surprised me and made me feel bad. "Do unto others as you would have them do unto you," I said to myself, the philosophy I repeated as a daily maxim and followed only until my desires told me otherwise.

Patrick, a Corona in his hand, told me not to give Ashley so much homework, that she spent all her time reading for my class. I was again surprised by his perfect, neutral Spanish, no accent, no idioms, and no mixing it with English, as if he had learned it in some generic Hispanic country. I congratulated him on his upcoming marriage and wanted to get away, but he wouldn't let me. He put a fluorescent hand on my right shoulder and asked me if I liked jazz. I told him I didn't but that the saxophone was OK, which was true. He stroked his beard and told me that he'd be playing sax next week at Lewinsky's, a bar near campus. He invited me to go; Yasemin and Joaquín would be going.

I told him I'd do my best but couldn't promise anything. He started to tell me about Chiapas. How he missed his fieldwork there. How the indigenous people were so generous to foreigners. How admirable their attitude toward life was in the midst of so much poverty. He asked me if things were the same in Bolivia.

"I hear they are," I said grudgingly. "I've never lived in a rural area."

"There must be indigenous people in the city."

"Lots of them. But it's not the same."

He told me that in Latin America, except for the odd city, all you had to do was drive for twenty minutes in order to be out in the country.

"You don't have to tell me," I replied. "Of course I know that. But it's one thing to pass through on a Sunday afternoon and another to live there."

He told me, without a trace of aggression in his voice, that he was surprised I gave opinions about the continent without really knowing it. He recommended I go live for a year in a campesino village sometime. That was the only way I'd know Latin America.

"It never really interested me," I said. "I'm too urban, but I don't think that disqualifies me. I don't know how to salsa either. And I've never visited the Potosí mines."

I left them with the excuse that I wanted a glass of wine. I wondered whether Ashley had said something to him. Whether she had asked him not to be so jealous and make some gesture of reconciliation. But the initial gesture had been defeated by his intuition, which told him to distrust all men who approached Ashley.

"Are you upset with Ashley?" Yasemin asked, sensing something.

"Not at all."

"She won't take her eyes off you."

I spent the evening turning my back on Ashley and at the same time unable to stop seeing her, her red hair falling over her green eyes, over her arched back at the instant of pleasure, whispering "I want more." I remembered nights like this in Río Fugitivo and Berkeley, when passion had been my driving force and threatened to flood the relative order of my days. It became more and more difficult to be so irresponsible when the consequences devastated the protagonists of the drama and all those around them. To top it all off, someone put on a Garbage CD and the not-at-all melancholy voice of Shirley Manson filled me with unrelenting melancholy.

It was very late when I went to the bathroom on the second floor. In the hallway I came across Joaquín kissing a guy from Spain. I looked at them out of the corner of my eye; they didn't even sense my presence. In the bathroom, in front of the mirror, I thought about what Patrick had said, feeling that my version of Latin America was no less incorrect than his. I had been wrong to think that six years of study at a California university was enough to make me an expert on Latin America. But had I ever really believed I was?

I was pulling my zipper down when I heard a soft knock on the door. "Just a second," I said, and the knocks were repeated. "Please," came a barely audible whisper. I opened the door: it was Ashley. She was drunk. She put her hand over my mouth and whispered that there wasn't much time. She kissed me while her right hand finished pulling down my zipper and began to play with my penis. I wanted her to kneel down and take me in her mouth. She didn't. She played and played, asking me to whisper in her ear how much I loved her; so, so, so much, I said, and just when I was about to come she stopped, smiling.

"How much?"

"So much."

"Like no one you've ever loved before?"

"No one."

"I wanted to hear that. But I want to hear more. If you ask me, I'm yours forever."

I wavered. My silence said it all. She kissed me and left, leaving me stranded. I pictured a fluorescent Patrick downstairs greeting her with a kiss.

She was waiting for just one word from me to leave Patrick. On the way home that night, shaken by anguish and, after all, by a bit of guilt, I decided it was time to end things with Ashley.

7

I T TOOK ME a week to read Villa's manuscript. I read it in his
study, every afternoon, while his secretary scrutinized me, soldiers came and went, and his wife wandered through the mansion listening to boleros that Luis Miguel had made popular again
— *Te vas porque yo quiero que te vayas* — which boomed out of a
stereo in the living room. His daughters seemed to have camped
out by the pool underneath a dovecote. Their bronzed skin betrayed the violence of the sun from noon until three, whatever the
season in Río Fugitivo. Once, on my way to the bathroom, the
younger of the two, with dyed hair and a flat chest, approached
and asked if I knew any narc jokes. I said no.

"Wanna hear one?" she replied with a hysterical laugh. Her
stepmother's appearance interrupted her and she ran back to her
sister's side.

"Excuse her. It's a silly way to relieve tension."

"She's a child; it's understandable."

"Not always," Villa's wife said, and turned away.

I took notes as I read in a large, well-lit room, its shelves
filled with videos (the majority of them action movies — he had a
weakness for McQueen and Schwarzenegger). The memoirs were
written in educated Spanish and had the dry tone of a legal docu-
ment. Villa told the story of his life from childhood on; a mere
chapter was dedicated to his drug trafficking, almost the same
number of pages given to his adolescence at La Salle or his cattle
ranching in Beni. I understood his strategy: to show that drugs

were just one part of his life, not the whole. Still, if anyone was going to read the book it would be because of his fame as the king of drug trafficking, not because he was a good father or a remarkable lover. When I finished reading, nervous about how he would react, I told him so. As usual, he was smoking and gathered the ash in the palm of his hand, then ate it.

"What are you trying to say, young man? That you don't like the book?"

The book? It was then I became almost certain (because of the learned words that had slipped onto the pages) that the secretary was the real author of the manuscript. Villa would have recorded his memories on cassette after cassette, and the secretary had given them a certain degree of coherence.

"I liked it, I liked it," I replied without much conviction. "I'm just trying to look at it from the point of view of a gringo editor. Didn't you say it wasn't for the local market?"

I had to watch what I said. Somewhere, a hidden microphone would be recording us. But surely the government's intelligence service had already read the memoirs, and if they had let Villa keep them, it was because they didn't consider them in any way compromising. They were right: it was a virtuous, repressed text full of circumlocution and formalities. In fact, maybe Montenegro was actually interested in having the manuscript published because it indirectly accused the military that kept him in power and not him. The military aided drug trafficking and had murdered Quiroga Santa Cruz and Reissig. His dictatorship seemed honest by comparison.

"People have to be called by name," I said. "Who is 'the Colonel'? And who is 'the General'?"

"I don't want to give names yet," he argued, worrying the rosary beads in his right hand. "They're still alive and would start an all-out war. I mentioned them as proof that I got into this for patriotic reasons, because people in power asked me to."

"Gringos like names, dates, details. If you're not willing to talk, why would they be interested in the book?"

Personally, I doubted an American publisher would be interested.

"My son had a similar opinion. It must be this younger, more . . . open generation."

He approached and grabbed me by the shirt.

"None of us will talk. Not yet. And whoever does, pow, gets shot, goddamn it!"

His face reddened in fury and his eyes bulged. I was intimidated. The secretary, stroking his mustache as if used to his boss's antics, handed him a glass of water. Villa calmed down. It was as if he were more scared than I was, that he wanted to be strong, act as if nothing were wrong, as if he were still in control. But he wasn't dumb: he was in a vulnerable position, at the mercy of others, as never before.

"And my philosophy, Pedrito? What do you think of my philosophy?"

His philosophy . . . was laughable. But it was the central theme of his memoirs, the method he had chosen to justify things to himself and to others.

"Because," he continued without waiting for my answer, "two decades ago, I was an innocent cattle rancher. Until I got that damn phone call from my cousin in the military, an important member of García Meza's government. He proposed that I take charge of drug trafficking to Colombia as an illegal, but necessary, way of raising funds for a government and a country that were floundering." He was repeating what I already knew; maybe he wasn't sure I had understood. "The way things were, the Colombians were keeping most of the profit. After thinking hard about it, I decided to accept my patriotic duty and go into drug trafficking as an intermediary between the Colombians and the government."

In the end, there was no intermediation: in just a few months the main Colombian drug lords in Bolivia turned up dead, until there was no doubt that the new strongman of drug trafficking in Bolivia was Villa.

"You're very clear about how you got involved," I said in a vain attempt at watching what I said, "but not why, once those military men were no longer in power, you decided to continue. Or was there still a patriotic reason?"

A paperweight was at hand and I thought he might throw it at me or strangle me with his rosary. He didn't, but frustration was written all over his face. He was a powerful man, not used to his subordinates being sarcastic with him. It wasn't my intention to be sarcastic: if I had thought about it a bit more I wouldn't have opened my mouth. Maybe I felt protected because there were so many soldiers around. Maybe.

"Explain it to Pedrito," Villa said to his secretary, crossing himself, as if throwing up his hands, confessing his inability to make me understand. The secretary, calm, could have been a member of a diplomatic mission or a stealthy black monk in the hallways of power at the Vatican.

"Don Jaime continued in the business" — great euphemism — "because once the dictatorships were over, he found that he could help the poor and needy directly. This was his new patriotic duty and that's what he did, don't you see? It's all in chapter ten, or did you skip that one?"

"Maybe I wasn't convinced."

"Then it will have to be rewritten."

"But without losing the essence, Pedrito," Villa added in a paternalistic, surprisingly pleasant tone. "Because my commitment to the people is the key to understanding me. Yes, I decided to work with the government, but I did it thinking about those who were most needy in this country."

The manuscript was, in the end, a pastiche of those made-for-TV, straight-to-video movies about courage and the triumph of the human spirit in difficult circumstances. Villa and his secretary, locked up in one of his haciendas, or maybe in this very room, had spent their Sundays watching those deplorable stories and had used that structure to outline Villa's life as a contemporary Robin Hood, a Scarface with a conscience, a misunderstood rebel who fought against the powerful and legitimated himself as a great defender of the people.

"So, then," I said, losing all fear, "if a bomb blew up a small plane carrying one of your business partners, it was for the oppressed. If you filled big American cities with drugs, it was to raise funds that would be invested in clinics and medical posts, electricity for the streets, and — why not — a soccer field for a forgotten little town. Then, in appreciation, statues would be built in small plazas and babies would be named after you, and a civic committee would nominate you as its chairman."

"Well done, young man," Villa agreed, nodding his head, showing signs that my words had affected him, or maybe he was thinking about how to get rid of me. "For a moment you reminded me of your dad. He wanted everyone to like him and still prove he was more intelligent. But at least you don't care what everyone thinks. I like that. We understand one another."

He'd come to the wrong conclusion: I had an exaggerated form of Dad's shortcoming, wanting everyone to like me, even people who offended me. It was blind egotism paradoxically coupled with a fevered sense of personal responsibility for every situation. There was one slight difference: Dad, they say, said or did whatever he wanted and then asked for forgiveness. In situations where I felt inferior or lacked power, I was sometimes able to control my words and actions. But it's true, there was something about Villa that forced me to be sincere. This wasn't a virtue of mine, but of Villa's. In any event, things aren't always what they seem.

"Your dad," he said with a sigh. "An interesting man. One of the first friends I made when my parents sent me here to study. I missed life in Beni; people are less friendly here. Pedro made friends with me. He wanted me to tell him about my village, the women there. He wanted to go there on vacation sometime. And he did. He was popular with the girls. A smooth talker."

"So why don't you mention him in your memoirs? I mean, if he was one of your first friends, he must have been important. That, for example, would interest readers. A new perspective on a famous politician."

"Not everyone I knew deserves a place in my book," he replied curtly. The secretary looked at me with contempt.

"He never had any money," he went on, "and was always borrowing from me. That has nothing to do with why I don't mention him, by the way. I always loaned it to him and he always had some excuse why he couldn't pay me back. He never came right out and said he didn't have it, just that he would pay me on such and such a day. But just then his brother would have had some type of emergency and he would have had to lend him the money. I pretended I believed him because I didn't need the money, but in truth it was because I liked him. He was a likable charlatan."

"He wasn't a charlatan," I burst out.

"Oh, yes, he was. But a likable one. He was a politician even then. He was class treasurer and our class never had any money. He organized Carnival parties and the tickets were expensive, but there was never enough to eat or drink. Don't ask me what he did with the money. I have no idea. His friends, his brother, we were all fooled. Small things at first; then they got progressively worse."

He went back to his seat.

"Once he told me he had a great plan and that he needed my help. It was to steal a painting from the school chapel. He knew a collector who would pay well and offered me thirty percent. I didn't need the money, but, what can I say, we were kids. So we did it. I never got a penny."

"We all make mistakes when we're young."

"Not always." He smiled. "Some people make mistakes and others, like your dad, downright sin. I'm only telling you the small stuff."

"I have no reason to believe you."

"You're right. And for precisely that reason you will believe me. But let's change the subject. I can see you're upset. Do you want to work on the manuscript or don't you?"

I would've liked to say no, quit ruining my reputation by association with such an evil person. But if I said no, that would end my relationship with Villa — no more arrivals at the mansion with police searches before I was let in, no more strange stories about Dad every now and then. I had to admit it: Villa repulsed and fascinated me at the same time. And what pushed me away and pulled me near was his evil, perverse side; it was my way of experiencing it. Never again would I be so close to the black hole of amorality. Someday I would go back to my academic life, but that was child's play next to Villa or, more precisely, the legend of Villa.

"Let me think about it."

"You'll have to decide today," the secretary said. "Do you think Don Jaime likes to wait?"

I accepted without really knowing how I could improve the manuscript. I wanted to talk to Carolina about it as we lay naked in bed, me smoking a cigarette and her sitting with her legs crossed (cellulite relentlessly building up on her thighs). We had been talking about my uncle: she knew about his plan to capture voices of the dead, too, but wasn't as shocked as I was.

"He's a conceptual inventor," I said. "I can't believe you take him seriously."

"It's not about taking him seriously or not," she replied, "but you can't just dismiss him without giving him a chance to prove his theory. One day I'll take you to my psychic. You'll be amazed at the things she can tell you about your life, and then you'll stop just dismissing anything that doesn't have a rational explanation. Because, let's be serious, rationality is a small island in the ocean of the supernatural. Don't you think?"

I didn't want to continue the argument. I put out my cigarette and embraced her warm body. The walls of her room were covered with posters of Everest and other mountains she would've liked to climb. The iMac on her desk was on, Scully on the screensaver. Around the edge of the mirror were black-and-white photos of her mom in a beauty contest when she was young and her dad wearing a racing suit, sitting on a white Honda. Next to the iMac were Riffard's esoteric dictionary and a blue pyramid of blown glass. Our clothes were scattered on the floor, on top of Web-design magazines and a newspaper open to a Cryptogram we'd been trying to do and couldn't finish. Borges's commentator in prison (seven letters)? Composed *Un brazalete tricolor?* A brown, green-eyed cat was curled up at our feet.

I told her about Villa. As I did, something unexpected (or maybe not) happened. Carolina started to say something, but I couldn't quite hear her. There was a ghost in that bed, more real than the physical body with its round, perky breasts in my line of sight. Ashley's ghost silently drowned out Carolina's words.

"Are you listening to me?"

"I'm sorry, what were you saying?"

"Nothing. It's not important."

I told my uncle.

"The master and his disciple," he said, walking around the patio with a glass of Old Parr in his hand, one eye looking at me, the other seeming to. "Like chapter thirty-six of *Berkeley*. You'll end up forgetting why you approached Villa and become his staunch defender. Be careful, he's very dangerous."

There was a long pause before he continued.

"Still, I'd do the same if I were you."

"What do you mean?"

"I only ever knew one man like that."

"Who?"

"Isn't it obvious?"

I was surprised.

"You can't compare him with Villa . . ."

"They're on different levels, of course. Your dad did or had others do brutal things, but as a result of the circumstances. Even then, what he did can't compare to Villa. Killed a couple of soldiers who he could have forgiven? A few comrades mercilessly shot as traitors?"

He went on:

"I can still see the afternoon that I confronted him, trying to defend those two comrades who didn't deserve to be killed in cold blood. 'We haven't completely proven that they're traitors!' I shouted in his face. We were in the basement of a country house on the outskirts of Río Fugitivo. 'And even if they are, shooting them is not the answer.'

"'So what do you suggest?' Pedro answered, bothered by my insolence. 'Let them leave, so they can go and reveal our location? Our strategies? Our plans?'

"'I don't know. But we're not supposed to be like the government thugs. We can't behave like them.'

"'Sometimes,' Pedro said, staring at me, 'there's no other choice.'

"Supposedly not," Uncle David went on. "We had ideals, we

were fighting for a just cause. But I saw hatred in his eyes. Real hatred. A desire for vengeance. It was as if it had never crossed his mind that someone might try to defend those traitors. Johnny, with his blue eyes, and Macario, who played the guitar so well. Just kids, both of them. They were so scared. If they had done it, why the hell had they? Who knows. And why was Pedro so uncompromising? I didn't understand. It took me a long time to realize that everyone's hands got dirty in that struggle. Even those who didn't participate were guilty, if not by act then by omission . . ."

"It was a difficult situation."

"It was war. But that shouldn't be an excuse. Circumstances required more than what some of us could give. Still, nothing compared to Villa. I was referring to their charisma when I said they were similar. Strange, isn't it? With their personal magnetism they could have done anything. They could even have exchanged destinies. But as you see, one made his life a constant justification for crime and the other didn't."

He paused, took a drink of his whiskey.

"Don't pay any attention to me. Just don't ever forget that Villa is a criminal."

"Of course not," I said, still bothered by the comparison.

"If I defend him it's for reasons of national sovereignty. As a person he doesn't interest me and, personally, I hope he rots in jail. I totally understand the group that's claiming . . . Did you hear the latest? What they suspected from the beginning — all the recent bombings came from one source. The members of something called National Vindication Commando claimed responsibility today. They said it was their way of protesting against the government, against Villa's imminent extradition."

"But why didn't they attack only government property? I can understand the post office, but a private TV station?"

"You'd have to ask them. In my opinion, that station deserved much worse. All they show is junk."

Channel Veintiuno showed the Berkeley video that freely interpreted the events of the Unzueta Street attack, the one that drove Uncle David crazy and that in the last few days had taken over my imagination. At night I dreamt I was in scenes from the video and got lost among geese and bayonets and children and trees in a park and helicopters flying over Río Fugitivo, while during the day I reconstructed the Unzueta Street attack using the video as a basis.

I should have asked him what really happened that day.

For a while I couldn't sleep without remembering one scene from Villa's memoirs: that of his religious conversion. The last dictator has already fallen, and Villa is in his hacienda meditating about which path to take when a voice orders him to go out into the empty field. He does and runs about two hundred yards, until he stops and falls to his knees, while in the cloudy sky a powerful light breaks through and comes to illuminate him. Villa feels the power of God for the first time and, at that instant, decides to continue with the "business," promising that all profit will be given to the poorest.

He was so megalomaniacal that a normal conversion wasn't enough: God had to intervene directly. I wondered whether God had left a card with his direct line.

I couldn't stop thinking about that scene, not even when I thought about Ashley.

I never managed to make that freezing cold, unattractive room where I slept or hid out during a migraine attack feel like mine. I spent as little time there as possible, preferring instead to go into the living room with my iBook or Palm Pilot. Early in the morning I went to the gym with Carolina (who I noticed was less and less patient with me, bothered by the fact that I didn't do anything to move our relationship forward). Later, while my uncle spent hours in the container or the study, I took refuge in the living room. Restless, forcing myself to articulate my ideas coherently, wanting to both stay in Río Fugitivo and return to Madison, I would sit in or walk through that museum of antiques presided over by the gigantic TV that ceaselessly vomited images, news programs, historical documentaries, and soccer, the screen the only light in this room with the curtains closed, where it was night even by day.

The living room continued to be the scene of my recurring vision of Dad's and Aunt Elsa's wake. I hadn't entirely been able to understand that vision and its particular scenography, but I thought that it likely had something to do with my childhood here and a present in which Dad's body had never been found, needing some religious ritual so it could rest in peace once and for all. In some way, through my coming back to live in this house, my memories and my imagination had been activated and had agreed to condense two different stories into one scene.

What was I going to do? I let the days go by, hoping they would provide me with an answer. I was the living image of passivity (if there can be such a thing). One weekend I let Carolina convince me to go camp out in a national park where there were eucalyptus forests and an icy lake. She was unusually somber and told me she wanted to forget about things. I wanted to do the same but couldn't escape entirely. Carolina kept asking me what was wrong, and I gave her evasive replies. I would go into the tent or the lake just to change the subject.

"You know what?" she said on our way back. "You're too caught up in yourself."

"You're referring to . . ."

"That you lock yourself up in your own little world and . . . other people." We were shouting on the motorcycle, some of our words getting lost in the wind. "And you don't . . . that other people have prob . . . too . . . office could have burnt down a week ago and you wouldn't have known. I could . . . bankrupt and the same thing."

"You would've told me."

"You don't understand," she said. "Forget it."

"Are you bankrupt?"

"Uh-huh."

"No way. Really?" I wanted to see her face. "I thought things were going really well."

"I thought . . . same thing. Which only . . . no one's immune to the crisis. Estela's moving to Spain — she has a sister there."

"I'm sorry."

"Forget it. You can't do anything. Neither can I."

"Debts?"

"Tons."

"So what will you do?"

"Survive, like everyone else."

Her brow was furrowed and her mouth set in an angry line when she let me off at the door to Uncle David's house. I invited her to come in, but she refused. I was sorry to see her so upset. I would have liked to help her, at least listen while she unburdened herself, but by the looks of it I was doomed to let her down.

I stood in the living room for a long time looking at that phantasmagoria of typewriters and radios. Uncle David would have liked to invent one of them or something better. An improbable radio whose waves were able to travel through time and capture, like a fisherman's net, the voices of our past — solid nuclei that would serve to reincarnate beings who had once lived and who still inhabited us. Maybe he couldn't sleep because those voices pursued him, because he felt that with just a little effort Dad and Aunt Elsa could appear in the doorway and be here in the present as if they had never left (and if they managed to appear, maybe the same thing would happen to him as happened to Randolph Jones when a long-awaited voice unexpectedly materialized and caused his heart to stop).

Maybe. He hadn't brought the subject up with me again and responded evasively to my questions about his progress with the project. He was a conceptual inventor — that magnificent excuse — and maybe the only thing of his that would end up on a pedestal would be his plans for that machine.

One morning in mid-July I found a copy of *El Posmo* on the table. The government had decreed a gas hike, and the official exchange rate had gone up; protests against Montenegro had resurfaced with unexpected virulence. Three soldiers had been killed in Achacachi, the nerve center for protests and blockades — the region's indigenous leader had become a national figure and now talked about forming his own political party — and two more in

Chapare; three university students had died in Cochabamba from bullets fired by plainclothes military snipers, and another had been blinded.

On the front page of the newspaper there were photos of protests being broken up by police and an inset containing a note from the National Vindication Commando to the press. One phrase proclaiming resistance to the bitter end caught my attention: *No nos daremos por vencidos ni aun vencidos*. Because of an inevitable association of ideas I remembered a recent Cryptogram that asked for the name, ten letters, of an Argentine poet. Federico had found the answer in a literature textbook — Almafuerte — and I had remembered the only verse I knew of his: *No te des por vencido ni aun vencido*. Did the Commando members know this verse? Were crosswords starting to define my vision of the world? I could no longer look at a computer without thinking about the name of the inventor, or watch a movie without trying to remember who directed it or did the cinematography, or hear the name of a city without asking myself what battles were fought there.

I put the newspaper aside. The same old problems, the exhausting routine. It had happened to me on other vacations: the novelty of Río Fugitivo lasted for about two months; then the city bored me and I wanted to break away again, until after a while Madison would bore me and I would want to return to Río Fugitivo once more.

I went to Villa's mansion several afternoons and suggested certain changes to his memoirs, which he immediately rejected: fear of reprisal prevented him from mentioning names, and his pride wouldn't allow him to see himself as a glorified drug lord. I knew he would reject my suggestions, but I insisted, knowing all the while the changes were just an excuse: deep down, I had been trapped in Villa's magnetic orbit and didn't know how to escape it.

We were walking in the garden. The mastiff followed us, indifferent. Villa held tightly to the rosary in his hand. He was smoking, letting the ash fall into his palm, and I wondered whether this had some meaning. Maybe his partners would see him on TV eating the ash and would get the message. Ashes to ashes, dust to dust . . . Villa was telling them not to worry, that he had kept quiet . . .

"Let me tell you, Pedrito, Montenegro is so worried about the image he's going to leave behind that he's no longer in control. Not a day goes by without strikes and protests. He's letting that Indian in La Paz have his way. Who does he think he is anyhow? Does he think this country is only for his people? And the gringos, making themselves right at home — *como Pedro por su casa,* no pun intended!"

He laughed out loud, threw the cigarette butt on the grass, and put the ash in his mouth. Ash, Asheville, Villa de Ash . . . Dad knew about Villa's habit and had coded it in his novel as that Villa de Ash — the scene of corruption, the place where Montiel hid out and spent his time on word games . . .

"I'm no fan of Montenegro's, you know, but he can't be blamed for everything. His hands are tied because of the recession."

"A person's true personality is revealed during difficult times. It makes me furious that I'm being used as the poster boy for change. I don't know, I just don't know. Sometimes I think that when this is all over I should go into politics."

I pictured him as a presidential candidate. The idea was comical, but I couldn't dismiss it. Anything was possible on this continent of ours, filled as it was with dictators who reinvented themselves as democrats, corrupt leaders who made themselves out to be masters of ethics, populist politicians who knew how to drive racecars and play soccer with their bodyguards but didn't have any idea what was needed to govern a country.

"I've been thinking about what you said about my dad," I said. "'A likable charlatan.' All right, maybe you're right. I know a few of his lies too. One of his weaknesses was to try to appear as if he were more than he really was. But I don't believe it was all negative. You're unsure of yourself when you're young, and need to project an image of glory and triumph in order to be accepted by your peers."

"Not even you believe that," he said, snorting. "You have to accept your dad as he is and that's that. And it's not all about his lies and word games. There are also the things he did. Things I haven't told you about and still haven't decided whether to or not."

His wife approached to tell us that his spiritual leader had arrived, a bearded Peruvian who combined certain Incan rites — worshiping Pachamama, or Mother Earth, and the protective spirits of mountain peaks — with an elastic New Age mysticism.

"I'm off, Pedrito. I'll pray for you and for me. Don't ever forget the one on high. I never did, but I should have been more insistent. There's always one more person who needs help, one more school I could have donated uniforms to, one more village I could have given a water pump to. No, I'm not happy with myself. Not even when so many humble people remember and stand by me today."

There was a touch of vulnerability in his voice. I was moved by his belief in an incoherent spectrum of religious causes. At night — he had told me this without a hint of irony — an ex-wife of his given to dealings with the hereafter came to lead sessions where those present held hands around the dining room table and asked to be freed from humiliating captivity.

I took my leave. The man of power was now defenseless, awaiting a miracle to free him from the helicopter that would one day touch down in his garden and take him to La Paz, then on to the North.

And at that moment they knew in unison, once and for all and forever, that they would soon be that which they had been born for and which a thousand permutations had hidden: ash. Like in the Villa de Ash. Like Ashley.

I was wearing a heavy sweater but still felt cold in the unheated house. I checked my e-mail and felt the urge to write or call Ashley. I resisted. How could I face her? I lay on the sofa. I played Dope Wars for a while, until the police caught me selling crack. I opened *Berkeley* at random and reread a few pages. What about those salamanders? I was being ridiculous, I told myself. It was one symbol no more or less important than the others; it wasn't worth obsessing about. Who had convinced me I would find one meaning that encompassed all the rest? Meanings, instead of leading to just one, could proliferate into infinity . . . It was getting late; the hallways and rooms in the house were getting darker. Now the only lights were in the living room and the container (a weak glimmer that hung around the crack of the door).

The light in the container went off. My uncle came to the doorway of the living room. Unshaven and with his hair in disarray, he looked older than he was. He gestured as if to ask me what I was doing.

"Thinking about a word. Salamander."

"Aren't you writing your book? Strange way of researching you have. You spend all your time reading. Shouldn't you be going to archives, interviewing people?"

Should I tell him that the so-called book would never be written?

"That's what I'm talking about," I improvised. "For a long time I thought that the bridges and crows and TV antennas that show up everywhere were the central symbols of the novel. Then it came to me that their abundance could be used to hide a subtler symbol. The salamander is mentioned seven times, always in connection with a street in Berkeley, and I think that's what it's all about."

He looked down at his old brown leather slippers.

"I've noted down the times it's mentioned . . . One after the other, they all have a different meaning. The seven of them together, I have no idea. And even less whether they're the central theme of the novel. Maybe it's some sort of secret wink, a message hidden for someone.

"That's the conclusion I'm coming to. Where's the best place to hide a book? A library. Where's the best place to hide a sentence? A book. I once heard an author say that he had to write a whole book just for the only sentence he really wanted to write. Dad wrote his novel to hide a message. To whom? And what was the message?"

The message is for me, I thought, but I didn't say it out loud.

My uncle took off his slippers and inhaled as if he were having trouble breathing. He looked at me sadly. "Your dad left us the pieces of a puzzle. Maybe some of those pieces have been lost and we'll never be able to completely understand the mysteries of the text."

"*No te des por vencido ni aun vencido.*"

He winked at me. "Other mysteries are more accessible and have an answer," he said. "It's a matter of having a good dictionary."

"And a nose for it. As with everything."

He sat down next to me. His gaze got lost in the hallway, as if anxiously looking for one of the Renaissance maps hanging on the wall (maps that in the darkness hid their magic power to make sailors disappear).

"Last night I dreamt about the Cuervos Anacoretas," he said without looking at me. "What a great character Montiel is! His dedication to language and words, at a time when all searches for meaning come crashing down, is moving. I can picture him walking through the streets of an empty city, wearing an old-fashioned overcoat and hat, murmuring verses of French poetry. 'Dressmakers, shoemakers, markets, stores. Items remain in shop windows for a mere moment in time before beginning their journey to dusty back rooms or the hands of those who will value and then forget them. People. Because time marches on, independent of us, despite our best efforts.'"

"Don't tell me you've memorized it?"

"A few paragraphs. It's enchanting prose. I wonder where Pedro got such rhythm. I have the words, but nothing else. That's why crosswords are ideal for me. You don't have to create rhythm there."

The Cuervos Anacoretas: Bernard, Montiel, and Xavier. In sixty-six quick, fragmentary chapters of two pages each, *Berkeley* narrates the history of these three friends from the time they form their group during the struggle for independence, through their later differences of opinion (allegorical reflections of the national and continental rifts in our history), until they are finally reunited in a dictator's jail 150 years later. In an oppressive and unstable atmosphere of revolution and repression, each one, in his own way, looks for the meaning of his life, trying to connect it to something larger, to the fervor for cause or country.

The novel ends with the failure of all three. Even so, there are small triumphs along the way. Montiel gives himself over to life through language and explores the world without leaving the corrupt Villa de Ash, practically a recluse in his own home except for his habitual walk through the semi-deserted city at siesta time. He is a character that would obviously interest Uncle David (sometimes I wondered whether Montiel wasn't based on him).

"I prefer Bernard."

Bernard, Dad's alter ego, is a metaphysical explorer who arrives in Berkeley in the sixties and finds a kind of nirvana there. His failure is that he feels responsible for what is happening in his country and returns in the seventies to fight against a dictatorship, with the subsequent loss of his ideals and a Berkeley that becomes, in the novel, at least in my reading of it, the Ithaca we all yearn for, the end that is the beginning, the lost paradise that inspires the journey. (At the end, in a moving scene, Bernard wants to leave all his responsibilities behind and return to Berkeley, only to discover that it's impossible.)

"That's the easy answer. Everyone identifies with Bernard. It's impossible not to. It would be more respectable if you identified with Xavier."

Xavier was the worst one in the brotherhood, the incarnation of evil. Like a Sade, although not through sex, he bet on the triumph of evil as a means of complete liberation from the moral conventions that rule our lives. The violence of his confrontations with society ended in nothing. As with the others, in the last chapter we find him in jail, about to be tortured or possibly killed. But there was a more positive interpretation of this ending: Xavier deserved it — you can't be a Xavier without paying the price, without dying violently or self-destructing. The final chapter suggested that Montiel and Bernard, members of the resistance against the dictatorship, were in jail because Xavier was a traitor, an ambiguous figure both for and against the dictatorship.

"As I came up the stairs," he continued — I could smell the alcohol on his breath — "I had a bad feeling. And it has to do with Xavier. What if one of us is a traitor?"

I didn't realize right away that he was talking about the Unzueta Street events. I shuddered.

"Pedro had called a meeting of the movement's leadership," he went on. "Of that MAS, *más,* that had become less. Ha. We were being defeated on every front and we had to regroup, organize ourselves better, unless we wanted the disaster to continue. I thought the meeting was a mistake — if something went wrong, they would catch us all together — but I didn't say anything. Still, it wouldn't have made any difference if I had. Pedro pretended to be flexible, but I have never known anyone more dogmatic."

He stood up.

"Nothing was the same after he had our comrades shot. I sound like a broken record, but in truth I stopped being as interested in the struggle. I can still see the hate, the vengeance in his eyes. I wanted to turn back the clock, go back to the days when I was innocent. Even more, I wanted to recapture the image I had of Pedro before that incident. He was a bit of a crazy, idealistic man, but not someone who could get caught up in the generalized, pervasive sense of loss. He talked so much about transcending, but I don't think he always searched for it the right way. Transcending doesn't just mean dying, leaving a diary behind for posterity. It means being able to see beyond the present, see what others can't see, not allowing yourself to be carried along by events around you. Pedro couldn't transcend his present and he lost his angel. The devil in him took over, and he wasn't the same as far as I was concerned. Over the years, it's true, I've learned to be more generous with him, to forgive his mistakes. I gave up the hero, recognized his humanity."

His left eye was restless. I rubbed the palms of my hands together; they were sweaty. I was afraid of what I might hear.

"I could have suggested we not meet. I didn't say anything and sometimes I regret that, feel guilty about the whole thing. But there was no reason not to trust anyone. We knew one another well, or that's what we thought. When I arrived, Elsa was already there, talking to Pedro. I went up and said hello. Then the others started to arrive. I still had that sinking feeling. Maybe it didn't have to be a traitor, maybe they had intercepted one of our messages and cracked it . . ."

He seemed to be reliving the moment and didn't care whether I was in the room or not.

"Everyone arrived. Almost everyone. Mérida was late, or at least that's what we thought at the time. We waited half an hour; then Pedro decided to start without him. Not more than five minutes had passed when the shooting started . . . They broke through doors and windows. I instinctively tried to protect Elsa, who was next to me. That was when I got shot in the face. I fell on top of her in a pool of blood."

There was a prolonged silence. I remembered that afternoon. I was playing with a soccer ball in the patio of our house when Mom came out crying with the news. She hugged me and said, "He's gone." Makeup was running down her face and she smelled of sweet perfume. That night I got my first migraine.

"The things that were said. So many stories, so many lies. It wasn't how they show it on the video, but youth today think it was. After the shooting I lost consciousness for a few minutes. Thinking I was dead, they left. When I woke up I was on a stretcher. I asked the nurses about Elsa, about Pedro, about everyone. 'All dead,' one of them said. 'All dead.'"

"And Mérida?"

"All dead. Eric, the blond who would have given you his last can of sardines and eaten nothing. Camilo, who spoke in parables and proverbs, who had stopped his theology studies but still went everywhere with his Bible. Barely twenty years old, he had a sweet face and a look of absorption about him. That wasn't his real name; you can guess in whose honor he took it. And if you tell me that we were all fragile and vulnerable and imperfect, that there were no heroes in that generation, I can name them both as examples that there were. Without a second thought. Eric and Camilo. Salazar was the orthodox Marxist, a bit hard to put up with — he never bathed and had so much plaque on his teeth that he would have lost them all by the time he was forty. He was self-serving, would eat the provisions when we weren't looking, and was very afraid. If it was hard for me to hold a gun, it was harder for him. Dominguez was crazy; he wanted to put bombs everywhere, loved the destruction and smiled when he heard the news about dead soldiers. He'd been a popular gynecologist who loved his work. I can't count the times I saw him put a gun to the head of someone we'd kidnapped and pretend to fire. Sooner or later the gun was bound to go off, I told myself, or he'd pull the trigger."

He turned his back on me, approached the window where the curtains were closed. I was no longer afraid and felt tenderness for that touching figure inhabited by living ghosts.

"Eric, Camilo, Salazar, Dominguez, Elsa. Everyone remembers Pedro. But no one remembers them."

"You do."

"I don't know. I never mention them in my crosswords. But I do mention your dad. I'm just as guilty of what I criticize in others."

He retraced his steps, looking at me as he passed, as if remembering that I'd asked him a question.

"I always suspected that Mérida was the Xavier of our group. We could never prove it. He turned up dead shortly after. The government got rid of him, we thought."

"People accused him of it."

"People are often wrong."

He left the living room and headed toward the container.

Later that night I was in bed replying to a questionnaire from *NewTimes* (they were obsessed with the idea that Bolivia would be the first country to break out of the cycle of cocaine) when I heard my uncle yell, throw books and glasses to the floor. The commotion made me go to the door, but I didn't open it. Instead I strained to hear the litany of insults.

I could hear Dad's name, I could hear insults directed at God. I pictured my uncle drunk, furious. I had seen him with a few drinks under his belt, his voice breaking and his words slurred, and I had occasionally seen his fits of rage, but that night something exploded inside. Maybe everything had converged and conspired to torment him, undermine the lucidity with which he seemed to contemplate the world even when sleeping.

He shouted for silence. He banged his head against the wall. He bawled. Plates were broken, and then, all of a sudden, there was silence. I went out into the living room. One of the digitally altered pictures, the one of Sartre at the Palacio Quemado, lay broken in the hallway. I jumped over it.

I found him sprawled on the floor, in his old blue checked robe, the smell of whiskey overpowering. He had passed out. There was something sweet about that defenseless giant curled up on the floor. I didn't try to move him; I wouldn't have been able to. I covered him with a blanket.

The next morning he spoke to me at breakfast as if nothing had happened.

8

IT WASN'T easy for me to break up with Ashley. I was on the verge of ending things several times, but my constant indecision prevented me from speaking the words. Sometimes in the afternoons I would see her lying on the sofa after we'd spent an intense hour together, with that ability she had to close her eyes and shortly thereafter exhibit muscle spasms from the depths of sleep, and I would feel as if I had a knife in my hands, was about to kill a person lost in angelic sleep. How could I feel so guilty and see her as so innocent when, after all, it should have been the other way around?

November was passing; we were already in an autumn of restless winds and trees bare of leaves. The cold hit harder on the hill where the campus was than in the city. Student activity on the Arts Quad was giving way to the desolation that would arrive in full force during winter. Coats, jackets, and overcoats were everywhere, even a scarf here and there. Ashley was one of the few in the Institute building who continued to wear light clothing — sandals, a sweater, sometimes skirts. I saw her often. As time went on, as if knowing that in any event it would all end on a December day that had already been chosen, she threw caution to the wind and visited me more urgently and more frequently. She would show up in my office on the third floor or when I was preparing class in the cafeteria full of freshmen anxious at the thought of final exams and projects. One morning as I was picking up my mail next to the secretary of the Institute — announcements on the walls of the office for Quechua classes at Cornell and seminars on Central Americans in New Mexico — she came up and kissed the back of my neck. One afternoon she followed me to the library, and in the Latin American history section, in a dark corner on the fourth floor smelling of old books, she startled me by touching my back with her cold hand and then made me lose control with her knowing, eager mouth.

They were the most agonizing days: I enjoyed being with her, but my pleasure was shrouded by an unsettling sense of guilt and paranoia. The phone would ring in my office or at home and I would expect an accusatory call from Patrick or Clavijero, even more so if there was no voice on the other end and they hung up (in that case, silence was the accuser). When Ashley arrived at my place, the first thing I did was anxiously go to the window to see if anyone had seen her come in. And when she came to talk to me in the hallway, I looked conspicuously left and right, feeling as if there were stares of reproach from colleagues or students. I had almost reached the point of wearing gloves or showering after seeing her so as to completely erase her fingerprints from my skin.

One afternoon I was walking with Yasemin to the library. The sky had clouded over and it would soon rain. The outlines of the Gothic buildings on campus were silhouetted ominously against the sudden darkness. The bell tower reverberated with the striking of bronze, announcing it was five o'clock. A few students were walking hurriedly from one building to another. A girl passed by carrying a Chihuahua. In the distance, at the foot of the hill, you could see the town lost among the trees.

Yasemin was telling me about Morgana.

"I'm going to leave her," she told me. "My boyfriend's coming to visit over Christmas. Morgana's falling in love and it's too dangerous," she said, emphasizing the last few words.

"I thought it was you who . . . well, you know."

"Lo estaba. But it's over now. In fact, I realized that I miss my boyfriend. This would never have happened if he'd been here."

In the entrance to the vast library, I asked her if she was referring to anything else with her "it's too dangerous" comment.

"We all like danger," she replied. "But some of us keep quiet and others don't."

Someone asked us to keep our voices down.

Yasemin whispered, "The students already know. The professors don't, but they will soon if you don't make a decision."

"Did she say anything?"

"She doesn't have to. It's written all over her face. That Patrick is either an idiot or pretends to be. Probably both."

"Quiet, please," someone studying at a nearby table said.

"Is she that good in bed?" Her whisper became an almost unintelligible murmur.

"It's not just that."

"Really."

"Would you please shut up?" came an aggressive, intimidating voice.

A pause. Then, in a provocatively loud voice, Yasemin said, "Hazlo ahora, before it's too fucking late. We don't want to lose you."

That conversation in the library was what decided me. The next time Ashley came to my apartment, I told her. I was unable to look her in the eye and concentrated instead on her obscene ring, as if to give myself strength. MTV was on — someone was singing "You got the dreamer's disease." She was wearing her black tracksuit, and her hair was in a ponytail. She had taken her shoes off and her toenails were painted red.

When I finished, she said, "Te puedo dar un first draft de mi paper? I'm writing on the connection between the Bolivian and Chilean military during Operation Condor."

"And your project on the Sandinistas?"

"I wanted to know more about your country."

"Don't you have anything to say to me?"

"Just that the Bolivian military wanted to ingratiate themselves with the Chileans in order to come to some kind of territorial concession. Access to the sea is an obsession of Montenegro's, isn't it?"

"Yes, and Pinochet used and abused him because of it. Once

our Secretary of State came back from negotiations with a contemptible phrase that's famous: 'I bring you the sea in my pocket.'"

"Maybe he was being literal — a few drops of water would be all Pinochet would give them."

"Yes, but that phrase was understood as a metaphor for our glorious return to the sea. From that failure on, the urban middle class withdrew their support for Montenegro and his days were numbered. But it's not only Montenegro's obsession."

"Or apparent obsession, mejor. Deep down they know that Chile isn't going to give them access, but no one can say that out loud because it would be anti-nationalistic."

"And it's one of the few symbols that really unites us. I would've liked to discuss your topic before you started to write."

"En diciembre se amontonan los papers. Better get rid of at least one while I can."

She didn't say anything more. She picked up her backpack, put on her shoes, and left. It was a disillusioning, anticlimactic finale; there was anguish but no tragedy. Perhaps I had hoped she would make a scene and refuse to accept my decision.

From the doorway I watched her disappear. She looked better with her hair down.

Ashley didn't come to my class for the last few weeks of the semester. I tried to teach *Berkeley* as if nothing had happened, in the midst of the first snow of the season — a winter that began at the end of November and lasted until April — but it was too late for that. Students exchanged looks and winks, and I couldn't help noticing that empty seat where, until not long ago, the woman I loved had sat.

Because by losing her I had discovered how fervently I loved her. Yes, I had known that I was in love when I saw her in class or naked in my apartment and her green eyes shone with love or desire. I just didn't know how much until the moment I lost her. Then I knew it wasn't just another of those fleeting loves I specialized in, as violent and intense as they were short-lived. Walking on campus in the snow, my face being caressed by downy flakes, I recalled her long red hair, the arch of her back, the braces on her teeth, and I told myself that she might well have been the one to spend the rest of my life with. I even remembered her ring nostalgically. I waited for an e-mail from her, but it never came. When the phone rang, I rushed to answer it, hoping in vain to hear her voice.

I spent more time at the Institute, wishing I'd run into her by chance. I didn't learn until later that Ashley had asked for incompletes in all her classes — except mine; maybe she felt sure I wouldn't fail her if she didn't do her final project — and had gone back to Boston to help her parents with the final wedding preparations.

No promises, no conditions.

Maybe it wasn't too late and I could call and ask her to cancel the wedding, leave Patrick, and be with me. Maybe this time pathos and melodrama were necessary, indispensable. Maybe I should assume my role as the perfect lover and jump onto the stage with a declaration of love, upsetting the established order. Didn't I like to defy convention?

I did, but only when there was a net to cushion my fall. This time there was no net. Not only would I lose my job, but I didn't know how long Ashley might stay with me. Because what assurance did I have that she wouldn't do to me what she'd done to Patrick?

None. Love is measured by the absence of calculation and reasoning. If I thought about the consequences, I was still very far from measuring up to the bar Ashley had set for me. Love wasn't about being a poet and a mathematician at the same time. It was about being just a poet.

I used her password to sign into her account and see how her Internet trading was going. I bought a Nomad and discovered that, thanks to her, I now had a fetish for technology. I learned to download songs from the Web onto my G3 at home. I bought an iBook. I started to look for a Palm Pilot.

The first thing Joaquín did when he got back from Georgia was arrange to meet Yasemin and me at Common Ground. We got a table in the corner, ordered a tea and two cappuccinos, and settled in to listen to him. He was ecstatic.

"So?" Yasemin said. "Was it worth it? Con cuántas business cards volviste?"

"Don't be ridiculous — I didn't go there to network. And of course it was worth it. It was incredible. There was a sea of people — men, women, adolescents, seniors, children — and a spirit somewhere between peaceful and religious."

"A very retro experience," I said. "Onda sixties."

"Something like that, but more of an ecological, religious version. I'd even go so far as to say Pentecostal or charismatic, with canticles and heated sermons from Baptist preachers. A noble desire to do something for our continent."

"Self-deceiving nobility, I'd say," Yasemin pointed out. "Would they commit themselves if the risk was too big? Oh, gringos. Most of them had never even heard about it."

"I don't know and it doesn't matter. The point is that I was moved by it. And Helen, what can I say, she was fulfilled. The funeral procession, the reading of the names of the dead and disappeared from Latin America before and while thousands slowly, calmly crossed into the fort . . . Finally, the display of joy and religious fervor once everyone had crossed over."

"I bet," I said. "They're not as somber as we are, not even in religious matters. Not even when they're Catholics."

"Did you see Martin Sheen?" Yasemin asked jokingly. "They were always showing him on TV. The fake blood, the masks, the coffins: it all seemed so theatrical to me. Although Fort Benning didn't impress me much — no high walls, no barbed wire."

"There was a bit of virtual conflict, scenes being created for television," Joaquín said as he drank his tea. "I would have laughed at it any other time, been ironic, cynical. But I let myself get caught up in the intensity of the experience, the collective moment. My distance became a sort of loving condescension for the innocence of almost all those who took part in the protest. Not all of them, because there were a few with a conscience and commitment to what they were doing. There were seventeen hundred arrests by the end of it."

"Now what?" Yasemin asked. "Are you going to join the Zapatistas?"

"Very funny. I don't know. I suppose I'll keep my distance, but in a different way."

I admired Joaquín's ability to let himself get caught up but still remain lucid. It had been a long time since I'd been so moved by political motives, maybe since those far-off days in Berkeley when I started to write my thesis.

"At least you'll have a good paper for class," Yasemin said.

The first week of December I got the happy news that my evaluation had been satisfactory overall, which surprised me. They asked me to speed up my progress with the book I had to publish if I wanted to be considered for tenure and take a more active part in the Institute and the university, volunteer on committees, and do the bureaucratic service work I detested. Everything else seemed to be in order. I would later learn that two of my colleagues, Clavijero and Sha(do)w, had voted against me. It was hard to feel proud knowing I didn't have everyone's support and that my contract would be renewed by a slim majority. Still, Helen convinced me that my case wasn't special: there likely wasn't an institute or department where everyone got along, approved of all their colleagues' work, believed that everyone was on the same intellectual level. You had to accept the rules of the game, learn to smile at the colleagues you hated and the ones who hated you — at least until tenure.

Despite my constant ambition to have everyone like me, I didn't really feel the blow from my colleagues' lack of unanimity about me. I spent my days in my apartment correcting exams and papers — snowed in during a three-day storm that turned Madison into a ghost town of dark afternoons where cars had to follow the single set of tire tracks left by other cars. I wrote an article for *NewTimes* that Silvana rejected ("but we're still interested in your opinion, Pedro"). I saw that Colombia had come into fashion again on CNN — guerrillas were gaining territory, the United States had decided to provide aid in the form of money, arms, and intelligence to fight the drug trafficking–guerrilla alliance — and sent a couple of opinions to *Latin American Affairs* and *Newsweek*. I also sent two more on the financial crisis in Ecuador and police corruption in Mexico to *Salon* and *The Nation*. Latin America was like a large forest in the middle of summer, with fires burning from one end to the other, furious outbreaks that were just barely contained before they flared up again or started elsewhere. It was easy to understand the generous impulse so many men and women had to put the fire out (or spur it on in order to bring the continent back to a tabula rasa, allowing rebirth). It was also easy to understand the not-so-generous impulse so many men and women had, preferring not to get involved, not to get consumed by the fire.

I tried to forget about the day that was drawing near, but couldn't. I would work up my courage and go to the phone thinking there was still time, only to change my mind.

One day before Ashley's wedding, I called Yasemin and said I urgently needed to speak to her. We met at Common Ground. It was snowing outside and the windows were steamy. The customers were all wearing boots that left pools of water in their wake. I had a cappuccino and M&Ms.

I didn't even wait for Yasemin to take off her snow-covered jacket before I started to unburden and tell her everything. She listened to me patiently and then declared, "Call her. There's no other choice."

"And my colleagues? And the students?"

"Fuck them."

"And my job?"

"Fuck it. No way around it. Si estás como dices que estás, it'll be worse in the long run if you don't."

"Would you do it if you were me?"

"It's a personal thing. But I'd do it. If I had to choose, I wouldn't think twice."

"Easy to say."

"Maybe."

I thanked her and went home, armed with courage.

But I couldn't call.

I spent the day of the wedding watching Orson Welles films on AMC, a bottle of Santa Rita at hand. I imagined Ashley dressed in diaphanous white, entering a church escorted by her father, while Patrick, wearing a ridiculously large tuxedo, waited for her at the altar. I imagined a Catholic wedding — even though neither of them was — with the rice and the Just Married sign on the car and the typical reception: the bouquet being tossed to single women, the garter that Patrick, on bended knee, would remove with his lascivious teeth from Ashley's right leg (which deserved other teeth).

I went out several times, without a jacket or gloves or a scarf, and walked through the park with the heavy snow falling incessantly on me and other blurry shadows in the streets of the ghost town. My steps sunk into a cottony layer, silencing the crunch. Paths of footprints crossed — the footprints of unfaithful husbands, women in crisis, and confused adolescents who were on their way to seek comfort in a lover's arms, at home, or with friends.

What was I doing in Madison, so alone and so far from my real world, in this voluntary exile? The snow fell and I remembered my days in Río Fugitivo. The snow fell and I remembered my days in Berkeley. That time, for example, when Elka and I were eating pizza in a restaurant and a homeless man came and sat next to her, lecturing us on how Western civilization was repressive by forcing us to wear clothes. He then took off his shirt and shoes, was proceeding to take off his pants when two waiters roughly pushed him out of the restaurant. Berkeley was repetitive in its originality, offering both perfection and its parody.

I fell asleep, drunk, before I could imagine the wedding night. When I woke up the next day, with a terrible headache and the television on, my first thought was that they were likely en route to their honeymoon in the Cayman Islands. I picked up the telephone, wandered with it through the apartment. I had lost my opportunity.

I spent the day rereading sections of *Berkeley* and missing the man who had written it. And where was Mom? In what European city was she forgetting her sorrows?

The urgent ring of the telephone woke me up early the next morning. I ran to answer it, no time for a premonition.

"Wake up, Little Ear."

9

Better than Chaplin. Photography theorist. ERP Commander in Oxford. Rosario Castellanos's character in *Balún-Canán*. Telegram that decided WWI. Contributed to the development of Colossus. Belgian expressionist. First Sandinista victory. Leader of the Mexican rebellion against secular law. Italian photographer. Local rock band.

Carolina had inserted herself into the weave of my days, and I, after initial resistance, had let her. Maybe I needed company to help heal my wounds, to help me recover before I got back into circulation. While the country floundered in its cyclical convulsions, abnormal situations that because of their frequency had become normal, we went to the gym, to the Twenty-First Century Mall for coffee and to window-shop, to bars and clubs on the weekends. One Saturday she convinced me to go with her to climb Angel, a barely visible snowy peak to the northeast of the city. We left in the early hours of the morning and it was ten o'clock when I gave up, halfway to the top. Still, we had fun: on the way down, we went into a bar in a little village and got drunk on *huarapo*.

At times Carolina would get depressed. She had dark circles under her eyes and was plagued by insomnia. She bit her brightly painted nails. She had been offered her old job at the Ciudadela but said she wasn't sure for ethical reasons — even though she needed the money. Estela had gone to Spain, leaving Carolina with debts. She said she thought a lot about her parents those days and missed them. She had the urge to show up on her dad's doorstep in Buenos Aires and say, Forgetting wasn't fair, Dad, I know how much it hurt to lose Mom, I know you loved her so deeply that you decided to erase everything from your life that reminded you of her, even me, but it's not fair, it's just not fair. She recalled the night her mom died.

"Toward the end they moved her into the guest room. I was hardly ever allowed to see her — she was disfigured, coughed up blood, and complained that she couldn't take it anymore, that she wanted to die. The room smelled awful — like mouse shit, I thought at the time. I jumped rope in the patio with my sisters, staring at the window of the room where my dad stood watch. My sisters were older and tried to distract me. At night I would take a blanket from my room and lie down to sleep in front of the guest room door. I heard her pitiful cries, her troubled breathing, as if she had something stuck in her throat, and I couldn't sleep. I wanted to go in but was afraid of what I'd see. That Saturday at three in the morning there was a different cry (almost a howl) that made me jump up. I heard Dad's footsteps and wanted to hide, but it was too late. He looked at me reproachfully, then ran into the room. And then there were no more cries, no more troubled breathing, and I knew she had died. I didn't cry until I heard Dad sob. I can still hear him sob."

In her room, I listened to her and consoled her. I tried hard to show her I wasn't indifferent; I softly kissed her ears, her neck, around her bellybutton. I told myself that everything would be much easier if I could just fall in love with her and forget about my life in Madison. She would look at me, wanting to get lost in my gaze, but couldn't because I would blink, because there were limits to the depth of my feelings for her.

One Sunday I gave in and went with her to see Cristina, the fifteen-year-old they said heard the voice of God in Latin. Her house was in the northern part of the city, in a neighborhood of old palm trees. I was surprised to see it was a two-story house, comfortably middle-class, with a big garden and large windows. (I would later learn that her parents had owned an advertising agency that they sold in order to take care of their daughter.) A lot of people were crowded around the door, and two women were moving forward on their knees while murmuring the Lord's Prayer over and over again. The sidewalks had been taken over by vendors offering candles, prayer cards, and skewers of *anticuchos*. It was a local fair, a syncretic ritual of Catholic faith and paganism. We got in line. There were sobs and the smell of incense. I felt uncomfortable but was so touched by the look of Carolina with her eyebrow ring, full of hope, that I decided not to protest.

We reached Cristina's room forty-five minutes later. Candles flickered on the bedside table, creating a moving half-light in that room of closed curtains and metal crucifix above the bed. We knelt down. I took off my glasses. Espresso-skinned, Cristina had black hair and chubby cheeks. She was fifteen years old but looked ten. The covers were pulled up to her neck, and with her right hand she was holding hands with her mother, who was sitting next to the bed. I was moved by Cristina's proximity.

Her manuscripts — sacred objects of devotion — were protected by a glass display case on a table to one side. The big, round handwriting was intelligible to those who could read Latin. I couldn't. Who in Río Fugitivo could? It was an old-fashioned cult without images, written in a prestigious language unknown to the majority of people. Maybe its power resided in its mystery, in its separation from daily life.

We didn't have much time. Carolina, overcome by fervor, asked if she could kiss her hands, and Cristina assented with a slight nod of her head. Then Carolina asked her to bless us, which she did. We recited the Lord's Prayer and an Ave Maria, and I silently prayed I would find Dad's decomposed body, his bones reduced to rubble. I prayed I would be reunited with Mom, lose myself in her embrace as I had when I was a child. I prayed that Uncle David would find peace in his world, so close and so removed. I prayed that Aunt Elsa would be a benign specter for him. I prayed that Ashley . . . I didn't know what to pray for her.

Cristina didn't write a single phrase in Latin for us, didn't hear a supernatural voice, didn't levitate, didn't resort to any one of those special effects that characterize miraculous beings. She didn't speak even a single word. Maybe that was why I had a bit of faith.

Carolina maintained my uncle's Web site, adding photos and new information. She had become friends with him and went to the house often (I would sometimes come home just as she was leaving). He seemed to reveal personal things to her, but not to me — I got only the barest of crumbs. She confidently entered the container and other rooms without asking for permission. I wondered whether she might have gone into my room to look for notes, photos, anything else that might put her on the trail of a supposed rival. (I was very discreet about things like that; there was no tangible sign of Ashley in my worlds — the marks she left behind were incorporeal. All right, I admit it: one photo in my wallet, but nothing else.) One day I found Carolina in the living room admiring the green Smith Corona that had been Dad's. She became very nervous even though I hadn't said anything. She commented that it was hard to believe that such a simple typewriter had become a museum piece. Then I became nervous too, as if the Smith Corona would suddenly start working like a telegraph and transmit, right in front of us, a passionate message from Ashley.

Caro was also the first to read my articles for *Digitar* (I had written one about Amazon and another on the role of political scientists in the Internet age). They were exercises that, above all, served as practice, since I still hadn't managed to achieve coherence and *NewTimes* would never have published them. At night, on the soft bed in her room, she would tell stories about her adventures with Estela, about recovering erased e-mails from lovers, disconsolate spouses who regretted having obtained such poisonous information: signs that came back from the dead to haunt them for the rest of their lives.

"Once a woman came to the office crying. She insulted Estela like crazy, threatened to kill herself, put on a whole show. I thought Estela had done something really awful. Nope. All she had done was find proof of the husband's infidelity in his e-mails. The wife had hired her to do that! People are crazy. If you're not ready to face the truth, don't try to discover it."

"And what happens when you think you're ready but find out that you're not?"

Sometimes it was hard for me to listen to her because I got lost in the memory of another voice in another place, but at least I tried. In bed, we understood each other better all the time, but I admit that sex had always been good between us: our bodies communicated better than we ourselves did. There was rhythm and a desire that, if not excessive, was constant, like a light guiding us on high seas. Her damp body shone in the half-light and fit harmoniously with mine.

Still, the sum of the parts never equaled the whole. I resisted commitment, calculating, balancing the effort, and she knew it, even though she didn't know why. She thought it was a matter of time and persisted in her efforts, becoming ever more disheartened. How could I tell her I would never completely commit, that she could never touch the center of my being? I couldn't. I was a coward when it suited me. At some point she would get tired, I told myself; at some point she would leave me of her own accord. As was my style, I let time decide for me. It was as if I hadn't learned a thing, quickly reverting after the fury and disaster of Ashley to my hardly original manner of conducting relationships with women. With my good-boy smile, I was a cynical, calculating opportunist who, having avoided commitment for so long, had forgotten how to commit and deserved every misfortune.

I decided it would be a good idea to talk to Carolina about my uncle. Maybe she could help me understand what was going on. I told her about what had happened that night.

"You *do* know your uncle's an alcoholic?" she asked. We were at the Mediterranean Café in the mall.

"Obviously," I said. I was so used to seeing him drink from morning until night that it seemed like a normal thing to do, like tying your shoes or washing your face. "But I don't think it all boils down to a medical diagnosis," I continued. "There's more to it, there has to be. Why is he an alcoholic? What brought him to that?"

"Of course it's more complicated. The question is: With all of our problems, why aren't we all alcoholics?"

"You're philosophical." I repeatedly took my glasses off and put them back on — no wonder the arms were always loose.

"Your uncle has suffered a lot. OK, it's pop psychology, I know, but put yourself in his place. Picture one afternoon, 1980, on Unzueta Street. Wouldn't that haunt you for the rest of your life? Wouldn't it have worn you out, made you turn to, I don't know, alcohol or drugs? But really, in the grand scheme of things, he knew how to deal with it. He was very close to your dad, wasn't he? And he was very much in love with his wife, wasn't he? All those years and he's never gone out with another woman."

"How do you know?"

"He told me. An old man, alone, tortured by memories, by nightmares. And to top it all off, the rumors. You saw the Berkeley video. Haven't you figured it out yet?"

"I don't know what you're talking about."

"What planet do you live on? Rumor has it he was the real Unzueta Street traitor. And that's why he was the only one who survived."

I was surprised. It was just a rumor, but I knew how much weight rumors carried in Río Fugitivo.

Through Ricardo, Caro got me an interview with the members of Berkeley. I had asked for the meeting a while ago, but after that conversation I became more insistent. We had to wait for their return, since they were on tour in Sucre, Potosí, and Tarija — aware that there was no such thing as too small a venue.

We met one night, at their request, at the Berkeley Café in Bohemia, a place packed with university students and foreigners, people wearing backpacks and alpaca vests who would never set foot in a place like El Marqués. It was smoky and smelled faintly of marijuana. A Rush CD was playing. Up close, the rockers were a bunch of baby-faced adolescents. Like everyone else, they had let themselves be seduced by American pop culture, but they had gone a step further than the rest and thrown themselves into the abyss of grotesque caricature. Maybe they were the distorted mirror of what was still to come: the younger they were, the more complete and irreversible the acceptance of values from the North. But there was no need to be apocalyptic or integrated — if our culture was as strong as I thought it was, it would withstand the onslaught.

They ordered tequila shots and drank them as they chewed gum. A pitcher of sangria came. The overweight waitress with a plunging neckline served us all a glass.

They were disappointed when they found out what I was looking for.

"What did you expect, a reporter from *Rolling Stone*?" I complained, irritated.

"Easy, boy," said the singer — dark glasses, plump lips, a straight nose, and high cheekbones. "We thought it was para algo más cool. Ricky told us you work for *Digitar*."

"I do, but that's not why I'm here. I'm writing a book about my father. Your video interested me."

The Rush CD ended. The place filled with the murmur of people conversing. Someone behind me was reciting a poem by Sabines. I didn't know the Mexican poet's work, but I did know this poem. Carolina had written it in a torrential letter after our first separation, when I called her from Berkeley to break up (I had left her to pursue in another body the same desires that had brought me to her, or at least that's what I thought). "The lovers wander around like crazy people / because they're alone, alone . . ."

Was I one of those lovers? Was Caro one too, and for a moment she had forgotten she was and I had made her remember it in some terrible way? I had never entirely understood why she sent me that poem in her final letter. There were so many gestures and words in the real world that I had never been able to understand, no matter how hard I tried. But there was no need to stop trying: signs were fragile butterflies that needed to be captured as soon as they extended their wings, or maybe later on.

Protected by the semidarkness, a woman with black curly hair was fondling her boyfriend at the next table.

"And who's your dad again?" said the espresso-skinned drummer with a perm that looked like crimped honeycomb.

"Pedro Reissig. Your video is an interesting allegory about his death."

I emphasized the word "allegory." Their eyes widened and they elbowed one another.

"You think we're dumb, huh, that we don't understand the word 'allegory'?" the singer said, sucking on a lemon and serving sangria to everyone. "Did it ever occur to you that the very name of our group suggests we know what an allegory is? None of us has ever been to Berkeley, but you know what it means in Río Fugitivo. What it meant, at least, to the previous generation and what we, you know, are trying to recapture."

I remembered one morning when I got to class at Barrows Hall. I couldn't get in because Ethnic Studies had taken over and demanded that the program become a department. Some of my classmates had joined in and urged me to pick up one of the placards protesting the university's discriminatory treatment of black students. I did, without much conviction, but admiring the few in my generation who were trying to recapture the argumentative spirit of the previous generation, of Berkeley (because by that time I knew Berkeley was a pale reflection of the sixties, a pale reflection of what the collective imagination had entrenched in the terrible world of stereotypes). The strike ended with the students' defeat: the administration, having learned its lesson decades earlier, wasn't easily intimidated.

"No, really," I said, trying to placate them, "I think you know all too well what it is. Your interpretation is so provocative that I decided to seek you out."

"So provocative," said the blond with a large, hooked nose (he'd definitely get a nose job with his first big earnings), "that the station decided not to play it anymore. There were too many protests and, to top it all off, the bomb."

"I thought the bomb had to do with Jaime Villa."

"The station has another theory. What does Villa have to do with a music station? The bomb was meant for someone there. It's not clear why. What is clear is that they used Villa as an excuse."

"But, tell me, why Kubrick and Buñuel? And why the geese? So much information in so few minutes and, as hard as I try, I can't put it all together. True, it's brilliant work. So much so that it's started to supplant reality, at least for me. When I think about what happened on Unzueta Street, the first images that come to mind are from the video."

"The person you need to talk to," said the singer, "is Ricky."

"Ricardo? Why him?"

"In reality it was his concept, his idea. Es un tipo muy cool. You'd get along well. He's, you know, hijo de . . ."

"Yeah, yeah, I know . . ."

"Everyone knows about Reissig, but not about the others."

An old woman approached and offered to sell me a rose for my girlfriend. I ignored her and Carolina looked at me as if to say that my lack of romanticism was predictable and depressing. She lit a cigarette.

"Ricardo," I repeated. "I didn't know he also directed videos. Or did he tell me? It doesn't matter. A one-man band."

"We've got no choice. In the States you can have one guy for each job. Here we've got to use what we can get. He didn't exactly direct, but he was the main creative force. He visually interpreted one of the biggest rumors about what happened."

"Which is . . . ?"

"It's just a rumor. You'd have to talk to Ricky."

I was bothered that they called him that. I looked at Carolina as if blaming her for not having told me about this side of her friend.

"He never believed the official version," the singer went on, "and set out to, you know, find another. Pero no tiene nada concreto. Just unfounded rumors."

"There was one informer in the group," the blond said.

"Exactly," I agreed. "Ricardo's dad."

"No, no. The group that was at the meeting."

"But then . . . ," I said.

"The crossword setter. David Reissig."

"Just because he survived doesn't mean it's him," the singer added, and waved a fly away with his right hand. "This has nothing to do with his crosswords, que son muy cool. A person learns from them. Just the other day I found out who discovered vitamin K."

"Or who invented the Walkman," said the blond.

"It might have been someone else," the singer continued, "maybe Mérida himself, you know? Don't tell Ricardo I said that. The government had to get rid of the informant, didn't they? That's the crossword setter's best alibi."

"Yes and no," said the blond. "According to Ricardo, he was the one with the motive. Your dad was doing his wife."

"And he told the government everything out of spite," I finished off. "So the political crime turns out to be a simple crime of passion. And my uncle asks them to take out his eye, to prevent suspicion. Straight from a soap opera. Maybe Ricky wrote the script? I thought I knew all the rumors. This one seems to have been invented yesterday."

"Se mantuvo underground, circuló word of mouth," the blond said. "In time a lot of things rise to the surface, you know."

"It seems like being shot in the eye wasn't part of the plan," the singer said. "That really was an accident."

"I see," I argued, "that Ricardo is very persuasive and has convinced you of his version. History, however, tells a different story."

I threw a few bills on the table and stood up quickly, gesturing to Caro that it was time to go. I didn't want to get upset but couldn't help it — that rumor infuriated me.

I left Berkeley with more questions than answers. Despite their foolish belief in unfounded rumors, the rockers had been intelligent and perceptive. Appearances deceive: sometimes the sublime could be found on MTV. Carolina told me to calm down, not to jump to conclusions.

I was upset, but knew I should get in touch with Ricardo to see where his version came from. It was unlikely and yet it fit perfectly with the strange sensation I got from my uncle. I had gotten to know him better and knew about his likable, everyday side — I had even come to care for him — but at the same time, I was sure he was hiding an enigma. Or *he* was the enigma and it was my mission to figure him out, get to the root of his relationship with Dad.

I should have talked to him, to that other man under house arrest around whom my world revolved these days.

The intensity of the present helped to control how much I missed Ashley.

I tried once again to find out what had really happened on Unzueta Street. I went back to the faded, yellowing municipal library on a hunch — silly wish, more like it — that maybe it had occurred to some reporter to hide events in the anonymity of a banal paragraph. No luck. Muted by military censorship, newspapers didn't reveal a thing — not even between the lines. Or maybe their writing was so secret that I would never uncover it. All I wound up with were hands stained from ink and the desire to never again see pages printed in such a rudimentary fashion (a press swarming with insomniac typesetters, letters being placed next to one another on a laborious metal sheet).

I searched out reporters, politicians. Their stories got lost in the dense mist of the myth. Dad and Uncle David emerged intact. Mérida was the obvious guilty party, the merciless informer. In what parallel world was the crossword setter guilty?

I called Ricardo and told him I wanted to meet. He replied that he'd love to, once he got back from a short trip to La Paz.

I wrote an insipid article about *Berkeley* for *Digitar* ("Humanism in Post-humanist Times"). I wrote Ashley a long e-mail, which I never sent.

One night Carolina and I met Carlos's wife leaving El Marqués with another man. Thinking I would quickly tell Carlos, she dared to introduce him as her cousin. She shouldn't have bothered — I wouldn't say a thing.

Federico called to tell me he'd been fired. He didn't seem upset.

"Look on the bright side," he said. "What kind of a life is that, traveling constantly?"

"Aren't you thinking about getting work with another airline?"

"You say that as if I had a ton of options. No, instead I think

I'm going to take this opportunity to find something else. It's impossible to have any kind of stability as a pilot. I'd never have been able to have a normal life."

"Do you think you will now? You might not get work and have to move to Santa Cruz."

"Don't burst my bubble, I'm trying to be positive."

"Sorry. I think you've got the right attitude."

There was silence on the other end of the line.

"Although, now that you mention it," he commented, "this recession is fucked. And there's not much I'd really like to do."

"I think pilots are the most admirable people in the world," I lied. "Co-pilots too."

"What if we opened a video store? I've got contacts in Miami, I could . . ."

Silence. I tried to imagine myself as his business partner, as if I had never left, but I couldn't. I realized that geographical distance was an excuse to justify my feeling of alienation. This would have happened anyhow, even if I had stayed, because life is unpredictable and can bring disparate beings together, but also separate them wherever they spend their days, whether in the same building or separated by a couple of continents.

"I'll be leaving again any day, Fede. I'd love to, but . . ."

Federico had only just realized the magnitude of what had happened. His positive attitude had helped him face being fired, but it hadn't lasted long. He said he had to go and hung up without waiting for me to respond. Ah, my friends: they were just like me, lost in the drama of their lives. When had the straight line become a dissolute labyrinth?

I went to Villa's mansion to tell him I was quitting. We had reached a stalemate and there was no point in continuing. They said he was busy, so I went to wait for him on the terrace.

I found a newspaper and decided to do Benjamín Laredo's crossword. Made King Alfonso swear the oath of Santa Gadea. Rivals of the Medicis, Florence. Canton of Switzerland. Elements in nitric acid. Famous violins from Cremona. "Bad money drives out good." Association of

American newspapers. Tango by Discépolo. I found it easier, more classical, less pop than my uncle's. I preferred the Cryptogram. I had often tried to do other crosswords in newspapers and magazines in other cities, only to lose interest after a short while, incapable of expanding my horizons. At times I played with the words in the grid in front of me, trying to configure them into something similar to my uncle's crossword. James Stewart must have felt something like that in *Vertigo*, when he decided to impose his sick obsession for Madeleine on redheaded Judy.

The mid-afternoon sun was strong and wrinkled the young body of Villa's wife, who was sleeping on an air mattress in the pool, on the verge of falling into the water. Two soldiers stood guard, distractedly staring at her oily back. Three ruffled doves in the dovecote looked bored.

Villa came up and apologized for the wait. "I see you're not very busy."

"There's not much for me to do. I've run out of ideas. Your secretary rejected all of my suggestions."

"Religious matters are not to be touched."

"I just said that your . . . conversion was a bit melodramatic and should be softened up a bit, that's all."

"If we took all your suggestions, not a single line would remain untouched. You have another vision of the book, so distinct that it would be better if you wrote it yourself. The idea was to improve it, not change it so it becomes unrecognizable."

"That's what I came to talk to you about. I don't know why I keep coming."

"Exactly. Why?"

We walked out toward the garden. Carolina's face suddenly came to mind. The night before, when I asked her what we should do on Friday, she told me she'd accepted an invitation from Ricardo. It was, I sensed, her way of forcing me to formalize our relationship, to take it more seriously. It wasn't enough that we spent almost all our time together: I had to give her a sign that I thought it was something more than just good company or gratifying sex. It was difficult for me to do that, but at the same time the mere mention of Ricardo stung me.

"The problem, Pedrito, isn't that you don't believe in the book. It's that you don't believe me."

"I wouldn't exactly say that."

"Call a spade a spade. Don't think I don't know why you sought me out. You wanted to hear something that would give you insight into your dad. And you did, but you didn't believe me then either."

There was silence. He asked me what I thought of the girl Cristina.

"I read one of the books she wrote. I don't know Latin, but damn it, you can't tell me that there's no divine intervention there."

I didn't comment. There were a lot of mysteries I would've liked to solve, but that wasn't one of them and I preferred to leave it that way — softly working away inside me, like a flame that refuses to be extinguished and that maybe, in the long run, would start a great fire.

"I'll save you the trouble," Villa said all of a sudden. "This is the golden rule to understanding your dad: you have to believe everything bad that's said about him. Absolutely everything. You have to remember that people are missing the whole story out of respect for his memory. Or feigned respect."

He put his right arm around my shoulders. In his expansive garden we looked like golf partners. The soldiers didn't let us out of their sight. The mastiff was sleeping on top of some daisies.

"I'm exaggerating. A lot of people respect him, but it's because they don't know the truth. Me, I lost touch with him after high school, Pedrito. You might say that what I'm telling you is schoolboy things. But damn it, you're never as real as when you were young, don't you think? That's my theory."

His hand squeezed my shoulder.

"Listen to me carefully one more time because I'm not going to repeat it. *Your dad was someone who took advantage of his smile.* He intentionally got into trouble, confident that he'd come out unscathed. And he did. Teachers, classmates, women all forgave him everything. I've never seen anything like it. The rest of us, we aren't forgiven a thing, but I tell you, if he were in my place they'd never consider extraditing him. It's unfair, absolutely unfair."

"Don't get worked up, Don Jaime."

"Don't worry, that's my style. He liked to get involved with his brother's women. I knew about three. Now it's all about Pedro, but back then David was more intelligent, more respected. Distant, not at all likable, but still. There was a strange rivalry between the two of them, most of all on the part of Pedro. He found his brother's weak spot and that was it. David was completely cuckolded and didn't believe what people said about Pedro. What's more, he defended him. Until he saw it with his own eyes. It was a scandal, but he forgave him in the end. He had to give in to that charisma."

"I've seen worse things," I said, trying to appear calm. Should I believe him? And if I did, was it important?

"Let me continue, I've only just begun. Have you ever heard of Miguelito Arnez? Of course you haven't, Pedrito. You didn't ask the right questions. No one asks the right questions. Everyone has forgotten about Miguelito Arnez. Pedro gave him a nickname: Salamander."

I looked at him, and he took his arm from around my shoulders.

"He was our classmate. The typical unpopular kid at school. He was extremely effeminate, to say the least. Pedro made fun of him behind his back but seemed to put up with him. He listened to his problems if nothing else."

Like me and Federico, I thought.

"Miguelito was full of problems. He came from a poor family, his dad beat him, and he wanted to run away."

He stopped.

"Salamander turned up dead in an empty lot one day, a bullet in his temple. Suicide, they said, and that was that. The police didn't want to look into it much. They weren't interested. I was the only one who knew the truth. I got the gun. I gave it to Pedro the night before. I was there when Pedro arranged to meet him at the lot, and I went with him."

The sun lit up his wicked face. I felt he was enjoying every word. I put my right index finger to the tip of my nose.

"And you know what's worse, Pedrito? There was no reason. It was gratuitous. Out of curiosity. To see what it felt like . . ."

"Were there other witnesses?"

"No. Only me. It's my word and that's it. You can disbelieve me again if you like. But I know that one day, when I'm no longer here, you'll wake up in the morning and you'll remember what I told you. And you'll believe me. Because I don't lie, Pedrito. It's not for nothing that the poor believe in me . . ."

Not wanting to hear any more, I turned and walked quickly to the main door. The mastiff stood up and slowly followed, not terribly interested in changing his somnolent routine. I cursed the day I had said I would be Villa's editor. He had hit me where it hurt most. Despite all the information I had about Dad, any story could fit into the empty space that was him.

It was impossible to be around evil and not be affected by it.

That night I showed up at Carolina's place. I made love to her so mechanically that she stopped and told me she'd rather not continue. It had taken her a while to realize my lack of interest and admit to it, but she had finally done so. I thought she would kick me out, but she felt sorry for my pitiful demeanor. She asked me not to lie to her anymore. I was unsure, but at last, gasping for breath, I unburdened and told her about my relationship with Ashley, how I ached with love for her and had so cowardly lost my chance, because time passes and we change, and in the blink of an eye our youth is gone, our delicious, scandalous attraction becomes ephemeral and fugitive, and sometimes love never comes, or it comes silently and then you have to listen to it, accept it, give yourself over to the enjoyment of day-to-day life. Oh, there was nothing I didn't tell her about Ashley! When it was over I sank into Carolina's sheltering embrace.

She sat on the edge of the bed and covered her body with the yellow sheet. The light from the lamp shone on her tense face and highlighted the ring over her eyebrow. She stretched her hand out to the bedside table, took the pack of cigarettes, and lit one.

"It was my psychic's fault," she said. "She assured me I would fall in love with a very good friend and that the attraction would be mutual. I was wrong. I didn't know how to read the signs."

The cat, lying on the bed, got up, meowed, and headed into the kitchen.

"I have a confession to make too," she said.

She took a long drag on the cigarette. I leaned up against the pillows.

"The whole time," she went on, "I've been seeing Ricardo. I started going out with him a few months before you arrived. Nothing formal, but we dated. When you arrived, I told him I had to deal with my situation with you, asked him to wait and see what happened. He accepted, but a week after you got here he made a scene. He was nobody's leftovers, et cetera. One thing led to another and, well, we got back together. Days went by and I just couldn't tell you. So you see, in a way you made my decision for me."

I silently processed what I'd just heard, then said, "Good to know I'm not the only son of a bitch."

I was exhausted and started to feel the stabbing pains of a migraine. I would've liked to hide my face in the pillow and forget about the world. Still, I couldn't stop talking:

"You're unbelievable. You had the nerve to introduce us, go out with us both, try to get us to be friends. I wonder what was going through your mind, whether you found the situation exciting."

"Don't blame it all on me." The ash from her cigarette fell onto the sheets. "That's just like you. Now I'm the one who's guilty and you're innocent."

Her voice broke as she talked, as if the initial strength with which she'd faced my story about Ashley had given way to anguish as the dream disappeared. I was leaving her life. I was no longer. I had played my part.

"What a great opportunity we lost, Pedro. What went wrong? We get along and would've had a beautiful friendship. That's not easy to find."

"You said it, Caro — a beautiful friendship. But now I'm not sure we even had that."

When she saw me lie back, she said firmly, "You're crazy if you think you're going to sleep here."

"Don't worry. I've already made that mistake before."

I got up in silence.

"Say hi to Ricky Martin," I said on my way out.

"Bastard," she replied.

I walked home to Uncle David's. I felt as if I were walking down the streets of Berkeley, just as Dad had described them, and got lost on Telegraph only to find myself on Unzueta, while geese — six? seven of them? — flew all around me and then all of a sudden there were shots and a salamander was following me and someone was shouting "All dead" and blood was flowing on the floor and a glass eye exploded. Anguish, agony. There was also a desperate sense of unreality. The barely lit streets and I both became ghost-like, suffered from a lack of substance.

10

OVER THE course of my life I've surprised a lot of people, not because I wanted to but because I had to — my girl-friends most of all. I've invited them out for coffee and they've arrived elegant and perfumed, unaware that the purpose of the date was for me to break up with them. I tend to hand back exams my students have failed with a smile, and for a moment they think they did well. It's not intentional; I guess it's nervousness. I don't like to surprise or be surprised. I try to control events. Like a chess player who can picture the next few moves, I approach people knowing I'll probably get a yes, not a no. Carolina always said I was missing out on the secret pleasure of life by trying to plan everything. Maybe I didn't understand what she meant until I met Ashley. And maybe, even then, I didn't get the full, delightful meaning of it until that morning when the phone rang and I answered it, my husky voice rising directly out of my larynx, shunning intermediaries, and heard the Spanish accent of a voice reply:

"Despierta, Little Ear."

It was impossible not to wake up and gain instant clarity. I gripped the handset, anxious and scared, and looked over my shoulder, expecting to see Patrick materialize and claim my soul.

"Ashley? Where are you calling from?"

"A pay phone outside the hotel. Don't worry, Patrick's sleeping."

"What if he wakes up and you're not there?"

"I won't be long. I'll just tell him it was such a special night that I went out for a walk on the beach in the moonlight."

She laughed sweetly, maliciously. I admit that I've done some things, but never, until that phone call, had I felt I'd done something so wrong. Maybe I had never been mature enough to realize what I'd done. Maybe I had finally discovered and crossed a line, one I could actually see. There was something intolerable about a woman calling her lover on her wedding night, from her honeymoon on a remote island, while the waves lapped the shore and her husband slept, exhausted from champagne and sex, before some of the guests had even returned home. It finally made me put myself in Patrick's shoes and feel for him. Ashley had definitely outdone me — she was far less scrupulous than I. Or maybe she was just more in love.

"He's so white. And he's gained weight lately, tiene unos rollos. His pudgy skin disgusts me. *He* disgusts me! What have you done to me, Pedro?"

"We shouldn't keep talking. What if he comes?"

"Do you promise we'll be together again when I get back?"

"We could go for coffee. You could take one of my classes."

"Right. Ni tú te la crees. I shouldn't have done it. Why? Why? Why me?"

"Calm down, Ashley. Go back to your room."

"What are you wearing?"

"The yellow boxers you gave me. And my gray Berkeley T-shirt."

"When we were fucking all I could think about was you: that you should've been him, here with me on our honeymoon. What the fuck have you done to me? What the fuck?"

"Ashley . . ."

She hung up. I was ten years older, I should've been the responsible one, the one to see things clearly and put everything right. But as I talked to her, wavering between delight and terror, between fascination and disgust, I knew that I would be unable to resist temptation and that I could only give myself over to Ashley, come what may.

▪ ▪ ▪

The next phase of our relationship began a few days after she got back from the Cayman Islands. She took advantage of Patrick's trust and invented a new time to go to the gym: from six to eight in the morning, three times a week. She would take the blue Saab that Patrick was still paying off and park it four blocks from my house. She walked on icy, snow-covered sidewalks, risking a fall, then opened the unlocked door to my apartment. Shivering, she took off her clothes on the way to my room and crawled into bed. I would wake up at the touch of her cold skin. Sometimes I had barely opened my eyes and she was already on top of me, kissing my chest with her slippery tongue or playing with my penis, her head down and her long red hair covering her breasts. They were wintry mornings of excess and I still don't understand how Patrick never knew, never saw a new light in Ashley's eyes, realized her moans were fake when she was with him at night, or discovered an almost invisible bruise or light scratches on her body.

The truth is that those days wild, unbridled sex, spiced with tenderness, took precedence over everything else. I knew it was better that way. By putting the carnal first we had little time to intensify emotional ties, and separation would be easier. We were in love, but we both seemed to have adopted a fatalistic attitude: this could end at any time and we should live as if each day were our last.

Or at least that was what I thought at first. A few weeks later came the inevitable question: "What are we going to do?"

"What do you mean?" I was playing with the leaves of a jasmine. Ashley had arrived with several pots one day, and now my apartment was full of wilted plants.

"No me estoy arriesgando just because I love to do it. There has to be something at the end."

"The Lord shall provide."

"Forget that. Let's not pretend to live for the moment anymore when we both know . . . Those were the worst days of my life when you broke up with me. Eso no se hace, Pedro. I don't know how I forgave you. Well, I know."

"It was awful for me too."

"And you wanted me back, didn't you? Well, here I am. But just to see each other in secret?"

"What else can we do?"

"How quickly we forget."

"We won't be apart again. I promise, Ashley. I'll think of something."

"Con ese tono no convences a nadie."

"Give Pedro a chance."

"This is your second."

"Second time lucky."

I didn't know what I would do. I had missed her when we were apart and believed myself capable of sacrificing my job just to have another chance. Now that I had it, caution returned, and calculation, and reasons, goddamn reasons.

There was also rest. Ashley would lie with her head on my chest while I caressed her back speckled with moles, telling me about her childhood and her plans to travel all over the world, never tiring of going to new countries. It was at those times, with the snow building up on the windowsill, my room a protective refuge from the battles waged in the world, that I realized how little I knew about her, her past, her dreams.

When she spoke of Patrick, I did all I could to make her stop.

"That night at the church, I saw him and wanted to run, esconderme. Not for me at all. And to think that at one time I was so in love with him."

"You'll say the same thing about me one day."

"I don't think so. Although you have gained a bit of weight," she said, smiling.

"It's winter," I said, pretending her comment hadn't bothered me. But it was true. My metabolism had changed, and I couldn't eat whatever I wanted without paying the price. I needed to go to the gym. I wasn't crazy about the idea but knew that, in the end, my vanity would force me to.

"You're different," she went on. "That night, it was a miracle I didn't escape. If it hadn't been for my mom, I would've. She looked so excited — her little girl. And my family and the guests and the cake. I might as well, me dije. And Patrick was . . ."

"We had a deal. No mention of Patrick."

"I'm a bitch, aren't I? Eso es lo que piensas."

"Yo también lo soy. You're nothing that I'm not."

"Will we go to hell?"

"Probably."

"I read *Berkeley* again when I was in Boston. I felt I owed it to you. And it was a way to stay connected to you. I understood it less than I did the first time. Don't even ask me what it's about now. I couldn't concentrate. I saw your face in every line I read."

"You said it the first time: it's a very romantic book."

"And these photos?" Ashley was looking at a photo album from my time in Berkeley.

"The co-op where my dad lived. It's abandoned now."

"Looks like it's about to fall down. Weeds have taken over the garden."

"It's near People's Park, where the homeless congregate. The university wants to demolish the building — just like they tried to get rid of People's Park by building student volleyball courts there. But there's a coalition of anarchists, old lefties, and leftovers from the sixties who say the co-op is a historical monument to the struggles of that time and should be preserved."

"How did you get inside?"

"There was a rave there and one of my students invited me. I went out of curiosity, when I still thought that going wherever my dad had been would help me understand him."

"And . . ."

"Kids getting high in every room. Pissing in every corner. An explosive odor of shit and marijuana. Broken wine bottles everywhere. I didn't stay long. Sometimes it's better not to try and see everything. Sometimes imagination and desire are preferable to reality."

"Still, it's hard to be happy with just desire and imagination."
"Unfortunately."

"Pedro?"
"Yeah?"
"No promises, no conditions. Don't ever forget."

The semester began. Those days of endless snow when night fell at four in the afternoon and the solitary, restored statue of Randolph Jones — a horrendous emerald green color, forever taciturn and in love, in search of the hereafter and afraid of it — reigned over an Arts Quad empty of people, I taught, somewhat detached, my usual introductory course and an advanced one called "Versions of Heaven on Earth in Leftist Discourse." The atmosphere in the Institute had really improved. Colleagues who opposed me had opted for indifference and, in the worst case, hypocritical diplomacy, the formality of circumstance. When I ran into them in the hallway or as I was checking my mail, they made the slightest facial gesture that could be interpreted as a greeting. It didn't bother me — in fact, I preferred it that way. We didn't have anything to say. Still, I didn't go into the building very often. I taught my classes, went to my office hours and only the most necessary meetings. Helen admonished me but didn't insist.

In academic matters, the most interesting thing at the Institute was a working group Joaquín created with Helen's help and to the disdain of Clavijero, to open dialogue with the Latino students from LSP. The group had managed to attract students from other departments and even some professors who took Latin America as a starting place from which to discuss postcolonial matters or to use for comparative studies. Joaquín had prepared a text containing readings from Latino/Latin American political scientists, sociologists, and cultural critics — Calderón, Bartra, Oppenhayn, Castañeda, Monsiváis, Sarlo, García Canclini, Alarcón, Stavans — and there was an ambitious list of speakers coming to campus. His energy, his faith in the academic world never ceased to amaze me. Would dialogue be possible? My skepticism said it wouldn't be.

Each group was in its discipline's own little world — academic work was ever further away from true intellectual pursuits. But there was no point in taking a comfortable stance and distancing oneself from the topic. At the very least an attempt had to be made to build bridges. Well, others should attempt what I never would.

Ashley was more and more daring in her show of affection. She came regularly to my office hours, arriving wrapped in a coat, gloves, scarf, hat, and boots (as with everyone else, winter had managed to cover her with layers of clothing). As soon as she came into my office she would comment on the magnificent sight out my window: the Gothic history and architecture buildings covered with snow, the fraternity and sorority mansions like an opulent belt around campus, the town luminous in its whiteness, green islands surrounded by white at the end of the valley. How many colors, how many shades did the word "white" encompass? She spoke as she slowly took off her coat, her gloves, and her hat and let her scarf fall to the floor. Then, with the door closed, a couple of students waiting outside, she dared to caress me, her hands sliding fluidly all over my body. I clenched my teeth and let her. Migraines, which I hadn't had for some time, came back with a vengeance, putting pressure on one side of my head, behind my right eye. I had to cancel a few classes because of them.

One night — it was only five o'clock, but already night — she was waiting next to my car in the Institute's parking lot. She was wearing her yellow coat and looked radiant, full of contained energy. I drove her home. As soon as I stopped the car she told me she wanted to say goodbye properly and asked me to go with her to the porch, where total darkness would protect us better. We kissed next to an incongruent hammock and an empty plant pot hanging from the roof. Locks of red hair fell around her expectant face. I asked her where Patrick was. She said she didn't know, either on campus or inside. We heard the notes of a saxophone and knew that he was in his study on the second floor. We kissed again, and I understood where this was leading. As at the Halloween party, Ashley grew more and more excited by risk, knowing that Patrick was near and could discover us. I thought back to those first cautious days when she was afraid to even come to my apartment. I wanted to stop, but tried without conviction. We ended up writhing against the wall while our hands smothered moans and the saxophone was our background music.

The previous cycle had started all over. Once again, Yasemin took notice and warned me. This time I didn't want to listen.

There was also desperation. One night when Patrick had to study late on campus, Ashley came to my place. We drank red wine and smoked a joint while she confessed her academic indifference. She was planning to quit university, said she didn't have the patience to do a Ph.D.

"I knew it all along, but now more than ever. Don't be disappointed in me, OK?"

"So what are you going to do?"

"Do I have to answer you right now? Podría dedicarme full-time al Internet trading. I think I'm good at it. This morning vi que the futures in NASDAQ estaban up and all my stocks were up but one, my favorite, Nortel, que estaba even. So I bought two hundred stocks in Nortel and got out. When I went back, NASDAQ seguía up, and my dear NT estaba up five percent, así que lo vendí for a quick profit. Me sentí muy inteligente porque I had guessed it right."

"Quite an expert. You're starting to get caught up in it. Weren't you losing money? The market has been disastrous lately."

"I told you, you don't lose money, stocks are just down. There's nothing concrete about studying. Internet trading is concrete. I know a lot of students who do this prácticamente full-time and they're not doing too badly. Claro que les iba mejor antes, before the bubble burst."

"I thought you weren't interested in money."

"I'm not interested in the money itself. Lo que estoy haciendo is very risky and that's what attracts me: the adrenaline rush. Ganar, perder dinero, that's secondary. But earning money does provide freedom. Just imagine never having to work again, being able to travel wherever you want."

Was I to take her seriously or laugh? She was lost, didn't know what to do with her life. And yet, maybe there was something coherent to her search. She longed for the materialness of experience, which wasn't in books but in travels and the ephemeral commitment to Chiapas, the money she won or lost with every second of buying and selling stocks.

We made love when the combination of wine and marijuana, which had put me to sleep, caused an explosive effect in Ashley. She held on to me tightly, said she couldn't make me stay still, that I was escaping through her fingers and multiplying into infinite Pedros in the swirling room. She begged me not to go, not to leave her alone. There was anguish in her voice and I didn't know how to calm her down. She vomited on my bed and came out of the trance somewhat. I bathed her, dressed her, and dropped her off a block from home, giving her instructions on how to get to her door.

By March, Ashley had articulated an escape plan. She would finish the semester and I would resign from the university. Then one day we would just disappear and go to Barcelona, where she had friends who could put us up until we found work and began our life all over. It was a crazy, romantic plan — out of this world, as Ashley would say. I wanted to object, but couldn't. I gave in to her impetus, the power of her love, and let her dream.

One day when a blizzard lashed the campus and neither scarves nor coats could stop the cold that froze any bare skin (my ears were like living stalactites), and I was damning Madison and missing Río Fugitivo, I found the door to my apartment open. The lock had been forced. I took off my gloves and went in. All the windows were broken, as were the TV and the G3. The plants had been ripped by their roots from their pots and my books were scattered on the floor, their pages destroyed. The walls in my room were painted with insulting, red graffiti. There was a pool of something on my bed — I didn't want to find out what it was. On my desk, I found a bill for the plants.

I sat on the floor of the bathroom, shaving cream on the broken mirror and walls. My confusion gave way to understanding. I wouldn't press charges. I understood Patrick better than he could ever think I understood him. It was about time. I wanted to find him and shake his hand. It could've been worse and I still wouldn't have complained. After all, there could've been a bullet that would've brought the unworthy rival to his end.

Ashley called me in tears. She told me Patrick had hit her and threatened her with the worst. She had moved out and would be staying with a friend for a few days. I told her what had happened to my apartment and said we shouldn't see each other for a while. She said she loved me, that this was just a test we would get through if our love was strong. Yes, yes, I said, and hung up.

That same day, I prepared my own escape plan. I spoke with Helen and asked for a leave of absence for the following semester: I needed to go to Río Fugitivo to finish the research for my book. She said I should have told her sooner. It would be hard to find a replacement this late, but she promised she would look into it.

In April, as spring tried to take over a still wintry land — the melting had only timidly begun and green vegetation was striving to return — everyone at the Institute heard about what had happened and added their own little twist to the facts. Patrick had hired a couple of hit men? Ashley had started divorce proceedings? I had been fired? Students looked at me mischievously and laughter disrupted the thread of my argument in class. The secretary cornered me with questions. Clavijero looked at me sarcastically, as if to say that the truth could not be hidden, that his intuition hadn't let him down.

Helen defended me at a meeting. She said that conclusions couldn't be drawn based on unfounded rumors and that while there was no official complaint the Institute couldn't do anything. In private, she told me she'd do everything she could to get me the leave of absence. Everything would calm down in a semester, and she hoped not to hear any more rumors.

"Why?" I asked her. "Why are you defending me?"

"I've been here for years. This isn't the first or last case of a professor getting involved with his student. If it's discreet and there are no complaints from either of the parties, there's nothing wrong with it."

"That's the official answer. Any other reason?"

She replied only after taking a while to decide whether or not to tell me. It was hard for her to open up; she was very reserved and it wasn't easy to get to know her. But I knew there were few people like her who could put themselves in another's shoes. She had a hard exterior and held a lot of power, but she didn't like to abuse it and tried to be understanding when the situation required. Students adored her, I cared for and admired her, other colleagues respected and feared her.

"Without meaning to," she said, "you got in the middle of a battle for power at the Institute. Clavijero dominated here for two decades and I was his faithful apprentice for years. Now things have changed. He's leaving soon, and he chose you to show us all that he still holds power. He doesn't realize he's already lost it. There's definitely a black mark against you, that's true. And if you keep doing stupid things it's going to become harder to defend you. I hope that what I've been told isn't true. Is it? No, don't answer that."

A friend of Ashley's called me a couple of times to say that Ashley wanted me to meet her. I avoided her, arguing that it was better to let things calm down. Ashley went back to living with Patrick.

One afternoon she showed up during my office hours, her body buried underneath a heavy gray overcoat. What had become of the moles on her back? I took my glasses off.

"How's the semester going?" she asked, staring at the bookshelves. Her gestures were vague and her voice shook.

"A little disorganized, but it's almost over. Yours?"

"It's going. No choice but to carry on: day after day, week after week. I have so many papers overdue from last semester."

"And your stocks?"

"Tech stocks are going down, down, down. Bad news todos los días. Soon there'll be nothing left. Another reason for Patrick to hate me. I'm investing the little that's left in stocks that have been destroyed, o por lo menos están como forty percent off their highs . . . but in solid companies con earning growth más de thirty percent y más de twenty-five billion dollars in market cap. Texas Instruments, Amgen, que es el granddaddy of all biotech stocks, JDS Uniphase, fiber optics. And I've still got Nortel."

Her voice changed when she talked about the stock market, acquired a sense of security and genuine interest that I'd never heard when she talked about her studies. That was what moved her, what touched her core. At least she had realized that.

"Fiber optics y biotech," I said. "Not bad."

"I haven't seen you anywhere. Are you avoiding me?"

"It's not that. Don't you think it's better this way?"

"For how long? I can't wait forever."

I was sitting behind my desk, my hands gripping the chair as if I were preparing myself for the moment of impact. She took a few steps around and then approached me.

"Si me lo pides, I'll leave him. If you ask me."

She rested her hands on my knees and brought her face close to mine. I smelled the sea breeze of her perfume, which always reminded me of the first time I drove her home, when everything was still new and nothing around us seemed to exist.

"What do we do now, Little Ear?"

We kissed passionately, tenderly. I realized, once again, what I already knew: even with my fear, I had never been as in love with anyone as I was with Ashley. She was the woman for me.

In early May, once I got approval from the Institute, I left for Río Fugitivo without saying goodbye to Ashley. It was the right decision, as much for her as for me. I trusted that distance would help me forget. I hoped she would forgive me. I was sure she wouldn't.

11

WOKE UP early, confused — I didn't know where I was. I
touched my damp forehead: I had had a nightmare. I was helping some soldiers excavate the patio in a military barracks and
bones kept appearing, bones that crumbled as soon as my hands
touched them. "All dead," murmured a lieutenant who had
Ricardo's face, over and over again. I went up to him and shouted,
"Who, you son of a bitch?" He looked at me sarcastically and repeated, "All dead."

My head hurt. I prayed a migraine wasn't on its way. It wasn't,
but I couldn't get back to sleep. I was distracted by the screeching
of a cat in heat somewhere on a neighbor's roof. Light slowly began to creep into day; the sun would soon rise.

I lit a cigarette. Maybe Dad's alter ego in *Berkeley* wasn't Bernard, the utopian dreamer, but Xavier, the incarnation of evil. Or
maybe he was both.

I took a couple of drags on the cigarette. I put the ash in the
palm of my right hand.

Then which was his brother's alter ego? Again, maybe both of
them.

Miguel Arnez was the salamander. Dad had left his body out in
the open in *Berkeley,* hoping someone would recognize it. If what
Villa told me was true, how could I justify Dad now? I could justify
his lies when they were to create the legend around him. I could

even rationalize a tense, warlike situation to understand how he'd had a couple of comrades shot. But a gratuitous death? There was simply no way.

I wished Villa had lied to me. I wanted Villa to have lied to me.

I put the ash in my mouth.

That Friday morning at breakfast, I started my day with the Cryptogram, asking myself for the name of the computer Von Neumann invented. Then, while my uncle showed me the latest improvements to his lawnmower motor in the garden, I heard on the radio that Villa had been sent to La Paz and on to Miami in an operation that was at once expected and a surprise. Later, as I walked to the building where the Channel Veintiuno offices were, I heard that a bomb had exploded at the offices of Digital Global Service, an Internet service provider. The National Vindication Commando had taken responsibility for it. I missed Villa, the ash from his cigarettes in the palm of his hand, his rosary as he prayed for help in the hereafter, his desperate attempt to recover an image of himself that would neutralize the picture of evil — a generous evil, but evil still — that he had built for himself over the last few years. I was sorry I hadn't said goodbye to him and regretted my ill-timed visit the day before.

I wondered what would happen to his memoirs. I tried once again to understand a man who was so generous to the poor and at the same time an amoral drug trafficker. I remembered the time I saw a bouquet of roses on his desk, sent by a thankful shoe shiner from Cochabamba. I remembered the burnt face of one of his men who had tried to betray him and in the morning was found hanging from a post in the plaza of a village in Beni. The contradictions of his personality would plague me for a long time. The contradictions of personalities always plague me for a long time.

Now I was left with more questions than answers, with one more piece to my shadowy puzzle: Miguel Arnez.

The blue Channel Veintiuno building, seven stories high with a huge parabolic antenna on the roof, was on Avenida de las Acacias.

I asked a police officer at the guard post for Ricardo Mérida's office. I was to go left down a long hallway, to the last door. He made me leave my ID card.

Villa's comments about my dad ran through my mind as I walked down the hall. I had tried to disregard them as a tall tale, but I couldn't. Why would he lie to me? The truth is that a part of me had always been capable of believing that Dad was guilty of what Villa said he'd done. How was it possible that, all of a sudden, both brothers had taken on a sinister air?

Who was Dad, for God's sake? Who?

When I went into Ricardo's office (a dark cubicle with no windows or ventilation), he was packing up his computer. His cheeks were red, his acne a living entity that threatened to take over his whole face. On the carpet there were four boxes filled with various objects, from videocassettes to paperweights and a picture frame from which Carolina smiled at us conspiratorially.

I shouldn't think about her. She had done nothing more than behave ignobly in an ignoble situation, one that I had created. I couldn't accuse her of having been incapable of transcending the situation. I couldn't accuse her of not having done what I hadn't.

There were photos of Ricardo's dad on the walls: black beard, untidy mop of hair, fierce eyes, thin lips. It was a common face, one more of those middle-class boys who want revolution, to change the structure of the continent with the fervor of their idealism and the blinkers of their ideology — at least in the beginning, before corruption inevitably takes over, affecting us all differently.

"You caught me just in time. I never liked this job. The *Digitar* offices are luxurious in comparison. Big windows, fresh air."

I looked at him without saying a word. I had come to insult him because I thought he was guilty of starting the rumors about Uncle David. The thing with Carolina had gotten in the way but wasn't important. After all, Ricardo was the only one who had benefited from the situation.

I didn't know how to begin.

"Did you need me for something urgent? Yeah, I know, we owe you for a few articles. Could you wait a couple of weeks?"

I sat down on the brown sofa with springs that sank under my weight. Ricardo continued packing. I tried not to fixate on his spotted cheeks but couldn't help it. I found them repulsive.

"I thought you were going to keep both jobs."

"*Digitar* is growing fast. And it was time for me to go. They never entirely accepted me here. They wanted me to take down the pictures of my dad, for example."

"I don't know much about him."

"Nobody knows about him. He ceased being a person and became the Traitor. Nobody knows that he would have sacrificed his life and family to achieve a more just society. That he risked everything to come and visit us, and when he was with us he acted as if nothing were wrong — he never even mentioned politics in front of Mom or us kids. He wanted to protect us through ignorance and would play with us, all the while keeping his problems bottled up inside. He liked Dylan and CCR. He read Cortázar and Dostoyevsky. He was shy with women. He admired Che, Frantz Fanon, and Juan José Torres. He had a brilliant strategic mind. Reissig took all the credit, but he gave only the general instructions and it was really my dad who planned the details of the attacks."

His voice threatened to break. He stopped talking.

"We weren't dealt an easy hand," I said. "I have to wrestle with being the son of a well-known person too. Sometimes I think that's why I stayed on in the States."

"It's even more difficult if the person everyone thinks is guilty is really innocent."

"Or vice versa."

"I wouldn't know anything about that."

"I heard a few things you've said about my uncle."

"Oh, so that's why." He stopped. "Things I supposedly said. I wasn't the first and I won't be the last. For every official version there's an alternative one."

"It's not about official versions. It's about what really happened."

Ricardo went and took one of the pictures off the wall.

"How do you know what happened?" He raised his voice.

"Were you there? And why does it bother you so much? Your dad isn't even the problem. I don't want to destroy him, all I want is to recover the real René Mérida."

"By destroying my uncle in the process?"

He opened one of the boxes that had already been closed, took out a file folder, and handed it to me. It was filled with typewritten pages.

"They're photocopies; you can keep them. I can show you the originals if you want."

They were letters. I read the first one, addressed to "My beloved Salamander." I got halfway through, then jumped to the end on the third page. It was unsigned. I continued reading. They were intense letters about a furtive love, full of a passion I had never felt and which made me painfully jealous. It wasn't hard to tell what this was about: Ricardo could immediately begin a scandalous rumor. The story of Dad and Aunt Elsa in the darkness of those violent times, while Uncle David looked the other way or pretended to. I suddenly felt the lack of air in the room.

"Your dad fell in love with your aunt," Ricardo said, savoring what was to come, his slow telling of the facts, rescued from the pool of conjecture for my benefit. "So much so that he decided to leave politics, run away with her to another country and start another life. It was a melodramatic plan, typical of your dad, who seemed condemned to grandiloquent gestures, to great declarations of love."

He paused.

"Isn't it clear at the end of his novel?" he continued. "Bernard, who resembles your dad, regrets having come back and wants to return to Berkeley."

"You're projecting a life onto a novel. *Berkeley* isn't my dad's memoirs."

"Don't we all project? Don't writers project? They hide their deepest truths in the most visible place in the text and then protect them by saying it's a work of fiction."

He poured himself a glass of water and asked me if I wanted one. I did, but said that I didn't.

"Your uncle," he went on, "knew about the relationship because it wasn't exactly hidden. Your dad did whatever he wanted and let others try to understand him and justify his actions. Your uncle didn't say anything until he found out about their plans to run away. That's when he decided to act and turned them in to the military. What did you think, that he was saved by pure luck? That they made a mistake and left him for dead? Something went wrong, that much is true. They had to wound him so it would look as if he had nothing to do with it, but they almost killed him."

"How did you get these letters?"

"Dad kept them hidden in a box. Mom never wanted to open it. I opened it a year ago. My dad was your dad's confidant, the person he trusted most."

"You could have made them public."

"They only prove that Pedro Reissig and Elsa had an intense love affair. That's it. I don't have proof that David did anything. What I tried to do, and thus the rumors, thus the video, was to make him nervous, let him know that I knew, see if that would wear him down and make him confess. I managed to unsettle him, that's for sure, but nothing more. Or do you think the bomb at the door here was a coincidence?"

"That has nothing to do with it. Up to this point, your story was believable. That's just pure paranoia. My uncle hardly ever leaves the house."

"I don't have proof, but I don't believe in coincidence. A bomb destroys the Jeep parked next to my car, minutes before I get into it, and people say it has something to do with Villa. Wouldn't it make more sense to think it had something to do with me? That the National Vindication Commando is a scheme of your uncle's to hide his attempt to get rid of me?"

I didn't answer. I felt very close to Ricardo. Something had made me identify with him from the moment I first met him, and that sense of identification had only deepened. I didn't believe all the details, but I did believe the argument of his story as a whole.

Before closing the door behind me, I couldn't keep it in any longer and said, "I know about Carolina. Don't think I'm upset with you. You have nothing to do with it. Anyhow, I learned a long time ago that it's not worth fighting over a woman."

"So what is worth fighting over?" he replied. "And if you're not upset, it's because you never loved her. It's that simple. Because I had everything to do with it. Everything."

Ricardo's response silenced me.

I left the office thinking that Villa hadn't lied to me either. It was no coincidence that Dad had called Elsa "Salamander." The act of treachery against his brother had been his way of redeeming a vile crime.

Like a paper that burns slowly in the ashes, Dad's image crackled inside of me and caught fire. The pain burnt my chest.

My uncle was in the container when I got back. I went into the living room, trying not to make any noise. Light streamed in through the open curtains, and I left them that way to see when he was coming. The enlarged shadow of the lemon tree lay over the messy patio.

The same misaligned letter *o*, the intermittent bar on the *t*. It wasn't hard to prove that the letters had been written on the green Smith Corona, now quiet on one of the pedestals. As if the traces of passion revealed by the hand can be hidden by typographical formality, by the technology of a medium that supposedly distanced the author from his product (and thus the trembling signature on all typewritten letters and documents, thus the personal ink after the attempt at impersonality). But these letters didn't hide a thing, and the typewriter served to transmit the product of a broken heart whose echoes were still heard twenty years later.

Something I still didn't understand was how Uncle David had been able to keep that antique which spoke to him of a horrific time, how he could arrange the living room in homage to *Berkeley* and take responsibility for keeping the memory of its author alive. Or maybe he could do just that because he had been capable of sending his brother, his wife, and other innocent people to their deaths? Maybe all of this spoke of a misguided attempt at atonement, a quest for redemption.

It wasn't important. I lived with my father's murderer and had better do something about it. I had to keep a level head.

I went to my room, where I had the file with the Cryptograms my uncle had given me and the crosswords cut out of the newspaper since my arrival. I looked for specific dates, then studied those crosswords.

Russian, true inventor of the television in 1908. Computer invented by Von Neumann. The three bombs had each exploded on a Friday, the day the crossword came out. I reviewed each one of them, and hidden among the many references to media I found: references to the postal system on the day of the bomb at the post office; to the television on the day of the explosion at the TV station; and to computers that Friday when the bomb went off at Digital Global Service.

He knew about the bombs beforehand: bombs that linked to form a chain, their true objective hidden in the guise of a protest against Villa's extradition. Despite myself, I had to admit that Ricardo was right. Only one bomb had been important — the one that destroyed the Jeep at the door to the TV station and failed in its attempt to reach him. The others had served to divert attention to a nonexistent National Vindication Commando.

I needed copies of the letters sent by the Commando to the newspaper. I remembered that *El Posmo* had printed a copy of one of them on the front page. I looked for it, then compared the letters with those from the Smith Corona. They weren't the same.

I realized I should check the black Underwood beside the Smith Corona. The tight *s*, the blurry *a*. They were the same. Maybe this whole museum of antiques was for no other purpose than to hide those two typewriters in the middle of the living room. *I only collect objects that allow communication at a distance. Because, you know, that's the best way to communicate. At a distance. The presence of people only blocks communication.*

There was more to it and, at the same time, it was only about this. It was about the breakdowns that are caused by the presence of other people, passions that are awakened and excesses that erupt at contact with another's skin, at the sweet tremor of a voice

197

in the same room or an inquisitive glance that can bore into us and we're lost. The presence of people is just an obstacle to communication, and yet, those obstacles *are* communication.

I pictured a man in a container building rudimentary but powerful bombs to carry out a plan to maintain his freedom. A man who feels that over time he has paid for all of his sins. He resists the idea of physical prison because he's already imprisoned by the voices of the dead that whisper his crime in his ear every day — voices that manage to materialize what has always been incorporeal and are the most concrete proof that his conceptual invention is real. The dead are never entirely dead; they float in the coordinates of space and time, in a past that at times interferes with the present and disrupts the future.

Should men be forgiven for mistakes they made twenty years before? Had Dad found redemption for a gratuitous crime committed in his adolescence through politics and, later, through love? Hadn't his brother already paid for all his guilty deeds?

I shouldn't feel pity. There were mistakes and then there were mistakes. Who was Uncle David's alter ego in *Berkeley*? Maybe, as it was for his brother, both Bernard and Xavier at the same time?

I sat down in one of the chairs. The case was closed. I had to go to the police.

But if I was to be fair, shouldn't I also make public what I knew about Miguel Arnez's death?

I would keep quiet on that matter. There was no proof; it was just the word of a drug trafficker. I could forgive Dad — that anguished hole in my chest that was Dad — for things that I could never tolerate in others.

No one could possibly understand how tired I was. It was time to leave Río Fugitivo and return to Madison.

"It's not all the way you think it is." The voice startled me. I hadn't heard him come in. He approached me with slow, steady steps. It occurred to me that he might be armed. I gripped the photocopies.

"I'm guilty of some things," he went on. "But rather than being guilty for what I've done, I'm guilty of not having done anything."

He looked around him, as if making sure we were alone. He seemed disoriented. His hair was messy, his shirt unbuttoned. I tried to control the slight trembling of my lips.

"I missed you this afternoon," he said. "I thought you were going to come back early."

"I had things to do."

"I went to the store to buy empanadas. I remember you used to like cheese ones. When you were a boy. Do you still like them?"

"I still like them."

Even though he was speaking softly, his words echoed in the living room. And he might have been saying inoffensive things, but there was something menacing in his tone of voice, or at least that was how I felt.

"One day . . . ," he said, all of a sudden. "René said he wanted to talk to me. He asked me to keep it a secret. I agreed. He was acting strange. 'I'm sure,' René said, sort of mumbling the words, 'that the traitor in our group is Pedro.' 'Why would he do such a thing?' I asked. 'He's tired of the struggle,' René said. 'He doesn't believe his own rhetoric anymore. And he wants to leave the country with Elsa. Yes, yes, Elsa, don't look at me like that. But he's not willing to give up his image as the great revolutionary. He's contacted the government to negotiate the conditions so he can leave. And they've told him they'll let him leave if he turns his people in. They're going to let him leave and they're not going to ruin his image.'

"Can you imagine?" my uncle went on, his gaze somber. "René was Pedro's confidant, he had to know what he was saying. I told him not to do anything until he was sure of the truth. Did I believe him or didn't I? Pedro was capable of a lot of things, but that? I decided not to believe René, although I must admit I wasn't convinced. I wanted to talk to Pedro about it but kept quiet. The day of the meeting, when I saw that René hadn't arrived, I had an inkling that something might happen. Once again, it was as if I were paralyzed and I didn't say a thing. I wish I had had the conviction. I wish I did."

He was a few feet away and the smell of alcohol assaulted me. I could see dandruff in his hair. His voice was firm — paradoxically, he spoke with conviction about his lack of conviction. I ran my hand across my forehead and shook my head, this time unable to believe. It felt like that big living room had shrunk, that there wasn't enough air for us both to breathe at the same time. I dug deep inside for the tenderness I felt for him, but couldn't find it, silenced as it was by fear and deception.

"I should have accepted the part about Elsa. It was what I deserved, after all, but I didn't and lost. And believe me, I've been paying for it ever since. Not a day goes by that I'm not tormented by an image, a word, a sound."

"What you deserved?"

"Something that was just between us, as brothers."

"Anything to do with . . . Miguel Arnez?"

"Who's Miguel Arnez?"

"You know who he is. Salamander. A kid from school that my dad . . . killed for no reason. Or at least that's what they say."

He laughed loudly and his laughter ripped at my chest.

"Oh . . . I had forgotten about him. But there's not much to remember. Such a long time ago and out of the blue you bring up a ghost from my adolescence. Miguel Arnez committed suicide. There was never any doubt. His fingerprints were on the gun, and he had more than enough reason to do so. Are you still on about the salamanders? You could say the same thing about the bridges. Deep down, did your dad want to commit suicide by jumping off a bridge? And why were the Cuervos Anacoretas always wearing something orange? And why . . . ? You're looking for one symbol among many. But the central theme of the novel, I think, is the impossibility of discovering meaning. We're lost in a sea of symbols and we desperately want to discover what really matters. But the years wear us down, and in the end every lead along the way is the same as all the rest. The salamander is just another lead."

"Like a crossword."

"Like a crossword you don't have to solve. A crossword that might be better not to solve."

"Miguel Arnez has to exist. Villa told me."

"Villa, Villa. I told you to be careful. Although I sent you to him, which was silly of me. He's an astute man, very astute. And you fell for the word of an untrustworthy man."

"Why would he have done it?"

"To feel like he was still in control of the puppet strings. That his words still held weight. You made him feel important, you went to listen to him; you were the audience for his outdated ideas, his delirious mystifications. He wanted to use you to justify himself. But it was my fault, I know. I told you to talk to him."

He paused, sneezed. The physical and emotional strain was mirrored on his face. He looked at me and I felt as if his restless eye was distracting me while the other, immobile one recorded each of my slightest movements — the laborious way the air flowed through my throat, my incessant blinking. I was exhausted too. I wanted to go out into the garden, fill my lungs with air, forget this whole thing.

"Salamander was René Mérida's nom de guerre," he went on. "Only those of us in the leadership knew that. In *Berkeley*, subtly, Pedro was showing who the real traitor was. The spy who had sold us out months or maybe even years before. Because in the end the story is the same as always. Pedro was a great hero of the resistance, but he made mistakes. His greatest defects were his unchecked ambition, his intransigence, and the fact that he fell in love with my wife. He betrayed me, but that doesn't mean he betrayed the cause."

I wanted to take a few steps back, gain some perspective. The facts were confusing and I was lost in a labyrinth of interpretations. I felt wretched that I'd been so ready to believe the despicable things Villa had said about Dad. I had failed the test. I hated that I had mistrusted Dad, had believed him capable of gratuitous evil. I should have trusted him blindly. I hated the fact that I had let myself like Villa.

If Villa had been able to seduce me with his story, I had to make sure Uncle David didn't do the same. I had to remember that his own Cryptograms, after all, suggested that he knew about the bombs. I gathered my courage. I tried to stop blinking, let my breath return to normal, stop the palms of my hands from sweating.

"That's not enough," I said, at last. "You, you were the traitor. Out of spite, you turned Dad in. Your own brother. Twenty years later, when you thought you were safe, Ricardo found you out and you wanted to kill him. You haven't finished paying for a thing. You never will. And to think, to think that I lived here and didn't know."

He sighed, shook his head as if incredulous at my credulity.

"So you also believed Ricardo's rumors," he said. "Oh, what am I going to do with you? Don't you realize that Ricardo is on a mission to clear his family name? A desperate mission, but understandable within his own logic. Not so much for his dad but for himself: to begin again, to live without the weight of being a traitor's son."

"The Cryptograms show that you knew about the bombs. And the letter from the so-called Commando was written on this typewriter. Now I understand your interest in Villa."

"On this one? Now that surprises me. He's smarter, or they're smarter, than I thought."

He cleared his throat. There was a long pause that felt interminable. My gaze focused on the Smith Corona, the machine that was capable of bringing together streets and objects and stories and wishes and ideals and nightmares with its ceaseless tap-tapping.

"But I won't say a thing," he said. His tone had changed; he sounded defeated. "I could give you a thousand explanations, but what I'm going to do now is more important to me. I've already told you what I'm guilty of: I didn't turn Pedro in, I didn't pull any trigger, but I didn't do anything to stop it. I didn't do anything that you're accusing me of. Do you believe me or not?"

Was this another test?

"The crosswords."

"Yes, I set those, but with no evil motive. It's a subject that has always interested me, and that's it. They used them to make me look guilty. I mean *it was the opposite of what you think*. I didn't put the clues in the Cryptograms to make fun of the police before committing a crime. Instead, they used my crosswords to choose their targets. Any casual association in them was enough."

"The letter from the Commando."

"I didn't write it," he said impatiently and with a certain edge of violence. "But enough. Enough. We could talk all day when it can all be resolved with a simple question: do you or don't you believe me?"

He looked at me, waiting for my answer. As if the meaning of his life hung on my affirmation or denial, as if all his actions had led him inexorably to this moment, condensing and explaining it. I didn't want to answer. I would rather have let the minutes tick by while we talked, rather wait for something unexpected to happen so that I wouldn't have to say what I had to.

"Just one more thing," I said. "The body. Where was it buried?"

"How should I know? And if I did, do you think you would find your father there? In some field? In some communal grave? Oh, Pedrito, you still have so much to learn."

There was tenderness in his voice. His calling me Pedrito reminded me of Villa. I also remembered the days I had spent living with him, our serious and inconsequential talks, how I had come to know him a bit better and learned to love him as I learned about his manual and verbal inventions and his magnificent homage to Dad and about those tortuous years of his life that were interwoven, accidentally, with the country's history. I told myself that rather than confront him, it was time for me to confront myself and answer his question.

"No," I said, emphatically. "I don't believe you."

"Would you really do that to me, not believe me?"

"I would."

He knelt on the floor and put his head in my lap. After a moment, surprised, I heard him crying. It was a weak, pitiful cry that ran through my body and made me close my eyes in a vain attempt to bring back the enchantment, at least for that exhausting moment.

Epilogue

I T WAS A LONG TRIP, or at least that's how it felt. Suspended in the blinding clarity of day, the American Airlines flight cut through the air, heading for the U.S. almost without noise or turbulence. My fellow passengers snored or read or watched the movie (a Tom Hanks one) while tired-looking flight attendants who hadn't been home in days prowled the aisles, feigning interest in what went on around them.

I wanted to sleep so as not to think, but I couldn't. I tried to watch the movie but lost interest in the soporific plot. I got only partway through a *New York Times* crossword on my Palm Pilot. I played Dope Wars without paying attention to the screen. I wanted to write on my iBook but couldn't even string two sentences together. I even resorted to conversing with an older divorcée who was drinking red wine as if celebrating the death of her ex-husband. Her gravelly voice hurt my ears, and after a few minutes I had to change seats.

I didn't want to think. I just wanted to get as far away as possible from Río Fugitivo, escape from that city as I had from Madison. It was as if some characteristic I had just discovered in the spaces I inhabited was enough to expel me, cursed, from them. Better yet, it seemed like it was a characteristic of mine to escape from the spaces I inhabited as if that would mean an end to my sorrows. But there had been no end and the stubborn wheel of life continued, its surprises crouched down ready to spring out at me as soon as I arrived at the airport, as soon as I returned to live with beings who were equally, or more, or less, fallible. Maybe I had lived for too long on borrowed time, with the wind at my back. Maybe it was true that, sooner or later, there was a price to be paid.

Carolina had shown up at the airport. I was surprised to run into her at a magazine stand while looking through the first Spanish edition of *NewTimes*. She looked beautiful, her gaze lively and her smile teasing. Tight black pants, a black leather jacket. The ring over her eyebrow pierced the skin poetically.

"Something of yours?" she asked. "A phrase to explain our problems, diagnosing them once and for all and forever? 'According to Dr. Mack the Knife, assistant professor of political science . . .'"

"Sarcasm doesn't suit you."

The indigenous leader from Achacachi stared at us contemptuously from the cover of a magazine. He had just founded his own political party, but the leader of the Chapare coca producers would not recognize him as the indigenous movement's representative. In a smaller headline, Montenegro (contradicting earlier declarations) affirmed that it was impossible to eradicate coca altogether. I should've written an article on it.

"Federico sends a big hug," she said.

"I stopped by his house to say goodbye. I'm worried about him. He told me not to be surprised if he shows up at my door in Madison one of these days."

"He'll land on his feet, you'll see. Let him enjoy being out of work. You're the only one who thinks he's suffering. Although he is spending all his savings pretty quickly. The recession . . ."

"I don't want to talk about that. Fede told me that Carlos found out about his wife, confronted her, and she didn't deny it. Poor guy doesn't know what to do."

"Poor nothing. Fuck him."

I would miss them until I got to Madison. Once there — since none of them e-mailed — I would forget them until one lonely night when too much wine would make me nostalgic or until my next trip back, which this time I felt would be a long way away. (I always thought that when I left. In a few months I would start to plot my return.)

"I decided to go back to work at the Ciudadela. I need the money. Please don't say a thing. I know what you think."

"I'm the last person to talk."

"So you're leaving. I thought they wouldn't let you go so soon."

"I made all the statements I had to. With the proof they found and the confession, they can figure it out. I told them how to reach me if there's anything urgent."

"It's a shame. I liked him a lot. I still can't believe it."

"That's what Federico said."

"He'll miss his crosswords. That's the least of it to me. Sorry for saying it, but despite the barriers he put up, he made you like him."

"That's what was so dangerous. That's what's always dangerous."

I had given the police all the proof I had. When they found bomb-making materials in the container, Uncle David said he didn't know who had put them there. Later, he wound up confessing to everything. It was a sad story. His confession hurt me in a way I hadn't expected, as if a part of me I didn't know existed had refused to believe in his guilt right up until the end. It was, perhaps, the part that knew about acrostics and crosswords and magic tricks thanks to him, when I inhabited the nebulous territory of childhood. It was the part that came back during those months to discover his likable side, his frustration as an inventor, his angst at the reality that surrounded him, and that was harder and harder to understand.

"I didn't really come to say goodbye," Caro said. "I just wanted to give you this."

She handed me a shoebox wrapped in newspaper.

"Sentimentalism doesn't suit you either," I said. "I don't know if it's worth it to hold on to keepsakes."

"Promise me you won't open it until you get home."

She made it seem very important. With any luck, I wouldn't have thrown it out by then.

She quickly kissed my right cheek — a furtive caress of the lips, like the touch of a butterfly's wings — and put something in my hand, then lost herself in the crowd. I was stunned, didn't know how to react at all. I opened my hand: it was the silver chain with the image of Cristina engraved on the pendant. I didn't have the courage to wear it, so I put it in my pocket. Maybe we had lost a great opportunity. Maybe we had no choice but to lose it. It wasn't strange — the chances of that were greater than of there being mutual interest. The world was filled with unrequited love, hearts that beat in indifference, lives dedicated to other lives in vain, or maybe not; maybe being true to the feelings themselves was an exalted form of redemption and on a higher plane than the banal, narcissistic search for reciprocity.

Later I became angry at holding a box in my hands. What the hell was I supposed to do with it? They were likely keepsakes from our time together, photos and a few letters she had never been able to send — the inevitable objects that accumulate in any relationship, even one of unrequited love. What stupidity. The necklace would've been enough of a gesture.

I put the box in my carry-on luggage, together with the copy of *NewTimes,* for which I would one day write again — great professional commentator on Latin America and its multiple crises, author of two-minute diagnoses and thirty-second prescriptions that didn't manage to scratch the surface of the problem (but if I didn't do it, someone else would, someone who might be more incorrect than I).

"Anything to drink?" the blond flight attendant asked. Her accent was Colombian.

"Whiskey, please."

In the Miami airport, surrounded by people from every part of Latin America, standing in line so the mustached Cuban or Puerto Rican customs agent could stamp my passport and give me permission to reenter, I realized that if he had lived a little longer, Dad might have given *Berkeley* another meaning. Dad wanted to abandon politics and leave, run away with Aunt Elsa — the Salamander — to Berkeley, his lost paradise. A utopian plan if ever there was one. Dad couldn't get back into the States, at least not legally. Would he have crossed the Rio Grande? Falsified his passport?

It didn't matter. Maybe you didn't have to go back to paradise to regain it. Maybe you didn't lose it just by leaving it. Maybe Dad had discovered sooner rather than later that he had never really left Berkeley, had never entirely lost it.

It was a long trip, or at least that's how it felt. The closer I got to Madison, looking out the window of the Embraer at interminable forests and lakes and little towns, I started to miss Río Fugitivo (despite my best efforts to try to forget everything that had happened there), and my desire to see Ashley again became a disturbing sense of panic. It was to be expected. What would our meeting be like? What would she do when she saw me at her door? Where would Patrick be?

I pictured her naked on the bed of a cheap motel room on Route 15, her long hair hiding her face, her skin damp, a wild sheen to it, her quick breaths drowned out by the voice of Shirley Manson on the TV. I looked in the mirror above the bed at her body finally at rest, reflected in all its vulnerable glory.

Yasemin was waiting for me at the airport — deserted around midnight. I had written an e-mail asking her to pick me up. Wearing a blue tracksuit and sandals, she looked as if she'd just gotten out of bed. On the way home she told me that her boyfriend had had to come here for her to discover she didn't love him anymore and that she'd moved in with Morgana.

"I thought you were just experimenting."

"Experimenting doesn't have to be the preparation for some future step. Experimenting can be an end in itself; one can live just for that."

Yasemin had a theory for every one of her actions. I didn't want to get into an exhausting pseudo-philosophical discussion right away — at least not that night.

"And Joaquín?"

"Anda a bit disappointed. Su working group fell apart. Los puertorriqueños tenían su own agenda. So did the Indians who said they were interested in Latin America. Al final, todo es quote unquote identity politics. No one can talk about a subject that doesn't directly relate to their local problems."

"That's what the new world order is like: more and more localist."

"That's why I stay out of it. But don't worry. Joaquín volverá a la carga sooner than we think."

She asked me to tell her about my vacation and so I did, selecting the most inoffensive parts of the story.

"That's all?"

"Pretty much."

"So why did you come back tan rápido?"

"Me aburrí. And there wasn't much more to research. I didn't discover a secret manuscript and I didn't find out anything too different from what I already knew. What else? Friends, food, social life, time spent at the library, interviewing people who knew Dad. That's about it. Río Fugitivo isn't New York."

"Tampoco Madison. You'll never convince me it's more boring than this place. Your book?"

"I did all the research. Now I just have to write it."

Why did I lie to her, to my friend? It obviously wasn't easy to get rid of certain bad habits.

"Are you going to teach this semester?"

"I have a leave of absence until December. I don't know. I have a lot of things to think about. Some important decisions to make. I'm not sure this is really for me. Don't get me wrong, me gusta enseñar. But I wonder if there are other things I'd like better than teaching."

"Your dream about politics."

"Why not?"

"Because it's just that — a dream that works because it's not real. We all like to have a Plan B, fantasear con el what if, about the possibility of reinventing ourselves. But that doesn't mean we should realize it. Its power is derived precisely from the fact that it's always there in our imagination, unattainable."

"I don't know, I just don't know. I have until December to think about it."

She offered to let me stay at Morgana's. I told her the last thing

I needed was for people at the Institute to find out I was living with two students. I asked her to drop me off at the Holiday Inn — I'd look for a new apartment later.

She dropped me off and a bellboy came to take my suitcase. As Yasemin was leaving, I couldn't resist asking about Ashley.

"I haven't seen her for a long time," she said, shaking her head resignedly. "I heard she left the program but that she'd be here until her husband finished his postdoc."

Husband. The word sounded strange.

"Brrr. Hace frío aquí."

"No te vuelvas a meter en líos, Pedro."

"I won't do anything. Trust me."

"Famous last words."

I made it as far as the door to Ashley's house a few times. In my car, parked at the curb outside, I lit a cigarette and remembered the night we made love on the porch while Patrick played sax on the second floor, the window lit up and the long silhouette cut out against the computer on the table (the last part was a lie, but that's how I remembered that night).

But those days were gone now. The porch was empty under the full moon, and the light in the window revealed shadows that came and went. It occurred to me that my behavior resembled that of a stalker: men or women who wander like delirious ghosts around the house where the object of their unrequited desire lives. But I wasn't like them, I told myself. Ashley belonged to me, and a single word from me was all it would take, or maybe a whisper would be enough, or a gesture, a finger on the nose in an attempt to share an old secret. But how many others knew that gesture?

I wasn't like them. And yet, I didn't have the courage to take the step I had to take, leave my pensive paralysis behind and get out of the car, cross the street, ring the bell, and face Patrick, tell him that it wasn't his fault or mine, it was just life and chance, which wants everything to be restless, perturbed, disordered. Or maybe Patrick wouldn't be home and Ashley would be waiting for me with her suitcase beside her under the failing light in the vestibule, ready to run away. Goodbye, Madison, goodbye: routine life was good while it lasted.

The step that needed to be taken wasn't and the days went by.

That's how the first week passed. Everything changed the second week when Yasemin called me urgently one night to tell me what she had just found out: Patrick and Ashley were leaving Madison forever the next day. As soon as he heard I was back, Patrick decided it was time to head for Amsterdam.

"They're leaving on the ten o'clock flight to New York. Try to confirm that yourself. All I've heard are rumors. I haven't seen her in ages and I don't think anyone else has either."

I should have gone to Ashley's house right then. Instead I decided to show up early, surprise them at the door as they were leaving for the airport, put off the moment of encounter as long as possible. I opted for melodrama.

I parked in front of Ashley's house. I had bought the *New York Times*, a cappuccino, and a chocolate croissant. A couple of toothless seniors passed by, then a young couple in shorts, jogging in the cold morning.

I didn't open the newspaper or try the cappuccino or croissant. I stared at the door out of the corner of my eye. Every now and then I would surreptitiously look at myself in the mirror, fix my hair and straighten the white Polo shirt that was becoming too small for me. I had put my contact lenses in and smelled of Boss. The old brown suede shoes I had on had worn out long ago.

Hours went by and the door didn't open. By mid-morning I realized there'd been a change of plans and decided to be brave. I went up and rang the bell.

Patrick opened the door. He was unshaven and unkempt; everything about him exuded slovenliness. He looked at me and went back inside, leaving the door ajar. His steps were tentative, or at least that's how they seemed to me. I followed him inside.

Patrick stopped on the landing and said no one had given me permission to come in. He wasn't upset, just indifferent. He was a man who had been through the worst and was completely re-signed. I asked him where Ashley was.

He told me indifferently — or feigning indifference, because deep down he wanted to tell me — that one day, a couple of weeks ago, he had come home to an empty house. Ashley had left in the Saab, taking all her things. He hadn't finished paying off the car. The police were looking for her, but so far there hadn't been any leads. He couldn't imagine where she might be. She hadn't gone back to her parents' house or even called them.

Patrick didn't know where to get the money to pay for the car. There wasn't a cent of his inheritance left. Ashley had lost it all Internet-trading.

He told me, stroking his beard, leaning a hand up against the bare wall, that he thought she'd gone off with another man, but that it didn't matter to him. He had given her everything and it still hadn't been enough. He had analyzed every one of his actions and was sure he hadn't done anything wrong. It made him think it had all been inevitable. He had already accepted his loss and suggested I do the same. I wanted to believe him, but I couldn't. People who say they've accepted their loss are usually the least accepting.

I thanked him and left. I asked myself whether that much guilt, that much anguish, had been fair. Maybe I had been more inno-cent than I thought. Or maybe not. I'd never really know.

The first thing I did when I got back to my room was to seek solace in the newspaper-wrapped box that Carolina had given me, which I had left unopened in the closet.

I hoped to find photos of the happy times I'd shared with Carolina. What I found, sitting on the carpet, were photos of the most enamored couple I had ever seen: Uncle David and my mother. Intimate photos in the twilight of a hotel room. Mom's letters were handwritten and Uncle David's were written on the Underwood typewriter — easily recognized by its faults, the uni-form and irregular letters trying in vain to hide the signs of pas-sion.

Uncle David and Mom, before and after my birth. The things the letters said were the logical, convincing conclusion to the story.

I felt as if I'd been hit in the stomach, and I was left winded, clenching my teeth. I stammered, "Uncle David . . . ?" I pictured him in jail and wanted to take the first flight to Río Fugitivo, tell him it had all been a mistake, that I never should have doubted him. I closed my eyes and told myself it was what I deserved.

Now everything became clearer and blurrier at the same time. The end was a new beginning and Uncle . . . *Dad* hadn't been far from the truth. Ricardo had discovered the letters between Pedro and Elsa. He was convinced his father wasn't the traitor and that mine was. He didn't have concrete proof and, maybe, had decided to fabricate it, using definitions from the crosswords to create a whole story around the bombs and incriminate him. Carolina must have helped him. After all, she had spent hours alone at David's house. And that time I found her alone in the living room, she was so nervous. I should have suspected something. She could have used the typewriter in the living room to write the letter from the Commando. She could have left the incriminating evidence in the container. She could have used me to get close to Dad.

But he wasn't the traitor in the group. Maybe it was the person who had been suspected all along: René Mérida. Mérida, the person in charge of strategic plans, had passed information on to the intelligence service. That was why the plans failed so frequently. When he heard that Pedro wanted to leave it all behind, leave the country in search of a new beginning with Elsa, he decided to turn him in. After using his information to break up the Unzueta Street meeting, the government intelligence service killed him.

I stood up. I wanted to talk to someone. I wanted to find Yasemin, tell her everything. She'd understand. But I stood motionless in the middle of the room, unable to make a decision.

I also thought about another possibility. The one insinuating that Pedro was the traitor, a person capable of handing over his own comrades to the government and fabricating his escape with Elsa just to keep his legend, plagued as it was with lies, alive. But something had gone wrong, or maybe the government had just made Pedro believe that everything would go according to plan, but they had decided all along that both he and Elsa would also be assassinated. Pedro would never go back to Berkeley, at least not the real Berkeley, much less after having paid such a high price for it.

Conjecture, pure conjecture. It all came to me — I was the meeting point for all the different versions of the story. I wanted to be left with just one version and discard the rest. That way my nights would be more peaceful. But I couldn't.

I took a few tentative steps, then sat down on the bed. I stood up again. I sat back down.

I continued unraveling the dizzying plot. David had always felt guilty for his brother's death, but when Ricardo made suspicion fall on him, he couldn't accept it. His guilt was intimate, not public. *He had killed his brother, but he hadn't killed his brother.*

The final straw came a little later: the moment I stopped believing in him, his life ceased to have meaning. The moment I stopped believing in him, I lost my father again. That was why, that was the only reason, he had confessed to things he didn't do.

I again pictured him in a cell and was overcome with despair: several things could be fixed — Dad would be freed; all I had to do was tell the authorities the truth — but other things, ah, other things were not so easily fixed. I felt breathless again and knew that this sensation would never leave me now.

I had looked for Dad in far-off, mistaken places. I should have looked for him in a house in Río Fugitivo while doing crosswords, as he told me about his brother and the never entirely forgotten voices of the dead.

That morning, I wanted to throw away my underlined copy of *Berkeley* and the only photo I had of Ashley, but I couldn't.

Ithaca, January 1999–March 2001